The Tipp Revival

RETURN TO GLORY
1987–94

SÉAMUS LEAHY

GW00702400

Gill & Macmillan

Gill & Macmillan Ltd
Goldenbridge
Dublin 8
with associated companies throughout the world
© Séamus Leahy 1995
0 7171 2329 4
Design and print origination by Graham Thew
Printed by ColourBooks Ltd, Dublin

A catalogue record is available for this book from the
British Library.

1 3 5 4 2

CONTENTS

To hurling men everywhere — especially those who have worn the Blue and Gold

PREFACE

It would be an understatement to say that hurling played an important part in our lives when we were growing up in Tipperary fifty years ago. To many of us it was everything. We played it from morning to night, we read the hurling reports in the national and local papers, we read *Carbery's Annual* at Christmas and we were authorities on games played long before we were born. There were no press sensations regarding players in those days. The game itself was what was important and if some personalities emerged in larger profile than others, it was generally because they had a larger profile on the field.

When I began to write the story of the Tipperary hurling revival I was advised to 'make a few sensational disclosures' in order to attract public attention. There are no startling revelations in these pages. There are no keyhole reports of board room or of dressing room intrigues. It is simply the story of a time of wonderful excitement in Tipperary. It is told from the point of view of one who believes that hurling is the greatest field-game in the world and that its well-being in Tipperary is of special interest to those who worry about its survival.

For me the writing of the story through the winter of 1994–95 renewed much of the excitement of summer days in Thurles and Killarney, and Limerick and Killarney and Croke Park and Killarney — and Killarney and Killarney. On winter nights I tasted again the glories of summer and I knew as I never knew before how much a part of my own self and my own experience the ancient game is.

Except for the final chapters, the book is mostly a straightforward narrative. The exception to this rule is chapter 14, where I deliberately pause to consider the career of Nicholas English, the outstanding hurler of the team.

If these pages help the reader to relive those days, I shall be happy. If they move a youngster in Boherlahan, Tullaroan, Carrigtwohill, Castlegar or Tallaght to take a hurley and head for the nearest field, I shall be happier still.

While I await that outcome, I should like to express my most sincere thanks to all who helped me along the way — Seamus King, Owen McCrohan, Seamus O'Doherty, Babs Keating, Donie Nealon, Liam O'Donncha, Jimmy Barry Murphy, Tomas O'Baroid, Sean Fogarty, Liam Fennell, John O'Neill, Theo English, Christy Ring, Jnr, Liz Howard, Enda McEvoy, Jerry Ring, Donie and Maire English, Johnny Clifford, John O'Grady, Donie O'Connell, Noel Morris, Justin McCarthy, Liam O'Duibhir, Eddie O'Donnell, Jerry Moynihan, Tom O'Donnell, Fr Tom Fogarty, Tom Ryall, Canon Ml O'Brien, J. J. Kennedy, Sean Carey, John Kennedy, John Kelly, the editors and staff of the *Tipperary GAA Yearbook*, the *Clonmel Nationalist*, the *Tipperary Star* and the *Nenagh Guardian*, the officers of the Tipperary Supporters Club, and my computer experts Fr Brian O'Connor and Frank McGrath. Finally my thanks to my wife Kay and the lads.

In July 1987 on a cloudy day that gave way to sunshine, against the glorious backdrop of the mountains of Kerry, a young man with blood-streaked face, wearing a blue and gold jersey, raised the Munster hurling cup over his head and shouted, 'The famine is over!' Then he led the crowd, delirious with excitement, in the singing of 'Slievenamon'.

This is the story of what led to that scene — and of similar scenes that followed.

Chapter One

KILLARNEY, 1987

There was a time when Tipperary's hurling supporters were generally considered a not too excitable lot. Over many years they took some pride in their ability to accept either victory or defeat with the minimum of fuss. Such is the privilege of those who are familiar with victory and who regard defeat as a temporary setback that will shortly be put right.

But the Tipperary supporters who flocked to Killarney on 19 July 1987 had little of the traditional aplomb. Sixteen years had passed since the county had won an All-Ireland or a Munster final. A generation were now adults who had only heard about their county's hurling greatness from their elders. It had all happened in the distant past and in recent years they had come to be dubious about a lot of things they had heard concerning the past. Tipperary's hurling story was history and history had nothing to do with the here and now. All that they had been told about how Tipp were never beaten belonged in the past — if it ever did belong anywhere.

So the hordes of youngsters who swept from north Tipperary along the Limerick road into Killarney and from south Tipperary through Mallow felt no monkey of history on their shoulders. With their flags, their badges and their neckbands of blue and gold they were as skittish as young colts on a spring outing. It was all new to them and it was great fun. They could not be expected to share the apprehensions of their elders who felt the ghosts of other times and other heroes breathing down their necks.

And if their elders felt the presence of ghosts, so did the lads who would wear the blue and gold jerseys on the field. 'The Three Wise Men' of the Tipperary dugout — Babs Keating, Theo English and Donie Nealon — had all played for Tipp during a period of dazzling achievement when the county had appeared in five All-Ireland finals in six years, winning four of them. They themselves had often sat in the dressing room before taking the field and listened while some star of other days spoke words of exhortation. And they had liberally spiced their own dressing room harangues with reminders of the county's traditions.

In the story of modern hurling, Tipperary-Cork games have always had a special significance. The rivalry began in a tournament played in 1886 before the GAA got its championships under way at all. By the 1920s games between the two counties were big crowd-pullers and a Tipp man's dream of contentment was to have 'Cork bet and the hay saved'. By the end of the 1940s Cork led in Munster titles, but Tipp cut it back and went ahead again until, inexplicably, the famine struck after 1971. Now, after sixteen years of hunger and frustration there was a feeling in Tipp that the time was ripe to set matters right.

Thus, when Richard Stakelum and his team raced on to the field on the afternoon of a day that would take its place in Tipperary legend, they carried a burden of tradition that was almost intolerable for young men to bear. That day and that game would be referred to subsequently by Tipperary hurling followers simply as 'Killarney'. In Tipperary's hurling parlance Killarney simply means 19 July 1987 when Tipp, replaying the game which had been drawn the previous Sunday in Thurles, trailed Cork for sixty-nine minutes and only drew level in the final minute of the game. Then in extra time Tipp turned on a magical performance which gave them victory by a clear margin of three goals. When a Tipperary man talks simply of something that happened 'after Killarney', he means it happened after the day the famine ended. It became like the 'night of the big wind', a marker from which all subsequent events were dated.

For at least twenty minutes and probably for longer that day it seemed that nothing had changed for Tipperary, that the end of the famine was as far away as ever. Pat Fox, so accurate with a placed ball, drove three frees wide before he scored one. Richard Stakelum tried and he too was wide. John Kennedy tried and failed. Meanwhile Cork's John Fenton, with effortless accuracy, was chalking up points from frees. After twenty minutes of play Cork led by seven points to one.

But still there were things to cheer about. A long ball from centre-back Jim Cashman to his brother Tom was flaked off the Tipp goalpost to be met on the rebound by corner-forward Kieran Kingston. Down on his knees went goalkeeper Ken Hogan to cover it; the moment was safe, and the ball was belted away up the field. A moment later Teddy McCarthy, until then impeccable, drove wide and it seemed that perhaps the Tipp bug had bitten Cork too.

Then came the first of the wonderful goals which would do so much to make the day a memorable one. Aidan Ryan, fifty yards from the Cork goal and in full flight, his hurley gone, kicked a long ball ahead to his brother Bobby who ran out from his unaccustomed corner-forward position to meet him. With Richard Browne breathing down Bobby's neck, Nicholas English, until now watched by all of the Cork full-back line, suddenly appeared behind the two. A quick shout and Bobby simply spread his legs wide, allowing the ball to pass without making any attempt to play it. English had a split second to do something. He put his hurley down and as the ball rose towards him he pulled without handling it. The Cork net shook and all Tipperary rose in a delirium of delight.

Cork were much too much in command to be put off by this one touch of genius and a minute later Kieran Kingston placed Tomas Mulcahy for another goal. Again Cork were rampant and in the 35th minute Tony O'Sullivan swung over his first point of the game as if to serve notice of the reserves of power still in Cork's arsenal. When the teams trooped into the dressing rooms at half-time the score stood Cork 1-10 Tipp 1-5.

History again. This Tipp team simply wouldn't be allowed to forget it. In the dressing room at the interval they were reminded of a day in Killarney in 1971 when they were six points down at half-time and came back to win. You are too tense to hurl as you are able, they were told. Just go out and be yourselves. Don't be so cautious. Forget about Cork and do the things you are able to do.

The sky had been overcast all morning but it had remained dry. At half-time there were a few drops of rain but that was all. Mother nature had changed her mind. The clouds would part in more ways than one and Tipp's golden moments would be drenched in sunshine.

But the sunshine did not come just yet. The second half was only fifteen seconds old when Pat Fox pointed, but John Fenton answered with a point from a 65. From out near the sideline English dropped a ball almost on goalkeeper Cunningham's head, only to have it cleared upfield. Tipp lived dangerously and John Heffernan intervened in time to save what would most certainly have been a goal from Tomas Mulcahy, so that Tipp were pleased enough to concede only Tony O'Sullivan's point. Then, as Pat Fox drove over a point from a free the sun came out and the crowd, as if sensing a change, began chanting 'Tipp! Tipp! Tipp!' Aidan Ryan drove over. Donie O'Connell began beating a swath through the Cork 40, making space for his wingers and putting new pressure on the Cork inside line.

Martin McGrath who had come on just before half-time at left half-forward would put over three points, two of them with fluid left-hand strokes. Pat Fox, taking a handpass from Nicholas English at full speed, drove towards the net. The ball rebounded; Fox and others would claim it had hit the stanchion supporting the net, but the umpire ruled that the ball had hit the upright. A long-range point from Pa Fitzelle a moment later was some compensation, but although Tipp were pegging back the deficit point by point, every ball was being contested by both sides as if it were the last. Now youngsters were perhaps learning the reasons for the mutual respect between Tipp and Cork.

In the 23rd minute of the second half, Tipp drew level with a point from Pat Fox and for the first time that day the challengers had drawn level with the champions. Now the pot was really boiling as it was supposed to in Cork-Tipp Munster finals. Teddy McCarthy sent a long ball floating goalwards and Tony O'Sullivan leaped high to touch it down into the net. 'In the square!' shouted the umpire, and the green flag which would have given victory to Cork was crossed with the white. A moment later there was a point to compensate, but a classic drop-puck from Richard Stakelum across the field reached Martin McGrath who put Tipp level again. Points were exchanged, the crowd cheered as they had never cheered before, and blue and gold clashed with red as if human energy was inexhaustible. John Fenton pointed another free and then, almost on the 70th minute, a 65 to Tipp was sent wide by Paul Delany. It looked like the gallant attempt at resurgence had failed.

Then Nicholas English gained immortality. As the clock registered the beginning of injury time, he dodged terrier-like through a ruck, collected the ball and made for goal, a red jersey thundering behind him close enough possibly to hook him when he pulled. But English made the decision which ensured that the Tipp hurling revival would not die an instant death as Ger Cunningham braced himself to save. There was no attempt to beat the Cork goalkeeper. Instead, with a mighty stroke of his hand he sent the ball soaring high over the bar. The crowd were already on their feet as the full-time whistle followed immediately on Cunningham's puckout.

While waiting for the teams to re-emerge for extra time, emotionally drained spectators of older vintage recalled a day in 1949 when Cork and Tipp, after 120 minutes of play, took a breather before going into extra time. The Cork team sat out on the field in baking sunshine. The Tipp team returned to the dressing room and were sponged with water brought in churns from Tipperary hills. Tipp were rejuvenated; Cork drooped; and Tipp took the first of what would be three titles in a row. Would Tipp have something similar up their sleeves today? They had nothing but youth and stamina, and that would be enough.

But the advantage of youth and stamina would not show until the second half of extra time. For the moment it was point for point as both sides fought out as dour a struggle as had ever been seen between these two storied counties. Extra time was only half a minute old when Ken Hogan was called upon to save. John Fenton resumed his relentless punishment of every Tipp lapse, but now Pat Fox had found his range and he too was showing something of his normal accuracy. For Cork, John Fitzgibbon retired and Mickey Mullins came on. Then came what proved to be a blessing in disguise for Tipp. A few minutes after pointing a 65 Paul Delany was seen to be suffering from cramp and was replaced by the veteran Michael Doyle. Bobby Ryan came back to centre-back, where he was always much more at home than in the forward line, and Mick Doyle took over at full-forward. Bobby would prove a steadying influence in the backline and Doyle would play a key part in the triumph of the forwards. Cork were two points up when just before half-time Aidan Ryan pointed to leave the score Cork 1-21 Tipp 1-20.

When the teams re-emerged for the last leg of the marathon, John Fenton had moved to corner-forward. Though his overall total that day would be thirteen points, all were from placed balls. He was now 33 years old and still one of the greatest exponents of the game. The second half of extra time was only two minutes old when time caught up with him. The teams were level when from fifty yards out he drove a free wide.

It was Fenton's miss which more than anything else gave Tipp the scent of victory. The break had come. Their tails were up. Two minutes later saw Donie O'Connell, who had battled heroically all through the afternoon, finish a solo run with a point which for the first time put Tipp ahead. There was blue and gold everywhere. The goals were coming.

The first came in the fifth minute. Colm Bonnar stormed down from centre-field and passed to O'Connell whose shot was blocked by

Cunningham. But Doyle, ever the poacher, was on hand to take it round the spreadeagled goalkeeper and palm it to the net. Now Tipp were ahead by 2-22 to 1-21. Cork were showing signs of muscle fatigue and, following a challenge on Colm Bonnar which he lost, Johnny Crowley retired to be replaced by Dermot McCurtain.

The second goal came in the 9th minute. The indomitable Browne broke upfield to be intercepted by Pa Fitzelle who sent a low ball unerringly to Mick Doyle. The big man dragged challengers and all goalwards and palmed the ball through to the net while Tipp supporters, displaying a most untraditional lack of restraint, burst on to the field in an ecstasy of jubilation.

That was not all. A sideline ball unexpectedly landed at Ken Hogan's feet; he fumbled it and picked it up off the ground. Up came John Fenton to blaze the free with all his Middleton might at the blue and goal wall. It was, appropriately, Richard Stakelum who saved it, and once again Tipp were on the attack. Mick Doyle, nothing going wrong for him, had a shot deflected for a 65, but now Tipp could afford wides from Pat Fox and Martin McGrath. Everything was going wrong for Cork. Ger Cunningham with a puckout failed to see Kevin Hennessy loose. The ball was returned and Denis Walshe retrieved magnificently only to be dispossessed by Fox. And then came the final golden moment when Fox, hemmed in by a wall of Cork men, parted to O'Connell whose momentum carried him into the net after the ball which he had palmed in front of him.

The long count was over. Tipp were three goals ahead and the celebrations began there and then in the Cork goalmouth, with Donie O'Connell mobbed by Tipp supporters. Never before had Killarney witnessed such a scene of unrestrained joy. As great moments tend to produce other great moments, a generation of Tipperary hurling followers will never forget the moment that bloodied, but certainly unbowed, Richard Stakelum, accepting the cup, announced in a voice that could be heard echoing from the MacGillycuddy's Reeks, 'The famine is over.' They had waited sixteen years to hear those words. But the wait was worth it.

The excitement was contagious. On the way back to our Gaeltacht holiday home in the evening, motorists coming against us, in acknowledgment of our blue and gold flags fluttering from the windows of the car, honked their horns and flashed their lights.

In Killorglin, realising that in our excitement we hadn't eaten since morning, we pulled in for a meal. Diners called congratulations and a Dutchman approached our table. He had been in Killarney and had caught the excitement in the streets during the morning. Having managed to get a ticket and seen the game, he had been enthralled. Would there be others like it? I was about to tell him that games like this don't happen everyday when I remembered Richard Stakelum's words. Indeed there will, I assured him — now that the famine is over.

TIPPERARY: CRADLE OF THE GAA

Tipperary, the sixth in size of all Irish counties, was originally carved out by King John in the early thirteenth century. Taking its name from the well of Ara near the Galtee Mountains, the county stretched from the Shannon and near the Bog of Allen in the north to within twenty miles of the south coast.

No sooner had the first Norman invaders arrived than the blood of Butlers, Fitzgeralds, Burkes, Purcells and Powers began to blend with that of the Gaelic inhabitants — Kennedys, Dwyers, Gleesons, Carrolls, Ryans, Meaghers and others. It blended so well that when, after nearly 500 years, Oliver Cromwell came calling he made little distinction between old Irish and new Irish. On the Rock of Cashel, from which Munster had once been ruled, the cathedral was the scene of a massacre that was calculated to impress upon those not already aware of it that those who were not in favour of the new Puritan order were against it.

But Tipperary folk were slow learners. At Clonmel, garrisoned by Ulstermen led by one of the truly talented soldiers of his time, Hugh Dubh O'Neill, they had the temerity to resist the Roundheads. Day after day, Oliver — pimples and all — rode in from Fethard to give the benefit of his genius to the battalions who traded shot with the men behind the walls. And each night he rode back to Fethard wondering when the job would be finished. But even the victor of Naseby and Marston Moor was worn down by the combination of Tipperary blood and Ulster muscle. He made peace with the town and hurried back to England where a sympathetic contemporary wrote: 'Cromwell found at Clonmel the stoutest enemy his army had ever met with in Ireland, and never was seen so hot a storm of so long continuance and so gallantly defended, neither in England nor in Ireland.' The story would not lose in the telling and a couple of centuries afterwards a versifier related how the garrison promised themselves:

> Before we go we'll make the foe
> Remember rare Clonmel.

But within a few years broad Tipperary acres were allotted to hard-faced men with money and sharp swords. This was a more thorough conquest than ever before and unlike Norman times there was a religious difference to add to the other lines of division between the conquered and the conquerors.

Throughout the eighteenth and nineteenth centuries Tipperary was in the front line of agrarian protest, of resistance to government repression and of attempted revolution, so much so that someone — nobody knows who — said, 'Where Tipperary leads, Ireland follows', and the term 'the premier county' was born. The Young Ireland Rebellion of 1848 was largely a Tipperary affair and the Fenians, successors to the Young Irelanders, flourished in the county in the aftermath of the Great Famine. It was one of the leading Fenians, a man from Mullinahone close to the Kilkenny border, who became the county's laureate. Charles Kickham, half-blind and almost wholly deaf from an accident after a day's wildfowling near Slievenamon, was consumed with love for his native place and its people. This love was expressed in his monumental *Knocknagow — or the Homes of Tipperary* in which he created a whole range of characters whose counterparts might be met in any Tipperary townland and who became part of Tipperary mythology. Among the ballads in which this gentle revolutionary, who went to his grave without benefit of priest or preacher, expressed the depth of his love for his own place and his yearning for his country's freedom was one that in time would come to be regarded as the anthem of Tipperary

> Alone, all alone by the wave-washed strand,
> And alone in the crowded hall,
> The hall it is gay and the waves they are grand,
> But my heart is not here at all!
> It flies far away by night and by day,
> To the times and the joys that are gone!
> And I never can forget the sweet maiden I met,
> In the valley near Slievenamon.
>
> In the festive hall by the wave-washed shore,
> My restless spirit cries:
> 'My love, oh my love, shall I ne'er see you more?

And, my land, will you never uprise?'
By night and by day, I ever, ever pray,
While lonely my life flows on,
To see our flag unfurled and my true love to enfold
In the valley near Slievenamon.

Decades later young fellows would march to a foreign war singing, 'It's a long way to Tipperary', with its condescending references to Paddy and his Irish Molly-O. But for those who stayed at home the British marching song had associations they had chosen to forget. It was not the one with the reference to Tipperary but the one that carried the name of Slievenamon that would be adopted by the hordes who would follow the blue and gold, and it was to the strains of 'Slievenamon' that Tipperary skies would redden when red barrels were lit to welcome home the conquering heroes of Gaelic fields.

In an age when books were passed from hand to hand in a way that is not done today, Charles Kickham's *Knocknagow* was increasingly influential in moulding a popular view of Tipperary. Matt the Thresher was widely recognised as a prototype of splendid rural manhood and his determination to beat his military opponent in the sledge-throwing contest 'for the credit of the little village' came to be regarded not just in Tipperary but elsewhere as the ideal of sporting behaviour and motivation. When Matt the Thresher eyed Captain French's mighty throw of the sledge-hammer and was undecided whether he should, out of courtesy to the visitor to Knocknagow, allow himself to be beaten, he was roused to a determination to win only by a fierce loyalty to his community. As he stood, hammer in hand, torn by indecision, Kickham described how:

> Someone struck the big drum a single blow, as if by accident, and, turning round quickly, the thatched roofs of the hamlet caught his eye. And, strange to say, those old mud walls and thatched roofs roused him as nothing else could. His breast heaved, as, with glistening eyes, and that soft plaintive smile of his, he uttered the words, 'For the credit of the little village!' in a tone of the deepest tenderness. Then, grasping the sledge in his right hand, and drawing himself up to his full height, he measured the captain's cast with his eye. The muscles of his arms seemed to start out like cords of steel as he wheeled slowly round and shot the ponderous hammer through the air. His eyes dilated, as, with quivering nostrils, he watched its flight, till it fell

so far beyond the best mark that even he himself started with astonishment. Then a shout of exultation burst from the excited throng; hands were convulsively grasped, and hats sent flying into the air; and in their wild joy they crushed around him and tried to lift him upon their shoulders.

'Oh boys, boys,' he remonstrated, 'be easy. Sure 'tisn't the first time ye saw me throw a sledge. Don't do anything that might offend the captain after coming here among us to show ye a little diversion.' This remonstrance had the desired effect and the people drew back and broke up into groups to discuss the event more calmly.

'Donovan,' said Captain French, 'your match is not in Europe. I was never beaten before.'

'Well, it took a Tipperary man to beat you, Captain,' returned Matt Donovan.

'That's some consolation,' said the captain. 'I'm a Tipperary boy myself and I'm glad you reminded me of it.'

The model of the sporting hero was all there — the intense spirit of competitiveness, the determination to win for the right reason, the magnanimity in victory, the instinct of the gentleman, but above all the affection for his own place and people.

It would be easy to suggest that the organisation which Michael Cusack launched, as he himself said to 'bring back the hurling', held its initial meeting in Thurles because of the strength of the game in that area. There were other reasons in Cusack's head for suggesting, six months before the meeting took place, 'some central place in Tipperary' as the venue, not the least of these being concerned with geography and accessibility. There was also, of course, the consideration that Maurice Davin, the man he had in mind for the presidency of the organisation, was a Tipperary man. But the fact that Tipperary had not alone a considerable reputation in contemporary athletics, but was known as an area where the ancient game of hurling had survived strongly, almost certainly came into the reckoning.

In various parts of County Tipperary hurling was played and had an established place in local tradition before ever Cusack held his seminal meeting in Thurles on 1 November 1884. Edward Carson, that unlikely member of the Trinity College Hurley Club — which pre-dated the GAA — had learned his hurling in Ardmayle in the parish of Boherlahan and he was sufficiently adept in the use of the camán to

11

earn mention in reports of a couple of Trinity's matches. Captain Tom O'Grady, the colourful local hero whose leadership qualities in his own Moycarkey made him captain of one of the two hurling teams which participated in the 'invasion' of the United States in 1888, once declared, 'There was hurling in Moycarkey before Solomon built the temple.'

Whether hurling in Moycarkey and other places in Tipperary pre-dated Solomon may be open to question, but it is certain that there was a rich tradition of hurling in the county going back a very long way. Before the founding of the GAA the game was very much alive, if not exactly well, in numerous places in the county. Moycarkey, Thurles, Boherlahan, Clonoulty, Youghalarra, Toomevara, Lorrha and Portroe are mentioned among localities where hurling survived the catastrophe of the Great Famine. Within a year of the birth of the GAA no less than thirty-five clubs were listed in the county, the majority of them hurling clubs. 'If you want to see the new Ireland that has arisen, go and look at Tipperary and hear the big drums of Knocknagow', exulted Michael Cusack.

For the first inter-county game played by Tipperary in February 1886 — played in Dublin against south Galway — the county was represented by a team chosen solely from its northern end. But it was mid and south Tipp that provided the four teams which travelled to Cork for a monster tournament a few months later. In that first of the modern Tipp-Cork games Killenaule were beaten by Aghabullogue, but Holycross succeeded in beating St Finbarr's. It was agreed then that only one more game could be played and, while Thurles sat it out on the sideline, Moycarkey, inspired by the redoubtable Captain O'Grady, proceeded to save the prestige of Tipperary by providing a whirlwind finish to snatch victory against all odds over Cork Nationals.

Little could the participants have guessed that day that they were providing a headline for generations of Tipperary and Cork hurlers. When the Tipperary team arrived at Glanmire station they were greeted with scenes of the greatest excitement and they were played into the city and to the field by four bands. When the hostilities on the field had ended the visitors were once again royally treated by their hosts as if bone had not crunched against bone — or ash against bone — an hour previously.

'Well done, noble and gallant Moycarkey!' said Michael Cusack, but the real victory that day was with the infant organisation which had brought together Cork men and Tipperary men in a spirit of friendship and rivalry that would outlive all those who were there to witness the event.

It was not Moycarkey, however, but Thurles to whom fell the honour of representing Tipperary in the first All-Ireland championship. And though the Cork-Tipp rivalry commenced with the GAA itself, while the Tipp-Galway rivalry belongs to recent times, it was Galway whom Tipp beat in the first of the All-Ireland finals. Victory in the first hurling final by the town in which the GAA itself had been founded would give Thurles and Tipp a unique place in the story not only of the GAA, but of the game of hurling.

Though Tipperary won its first football title in 1889, it would not win its second hurling title until 1895; in that year it became the second county to win the hurling and football titles in the same year, Cork having done so in 1890. The team which represented Tipperary in 1895 was one of the most remarkable ever to grace the Gaelic arena. From the parish of Boherlahan on the road between Cashel and Thurles, the tiny townland of Tubberadora — the 'well of tears' which is linked with an old local tradition concerning St Brigid — put out a team which won the county championship of 1895, 1896 and 1898. Then, reinforced by a few players from the other end of Boherlahan parish and a few from neighbouring parishes, they went on to win the All-Irelands of those same years.

Led by the towering Mikey Maher, who played at centre-forward and who shares with Christy Ring and Kilkenny's Drug Walsh the distinction of captaining three All-Ireland winning teams, Tubberadora captured the imagination of the hurling public in a way that was not to be repeated until the advent of the Tullaroan and Mooncoin teams in the decades following. Much of the credit for the success of the wonderful combination was due to the leadership qualities of Maher himself; but it says much for their combined individual skills that a number of players, after the demise of Tubberadora, won All-Ireland honours with other Tipperary teams: one of them, Denis Walsh, figured in the Tipperary team which defeated Sim Walton's Kilkenny men in 1916 — twenty-one years after he had won his first All-Ireland.

When Tipperary, with teams drawn mainly from Moycarkey and Two-Mile-Borris, won the All-Ireland in 1898 and 1900, they

13

established a record in being the first to have won three in a row and to have won five in six years. Not until 1949–51 would the former achievement be repeated by the county, and never again the latter.

Tipperary entered the twentieth century, then, well in the lead on the list of national title-holders. But Jim Kelleher, the formidable Dungourney man, with his fine Cork stickmen, had arrived on one side and on the other Kilkenny, with the most star-studded team that would ever represent the county. It was six years before Tom Semple with his Thurles 'Blues' again raised the Tipperary banner at Jones's Road. They would appear in three All-Irelands, two of which they won — 1906 and 1908 — and the other they lost to Drug Walsh's great Kilkenny combination in 1909. Once again leadership qualities were an important factor in these Tipperary victories. Like Mikey Maher, Semple was a strikingly powerful and graceful figure who ruled his squad with an almost military insistence on discipline. He himself played at wing-back from where his long raking pucks were a torment to opposing backlines and from where his voice could be heard in every quarter of the field. Authority came naturally to him and twenty years later the manner in which he disposed stewards at a Munster final in Thurles was remarked upon, men rushing to do his bidding as he pointed with a stick to wherever order needed to be asserted. He did well to snatch two All-Irelands at a time when Kilkenny were on a rampage of unparalleled success, winning seven All-Irelands in nine years, with names that will be remembered as long as hurling is played — Graces and Doyles, Walton, Rochford, Gargan and others.

The next Tipp team to carry the banner to Croke Park (as Jones's Road was now called) came from the north-east end of the county, bounding on County Offaly. The Toomevara Greyhounds came at a time when Kilkenny were in the ascendant and, although they won everything else that was to be won, they were defeated in their only appearance in an All-Ireland final by Kilkenny. In his old age the legendary freedom fighter Dan Breen described how as a 19-year old he stood on the platform at then-Kingsbridge Station waving to the Tipp hurlers as they went home defeated, trying in vain to hold back his tears. Thirty-two years later, when the rest of the world was still preoccupied with the awful events at Hiroshima and Nagasaki which had just brought an end to the World War, he rushed a new set of jerseys to Tipperary so that they would not have to line out against

Kilkenny in the All-Ireland final in the tattered jerseys which war shortages had compelled them to wear since their last All-Ireland appearance in 1937.

It was unfortunate for the Greyhounds that they should arrive on the scene at the same time as another wonderful squad from the parish of Boherlahan. Johnny Leahy, son of one of Captain O'Grady's veterans and the eldest of five brothers, four of whom would win All-Irelands, had his first games in the county colours with Greyhound selections, but under him Boherlahan would replace Toomevara as the county's leading hurling parish. Under him, too, Tipperary would be kept firmly in the forefront of the national hurling scene. During the dozen years of Johnny Leahy's captaincy — like Captain O'Grady, he would carry the title Captain to the grave — Tipp would win five Munster titles and two All-Irelands. They fell to Galway in the semi-final in 1924, but their two All-Ireland final defeats — the first by Dublin in 1917 and the next by Dick Walsh's Kilkenny men in 1922 — were regarded as among the great hurling classics of the GAA's first half-century. In 1926 Tipp toured the United States in a six week tour that took them to the West Coast, and when they returned they played Cork three times for the Munster title. With men playing on both sides who had been comrades in the War of Independence, a new ingredient was thus added to the Cork-Tipp rivalry which had begun with the famous 1886 tournament.

In 1930 Tipp achieved the hitherto unknown feat of winning senior, junior and minor All-Irelands, and such was the jubilation within the county that a cash prize was offered for suitable verses to commemorate the event. But emerging on Shannon's banks was a crop of young hurlers who would for a number of years dazzle the hurling world with their brilliance. Mick Mackey and his men brought a new colour to hurling and a new type of forward play which the traditional type of Tipp backline could not handle. Nevertheless, while Limerick took five National Leagues and four Munster championships in a row, Tipp slipped in to surprise them in the 1937 Munster final and then went on to give Kilkenny a fearsome trouncing in the All-Ireland final played in Killarney. It was a victory which gave particular pleasure in Tipp, it being the fiftieth anniversary of the first All-Ireland which had been won by Jim Stapleton's Thurles men and, by coincidence, it was Thurles who again had the responsibility of selecting the Tipp team.

Eight years would pass before Tipperary returned to Croke Park and in between there were hard luck stories which became the stuff of folklore during the war years. In 1938 the county, although reigning champions, were ruled out of the Munster championship because one player — Colonel Jimmy Cooney — had played while under suspension for having attended a rugby game. In 1941 the county was again ruled out of the Munster championship because of foot and mouth disease regulations. Cork were nominated to represent Munster in the All-Ireland which they won by beating Dublin; but when the Munster final was played in October, Tipp beat the new All-Ireland champions 5-4 to 2-5. If it was a bad luck omen for Tipp, it was a good luck one for Cork; they went on to establish a new record by winning four All-Irelands in a row. By the time Tipp returned to beat Kilkenny in the first post-war All-Ireland final, the disgrace of not having won a title for eight years was held out as proof of the deterioration of the quality of manhood within the county. For many, the bad luck of the foot and mouth disease in 1941 was not an acceptable excuse for the longest absence of the county from an All-Ireland final in the history of the Association.

Holycross, in the dead centre of mid-Tipperary, won the county championship in 1948 to usher in another successful period. Abolished forever was the system of giving to the county champions the right to pick the county team and, with a new openness to players from less prominent clubs, the county set out on a winning streak which brought three All-Irelands in a row. It brought, too, a series of six-in-a-row enthralling championship games against Cork which between 1949 and 1954 added a fresh dimension to the old Cork-Tipp rivalry and created hitherto undreamed of attendance records. It brought, too, in the playing life of one Holycross man, John Doyle, eleven National League titles to the county.

Those were the years when Tipp teams, no matter how under strength, no matter how insignificant the occasion, were under instructions to win at all times. There was no such thing as a Tipp team that did not try.

Between two great years for Waterford, 1957 and 1959, Tipp took the All-Ireland of 1958 and then, with many new faces, they returned to Croke Park in 1960 for the first of seven All-Ireland final appearances in nine years. In four of these they would be winners. Those were the days of John and Jimmy Doyle, of Mick Roche and

Theo English, of Tony Wall, Donie Nealon and Babs Keating, of the 'hell's kitchen' backline and a forward line of six possible match winners. Those were the days when the trip to Croke Park in September became an annual pilgrimage for Tipperary supporters and one which gave others the impression that Tipp folk felt they had a divine right to be there. It was not that Tipp folk felt any such right. It was simply that they were there more frequently than anyone else. Tipp hurlers appreciated more than most that the ones with the right to advance to the next round were those who were ahead on the scoreboard when the final whistle blew. They had learned that lesson throughout many decades of experience.

When Tipp went to Croke Park to beat Kilkenny in the 1971 All-Ireland they again had many new faces. The old reliables, Babs Keating, Mick Roche and Len Gaynor were still there, but the bulk of the team were new to All-Ireland success. It seemed that the torch had passed to new hands as had happened so often in the past, and there were those who saw this as heralding a new period of Tipperary success.

It was indeed the beginning of a new period. But success . . ?

THE FAMINE, 1971–86

On the morning after Tipp beat Kilkenny in the All-Ireland of 1971, I drove from Clonmel to Nenagh, a journey of fifty miles that takes one through some of the towns and villages that are part of Tipperary's hurling tradition — Cashel, Boherlahan, Holycross, Thurles and Borrisoleigh, and the end of the parish of Toomevara. It was a beautiful sunny day and along the way, as the children waved their blue and gold flags from the car, people waved in return. An occasional house flew the blue and gold and here and there children shouted, 'Up Tipp!' as we passed. There was no sign of ungovernable excitement, just satisfaction at a job well done. The All-Ireland cup would be back in the county in the evening, as it had been on twenty-one previous occasions. By the following day the county would be well on the way back to normal. Yet there was a discernible difference from previous occasions, as if there was an unrealised consciousness that this would not happen for a long time again.

In the evening I returned to Thurles so that the children would see the team arriving on the Dublin–Cork train. Perhaps it wouldn't be convenient for me to come next year, I thought, or the year after. When the train pulled into the station there was appreciative applause and cheering from the small crowd that had gathered. The team climbed on to the back of a lorry and they were driven through the town to the Archbishop's residence to make the presentation of the cup and hear the traditional words of praise. If there were no scenes of frantic excitement, there was solid appreciation from those present. Many of them were hurling followers of long experience. They had seen teams come and go. They knew the short-cuts to all the great hurling venues; hurling was part of the fabric of their lives; the walk from Thurles station to the Archbishop's residence was a well-worn one for them.

Few could have forecast that night that almost a couple of decades would pass before the scene would be repeated, that the young boys waving their blue and gold flags would be in their mid-20's before the McCarthy Cup would pass that way again.

The famine did not happen suddenly and there was nothing to indicate that it was on the way. After coming back from a trip to San Francisco, where they had played the All-Stars in the spring of 1972, Tipp were beaten by Cork in a rousing game and again fell to Cork in the championship. But they returned in the autumn to beat Kilkenny and Wexford in turn for the county's eighth Oireachtas title. The county also won the last All-Ireland Intermediate hurling championship, beating Galway in the final, and Roscrea won the first ever All-Ireland club championship. There was no sign of a crack in the premier county's structures.

In the following year Tipp fielded with the legendary Jimmy Doyle in goal for the first round of the championship against Waterford. His inter-county hurling career had begun between the posts a long nineteen years before in the first of four All-Ireland minor appearances. Now, at the end of a brilliant career as a forward, he was back in the position from which he had started. It was the swansong of a man who had delighted a whole generation of Tipp followers as he was not retained for the next round against Cork, the regular goalkeeper of the time, Tadhg Murphy, having returned by then.

The Munster semi-final of 1973 was long remembered for the storming finish which depicted Tipperary hurling at its best. Cork appeared to have the game well in hand when, at the end of the hour, Tipp unleashed a hurricane of power which, beginning with a goal from John Flanagan, produced four goals in seven minutes to bring victory to Tipp at a time when even their most ardent supporters had given up the ghost. A Tipp follower who had suffered from the ribbing of Cork men during the game, as astonished as they were by the turnabout which left the scoreboard reading at the end Tipp 5-4 Cork 1-10, was heard to declare, 'That's the way to beat them. Give them a smell of it and take it away again.' For many it was the most satisfying victory of all in the ongoing Tipp-Cork saga and, had they been able to see into the future, their jubilation would have been even greater. Many in the crowd would never again see Tipp beat Cork — or anyone else for that matter — in a championship game. That result would not be repeated until the glorious July day in Killarney in 1987.

The Munster final at Thurles, too, was of epic quality. Tipp were leading by four points at half-time, but in an utterly thrilling second half Limerick went ahead. In the last minute fair-haired John Flanagan fired over the equalising point from midfield, but Limerick came at them again and forced a 70. The referee told Limerick's Richie Bennis that he must score directly as time was up and, as one Babs Keating walked past to take up his position facing the free-taker, legend has it that a quick bet was offered against a score. Whether or not, over 40,000 hearts missed a beat as the Patrickswell sharpshooter stooped and drove over the bar for the winning point for Limerick. With that one calculating strike, Bennis effectively won Limerick's 7th All-Ireland title and their joy in the achievement was not begrudged in Tipperary. A county with twenty-two All-Irelands behind it could afford to be magnanimous in defeat. Over the next fourteen years that magnanimity would be worn thin and the characteristics of habitual champions would be eroded.

When Tipp got a bye in the first round of the Munster championship in 1974 and found themselves facing Clare in Limerick, there was a feeling that whoever presented them with problems, it would not be Clare. They had performed well in the League and had been unlucky not to have beaten Limerick. Waterford had caused a sensation in their first round by defeating Cork who had beaten Limerick 6-15 to 1-12 in the League final only a few weeks earlier. All in all, things looked well for Tipp. But such confidence proved ill founded. Tipp performed abysmally and Clare, seizing their opportunity, defeated them by a single point: 1-8 to 1-7. And with that game may be considered the beginning of the famine years for Tipperary. Clare were hammered by Limerick who, in turn, were beaten by Kilkenny.

Ten years would elapse before Tipp won another senior championship game. It was an intolerable deprivation for a county which, since the founding of the GAA, had never failed to win at least one All-Ireland in every decade. The 1970s was saved from total disgrace by a victory in the first year of the decade and the 1980s would be saved by a victory in the last year. In between lay the bleak years of the famine.

Even with the benefit of hindsight it is very difficult to explain the reason for Tipp's failure during those years. It can hardly be said that there was a dearth of hurling enthusiasm in the county. Three times during this worst of all possible periods the county's minors and four times the under-21's won the All-Ireland. Even the seniors were not entirely without achievement, since they won the League in 1979. But expectations are always high in Tipperary. Other achievements are fine as long as they are fronted by the only achievement that really counts — winning the McCarthy Cup.

There were times when Tipp were tantalisingly close to success. In 1976, with Cork goalkeeper Martin Coleman wrong-footed, Seamus Power unleashed a thunderbolt that went off the wrong side of the goalpost. In 1979 rising Tipp star Pat O'Neill steadied himself out on the wing and sent goalward a shot that would have drawn with Cork; it went straight as an arrow only to tail off wide in its final yards of flight. Three times they drew — in 1975 with Limerick, in 1977 with Clare and in 1981 with Limerick — but they lost all three replays. There was a formidable list of might-have-beens, but these are the memories of losers. In times past there were victories to balance the near-misses, and there were victories which were achieved at the expense of near-misses by opponents. It is only with congenital losers that the best memories that can be summoned up are of might-have-beens.

So Tipp staggered along from championship defeat to championship defeat through the 1970s and 1980s. As the gap widened and the memories of victories receded, a note of near-hysteria entered into arguments on the situation. Discussions were held by the County Board — on one occasion two hours were set aside at a meeting to discuss the deterioration — by divisional boards, by club committees, and weird and wonderful remedies were suggested. Frustrated followers voiced their feelings in the letter columns of local papers and sports journalists found in the decline of the premier county a never-failing subject when another few hundred words were needed to fill out a column. One letter-writer to the *Tipperary Star* called for mass meetings 'in halls in towns and villages to see how we the supporters could contribute to the return of Tipperary to its former glory'.

From Christy Ring, the man who had done so much to deprive Tipperary of additional honours, came an expression of regret which, more than any at the time, tugged at the heartstrings of older Tipp followers: 'The GAA without Tipperary is only half dressed.' The greatest hurler of all appreciated that the game of hurling could not afford to lose Tipperary from its front ranks. Nobody had been more often at the receiving end of Tipperary brawn — and occasionally Tipperary ash — and nobody revelled more in the peculiar fire that Tipp-Cork clashes can spark. Paradoxically, nobody had closer friends among the hurling fraternity in Tipperary than he. He was a frequent caller to the home of his old opponent Tommy Doyle in Thurles and roadworkers on the main Cork–Dublin road near Horse and Jockey told of how they once saw a familiar figure kneeling at the grave of the Tipp wing-back Tommy Purcell, at the time dead for nearly thirty years. It was the once-dreaded wizard of Cloyne who, on a far-off day in 1945, had been held by the fair-haired Purcell when Cork were stopped on their march to five All-Irelands in a row.

At every meeting of Cork-Tipp veterans there were worried enquiries, 'When will ye be back?' And if Cork veterans could mourn for Tipp's apparent demise, what was it like for the county's own veterans? At funerals, which tend to be the focal points for gatherings of old hurlers, the reaction changed from one of mild amusement to despair. Some eventually dropped the sardonic 'Will we see them win one before we die?' as the years passed and it was felt to be getting too near the bone. A universal gloom descended which was not in any way alleviated by minor and under-21 successes. The failure was underscored by television which, while bringing to the older generation the previously unimaginable luxury of allowing them a front row seat at big games, never showed our own lads for the simple reason that our own lads never got far enough to merit notice on television. For the first time in a century Tipperary was one of hurling's poorer relations.

In 1979 Tipp emerged from Division 2 to win the League for the first time since 1968 but, as if to belie raised expectations, they went down to Cork in the first round of the championship, Pat O'Neill's last-minute near-miss possibly giving Tipp's performance a colour it did not deserve. It was four more years before they won their first championship game in a decade by defeating Clare by three points in 1983. The kiss of life lasted for only three weeks for they were defeated by Waterford in the next round.

As the celebrations to mark the GAA's Centenary Year in 1984 loomed ahead, a new spirit of resolution seemed to take hold in the county. Semple Stadium had been developed at huge cost in terms of money and effort and the GAA had shown a commendable desire to remain in touch with its roots by agreeing that the All-Ireland Hurling final would be played there. Through the county there spread the feeling that a year in which there was so much talk of tradition was the ideal time for a Tipp comeback, and if tradition was to count for anything at all the hurlers would rise to the challenge by contesting the Centenary All-Ireland on their own ground. They nearly did.

The 1984 Munster final will be remembered as one of the great hurling games of recent times. Tipp had given indications of being ready to claw their way upwards again by beating Clare in the semi-final into which a lucky draw had given them a bye. But it was more in hope than expectation that they lined out against Cork at Semple Stadium. The backbone of Cork's team had already played in two All-Irelands; only one of Tipp's team, Noel O'Dwyer, had ever played even in a Munster final. Nevertheless, as if drawing strength from the 50,000-plus crowd, the great majority of whom were home supporters, Tipp turned on a display which was reminiscent of the county's great days and which brought them tantalisingly close to victory. All the dreams were on the verge of realisation with five minutes to go and Tipp four points ahead. Then disaster struck to rob Tipp of victory. John Fenton pointed a free and a minute later Tony O'Sullivan was on the spot to ram home a rebound from goalkeeper John Sheedy's save of what seemed an unstoppable shot from Pat Hartnett. Incredibly, the sides were level. Then big Michael Doyle soloed in from the new stand side at the Killinan end and, with the option either to take a point or keep going and hope to be fouled, he chose neither but instead palmed to Nicholas English. There was a flash of magic and Denis Mulcahy was there to intercept and belt upfield a ball which, by all the laws known to hurling gods, should now have been nestling in the Cork net. The clearance went to the unmarked Tony O'Sullivan who drove low for a point — low enough for John Sheedy to hurl himself aloft and save what would otherwise have been the winning score.

Fifteen minutes previously Tipp captain Bobby Ryan had gone off injured and Seamus Power of Boherlahan, bred of two generations of All-Ireland winners, who was having such a thundering game at full-forward that his marker Donal O'Grady had been withdrawn, was brought back to left corner-back. It proved a disastrous move by Tipp.

Now Seanie O'Leary, another man in whose veins ran the blood of All-Ireland winners, was loitering with intent outside the Tipp square and when he read Sheedy's decision to pull down the point he saw his opportunity. Like a flash he was under the ball as it hit the ground off Sheedy's hurley and before the crowd understood what was happening it was in the net. From the puckout John Fenton pointed a free and a lead of four points to Tipp was thus converted in the space of five minutes into a deficit of four points. This time the Cork men were even more astounded, if such were possible, than the Tipp supporters.

But as the Tipp supporters stood around, struck speechless by the turnabout, even those who had been most sanguine before the game had to admit that this had not been famine fare. There had been a touch of old times about the entire proceedings and in a sense mutual Cork-Tipp respect had been restored. Cork went on to win the coveted Centenary Year All-Ireland, but they knew that the hardest challenge they had met had been in Thurles on 15 July.

By beating Galway, Tipp won the Centenary Cup competition which was continued in 1985 as the Ford Open Draw. But championship success was what was needed and they didn't get it. They drew with Clare and won the replay, thus making it three championship defeats of Clare in a row. Once again they perished in Pairc Ui Chaoimh at the hands of Cork and when they went out against Clare in the championship of the following year, any idea they might have had that meetings with Clare might be taken for granted were demolished at Ennis. On a day which would be remembered as one of the worst of the famine years, Clare pulled back a half-time deficit of seven points and sent Tipp home dumbfounded by a two point defeat. Following on a miserable League performance, there were those who felt that the blinds might be drawn again on Tipp hurling for some time to come.

ALONG CAME BABS

Faced throughout the early 1980s with the spectacle of minor and under-21 All-Ireland successes side by side with the failure of their seniors, Tipperary turned its attention to the matter of its selectors. As defeat followed defeat and frustrations multiplied, it was inevitable that a portion of the blame should land at the feet of those with responsibility for picking the team.

Until as late as 1948 the tradition of the senior team being picked by a committee comprised of the county secretary plus four represent-atives of the club which had won the county championship the previous year had survived in the county. This was, of course, a throwback to the early days of the Association when the county team would in fact be composed chiefly of members of the winning club, strengthened by the addition of a few guest players from other clubs. This system having served well, it didn't strike anyone that there might be one that would work even better until, with the advent of Holycross as county champions in 1948, it was decided to change. The new system that was introduced was a selection committee of five, two of whom would be from the county champions' club. It produced the goods in terms of All-Ireland and League successes and, consequently, never came under public scrutiny. It was only when the bacon was no longer being brought home that the selection process came under severe examination and pressure.

There had been a tradition in Tipperary from the beginning of involving past players as selectors. Big Mikey Maher, Tom Semple, Johnny Leahy, Jim Lanigan — all captains of All-Ireland winning teams — had helped bring other teams to All-Ireland honours. In the 1950s the names of selectors would have been well known as past players — county secretary Phil Purcell, John Joe Callanan of Thurles, John Joe Hayes of Moycarkey, Martin Kennedy of Toomevara, Paddy Leahy of Boherlahan and so on. The last mentioned of these, a veteran of the 1916 and 1925 All-Ireland winning teams, having first become a selector in 1949, became chairman of the selection committee in the 1950s and by the time of his death in 1966 had been part of eight All-Ireland victories and eleven National Leagues. He had a reputation as an expert in the handling of players and as an astute matchplay tactician, but in an age when there was deference to age and experience, the fact that a couple of generations separated him from the players under his control was probably to his advantage. He was 76 at the time of his death and was involved with the Tipp team to within months of his end.

This custom of finding selectors from among the ranks of past players continued into the famine years and among those who served on selection committees at different times during that period were some of the great names of Tipp's hurling story — Pat Stakelum, Tony Wall, John Doyle, Paddy Kenny, Len Gaynor, John Kelly, Ray Reidy and Liam King. With repeated failures creating a mood in which any new idea would be entertained, the experiment was tried during the 1981–82 season of giving the entire responsibility of selecting the team over to those selectors who had been successful in winning All-Irelands with under-21 teams. This neither produced the goods nor inspired confidence and was terminated after a single year.

When Tony Wall was introduced as coach after the disastrous summer of 1985 it was widely believed that Tipp had the answer to all its problems. Many would still consider him the greatest centre-back the game of hurling has produced. He had been very much in contention in 1984 when hurling followers around the country aired their opinions as to who should be included in the 'team of the century'. Four other Tipp men had been selected for the final honour — Tony Reddan, John Doyle, Jimmy Finn and Jimmy Doyle — but it was widely recognised that Wall's claim had been a challenging one. He had been not alone a hurler's hurler but a thinking man's hurler and he had written one of the most authoritative books on the skills of the game. He was now a senior army officer, accustomed by training and experience to handling men. He seemed to be the ideal man for the task of retrieving Tipp's fortunes and when he agreed to take the job of coach a great sigh of relief went up through the county.

The experiment did not work instantly and, by now impatient with anything short of instant success, the County Board and its chairman, Michael Lowry, turned to a Heffo-Mick O'Dwyer style of management. The man they chose was Babs Keating and they gave him the right to choose two selectors to help him.

On the road from Clonmel to Ardfinnan, Clogheen and what is now known with tongue in cheek as Ronald Regan country is the rich farmland of Grange which was home to Michael 'Babs' Keating. It was not an area in which hurling was seriously played and the only local hero of real proportions was Tommy Ryan of Castlegrace, a granduncle of Babs, who had won a football All-Ireland with Tipp and had played on Bloody Sunday when his team mate Mick Hogan and thirteen spectators had been shot by British forces in Croke Park. Tommy Ryan was also a legendary figure in the War of Independence and such were his qualities of character and his ability to forget old wounds that in later life Dan Breen and others who had fought against him in the Civil War were among his closest friends.

In school in Grange there were three Michael Keatings and, in order to differentiate between the three, the teacher called the eldest Benny and the youngest of the three, Babs. The name stuck and by the time he moved to secondary school in Clonmel he was known even in family circles by the nickname. It was this same teacher, Kerry man Paid O'Shea, who introduced hurling in a serious way to a locality where football had previously been the principal game, and it flourished to such an extent that the youngsters contested an under-14 county final. But football had been Babs' first game and it was not until he went to secondary school in Clonmel that he was made to change his hurling grip to the orthodox right-over-left. He was a natural ball player, with the swerve of the complete footballer and the wrist action of the born hurler. He would play both hurling and football in all grades for Tipperary and by the time he was out of minor grade he had played in and lost three All-Irelands. He went on to win All-Ireland medals in intermediate, under-21 and senior hurling grades (3). He won Railway Cup medals in both hurling and football, played on Munster football teams over ten years and Munster hurling teams over five years. He played in every single position in the forward line for Tipp, was on the first Carrolls All-Stars selection in 1971 and in that same year he won the Texaco 'Hurler of the Year' award.

Coming from an area which had not been in the habit of producing sporting heroes of these dimensions, Babs was early on regarded in his own place as something of a folk hero and over the years this was the image that spread through the rest of the county. He was the original 'broth of a boy', always newsworthy, as likely to sink a birdie putt on the 18th as he was to split the net with a 14 or a 21 in the last few minutes of a game. He had a polite interest in horses and dogs and there were occasions when his 'flutters' were the subject of admiring whispers. He was a successful businessman who always seemed to have time for the things which interested him. He was a modern sporting figure rather than of the traditional cut. He belonged in the fast lane; he was a born winner and he carried excitement with him.

He was exactly what Tipp needed after all the drab years of dull despair — someone who radiated colour and who couldn't but know what he was about. He hadn't been particularly successful as manager of Galway in 1979 but that was Galway.

With Tipp, as with every other county, the financing of the county team had always been a problem. In the old days when National Leagues came almost with the regularity of late spring, the senior team could always be depended upon to pay its way. But those days had gone and Tipp had never quite adjusted to the expectations of a new breed of player. As soon as Babs arrived there was talk of money and it was not of tapping traditional sources. Gone were the days of church gate collections and their associations with backside-to-the-ditch dressing rooms and meat teas after games. When there was talk of Babs introducing a new style, what was meant was style. There was mention of foreign trips, of sponsored golf outings and sponsored horse racing. There were raffles, sponsored photographs and sponsored calendars. Commercial concerns which had never before opened their coffers to Tipp or any other hurling team were brought into the net and Babs figured as much in fund-raising activities as on the training pitch. If it took money to put Tipp back on the hurling map, then money had to be collected and there were times when people wondered how one man could stand the strain of the mixed demands of fund-raising and team management — and at the same time discharge the duties of his senior executive position with Esso.

In his launching of the Supporters Club, Babs introduced what was to be the most controversial of his fund-raising enterprises. Harnessing the goodwill and the financial possibilities of Tipp folk who would not normally be involved in GAA affairs and who mainly lived outside the county, he provided a financial pool which would bear the burden of the cost of treating the team in the style which he considered their due. The Supporters Club in turn got less credit than was their due and when the financial support had come to be taken for granted there were complaints about the high profile which the organisation was given in team affairs. Particular exception was taken to the appearance of prominent members of the Supporters Club in the dressing room and dugout on big occasions — an intrusion which traditionalists found hard to take, though nobody complained about the financial support.

From the point of view of the players, the advent of Babs as manager was a godsend. There had never been a time when being on a county panel did not carry its own prestige, but now there were the trimmings to suit that prestige. If Babs was not one to throw tradition out the window for the sake of exercise, neither was he one to be tied to traditional patterns of behaviour in handling teams. There appeared a sartorial elegance that had not always been evident with previous teams and money became no object where the general treatment of players was concerned.

If the choice of Babs as manager had been slowly arrived at, in giving him the right to choose his own selectors Tipp's County Board had given him the ultimate vote of confidence. It was one thing to make him manager; it was quite another to hand over the selection of the team entirely to him. But his choice of co-selectors could not have been better calculated to allay disquiet. Both of his choices had shown management skills with club teams. Both had impeccable hurling credentials. Both were nationally known as former hurling stars. Theo English and Donie Nealon needed no introduction to hurling followers anywhere.

Theo, like Babs himself, came from an area which had no great hurling tradition behind it, but by earnest endeavour and by his own personal commitment to sharpening his hurling skills he had become one of the great midfield players of his time. A stocky man of medium height, he won an All-Ireland junior title in 1953 and in the following year appeared at midfield on the senior team which won the League and went down to Cork after a brilliant display by Christy Ring in the Munster final. He maintained his place at midfield until, several Leagues and All-Ireland medals later, he appeared in his last major game with the county in the All-Ireland final of 1967. Few players in the history of the association have played in the demanding midfield spot over such a long period at such a high level. He never drank and he himself would be the first to admit that much of the secret of his survival lay in maintaining a superlative level of personal fitness and in 'letting the ball do the work' on the field. He had lots of experience in handling teams and he had been a selector at the time of Tipp's last All-Ireland win in 1971. Like Babs, he was known to be fond of a flutter on the horses and Babs' choice of him as a selector was widely approved.

Donie Nealon had already been involved in coaching and selecting Tipp teams, but it was as a flashing forward in the 60s that he was known to hurling men everywhere. He was the purest type of forward, possessing a lightning sprint and all the skills, with a first-class hurling brain. Like his fellow mentors, he had a pocketful of All-Ireland medals and in his long playing career he had never as much as been warned for any unsporting behaviour. Hurling was his entire life, and the fact that he was secretary of the Munster Council was not seen by him as an obstacle to serving his county as a mentor. To many it seemed that if this new set of mentors could not come up with the goods for Tipp, nobody could.

But whatever the qualifications of those he had selected to help him carry the burden of Tipperary's ambitions, it was Babs himself who would carry the major share of the load. He was the one in the public eye. 'Babs can do it' was the heading of an article in the *Tipperary GAA Yearbook* by Liz Howard in which the immediate task of the new team was spelled out as gaining promotion from Division 2 of the League. Other good things would follow.

THE ROAD TO KILLARNEY, 1987

The measure of mild excitement which greeted Tipp's promotion from Division 2 of the League is a measure of the fall in Tipp's self-esteem over the years of defeat. 'Mission accomplished! Barring an unthinkable slip against Mayo on Sunday week, Tipperary are back among hurling's elite in Division 1 of the National Hurling League', trumpeted the *Tipperary Star* in its report of Tipp's victory over Waterford in February 1987. Tipp had already beaten Antrim, Kerry, Meath and Dublin and had sustained a thumping eight points defeat at the hands of a Laois team trained by the Tipp maestro Jimmy Doyle. The unimaginable defeat by Mayo did not materialise and Babs' first obstacle had been overcome.

Moving up among 'hurling's elite' for their quarter-final draw with Limerick, Tipp discovered the difference between Division 1 and Division 2 in a bone-crunching game which Nicholas English turned into a draw with a point well into injury time. An interesting situation had arisen when Limerick's Jimmy Carroll was sent to the line in the second half for a foul on Michael Scully who was stretchered off. But Tipp had already used up their three subs, so that the Limerick man's dismissal merely left both sides with fourteen men.

It was the first of Tipp's many draws of the year and when the two teams resumed after ten minutes' rest for an extra thirty minutes, spectators realised that teams are not quite ready in mid-April for that kind of physical endurance test. Tipp increased their lead by seven points, but in the second half of extra time Limerick drew level. The last four minutes of the game was a struggle to see which side would crack and when Pat Fox grabbed a Tipp puckout and, having made about twenty yards, shot over the bar, it was all over. Tipp had beaten Limerick for the first time in a knockout game since the 1971 Munster final in Killarney. But lest the event would go to anybody's head, Babs made it immediately clear that while Tipp would do their best, injuries notwithstanding, in the League semi-final against Clare the following Sunday, the championship was the real target.

It was as well that Babs had entered reservations. Still the worse for wear after the encounter with Limerick, Tipp, short Nicholas English and Richard Stakelum who were still nursing injuries, went down the following Sunday by 2-11 to 1-11 to a Clare team that went on to lose to Galway in the League final. It was a disappointment, but Tipp's confidence was still rising and there was a feeling abroad that this was no more than a temporary setback.

By the time Tipp lined out against Clare again in the championship it was realised that the League defeat had been a blessing in disguise. Famine years apart, championship meetings with Clare tended to be regarded in Tipp with not quite the same degree of seriousness as meetings with Cork or Limerick. The League defeat was precisely what was needed to put Tipp on guard and in the proper frame of mind for the championship meeting.

But before they met, Tipp had to dispose of Kerry and, if they did it in a manner that looked convincing on the scoreboard (1-21 to 2-6), it was less convincing in reality. So much so that after the game Babs was able to tell the Kerry team, 'Ye scared the living daylights out of us.' The Killarney venue had a significance, however, which would become apparent later.

They came back to Killarney to play Clare with a team which, as soon as it was announced, caused not a little controversy. Bobby Ryan, All-Star half-back of the previous year, was placed at full-forward and, with Noel Sheehy sidelined by injury, two new half-backs, John Kennedy and Paul Delaney, were introduced. In the event, though, Bobby failed to function as was hoped in the unaccustomed position and was substituted. There could be no complaints at all about the new-look half-back line and Delaney in particular gave promise of great things to come.

Just as in Ennis the previous year Tipp almost left it after them. Chances were missed by forwards, backs were lucky in their escapes and even when playing against fourteen men in the last quarter, Clare man Tommy Guilfoyle having been put off for a second-warning offence, they still could not put Clare away. Then in the dying seconds of the game, with Tipp leading by three points, Clare sub Leo Quinlan centred for corner-forward Gerry McInerney to ram home the equaliser and send both teams home dissatisfied with their display but relieved to have qualified for another meeting.

When they met in Killarney again a fortnight later the Tipp line-out had become roughly as it would be familiar to hurling followers for a while to come: Ken Hogan in goal; John Heffernan, Conor O'Donovan and Seamus Gibson; Richard Stakelum, John Kennedy and Paul Delaney; Colm Bonnar and Joe Hayes; Gerry Williams, Donie O'Connell and Aidan Ryan; Pat Fox, Bobby Ryan and Nicholas English. Joe Hayes was brought in instead of John McGrath of Borrisoleigh at centre-field on the basis of performance in practice games and form in training.

If Clare were a mere shadow of the team which played in the drawn game, Tipp made everyone's dreams come true. With all the controversial placings working out, the game was a triumph for the Tipp selectors. It was only two minutes old when Bobby Ryan picked a ball which had been kicked into his path by Donie O'Connell and raced towards goal avoiding the hook from behind and driving low to the net. And Joe Hayes, who would not have been everyone's choice at centre-field, didn't put a foot wrong.

The trouble with a cricket-score victory is that it is of benefit to nobody and is all too often not a true reflection of real ability either of winners or losers. Winners play above themselves, their weaknesses do not show up, and losers do not rise to their real ability. In this case it gave Tipp a feeling of superiority that would do them no good when they came up against Cork. Such was the self-confidence now felt that Babs expressed his preference to meet Cork in the Munster final. And Cork duly obliged by winning their replay against Limerick in much the same fashion as Tipp had won theirs against Clare. The game was effectively dead by half-time and was made memorable only by the classic ground stroke which John Fenton hit from near midfield to the Limerick net. For those traditionalists who lament the disappearance of ground hurling it demonstrated that the real top quality players can play ground hurling whenever there is an advantage in doing so.

The Limerick-Cork replay had necessitated the postponement of the Munster final, with the result that tension and excitement mounted over a longer than usual period in Tipperary. Cork were going for an unprecedented six-in-a-row Munster championships; Tipp, now the poor relations of hurling, had not won one for sixteen years. Not one player of the entire Tipp panel had ever won a senior Munster championship. The nearest any of them had come to a Munster final victory was that exciting but disastrous day in 1984 when Cork's Seanie O'Leary had shown them that a game is never won until the final whistle. But confidence was evident in the words of the *Tipperary Star* columnist Culbaire, who had himself been a goalkeeper for Tipp in its great days, who found encouragement even in the inexperience of the Tipp side. In his widely read and authoritative column he remarked: 'We have several new players. This can be a beneficial element — inexperience means lack of acquaintance with losing to Cork. One thinks here of Heffernan, Delaney, Kennedy, Stakelum, Hayes, Bonnar.' In other words, their lack of experience of the power of Cork might help to steady them. If they knew Cork better, they might be unnerved.

In the meantime the excitement grew with every day. Tipperary emigrants suddenly discovered that they would be better off to take their annual holidays in July; Thurles battened down the hatches for the greatest influx of visitors since the All-Ireland in 1984 and Babs appealed to the general public to stop badgering the players for tickets and let them concentrate their minds on the game itself. For the Tipp supporters this had all the ingredients of a classic game.

It has become fashionable in recent times to play down Munster hurling and to assert that there is nothing special about Tipp-Cork meetings. That may be so, depending on one's point of view and on one's purpose in making the assertion. But for Tipp and Cork folk whose first allegiance in games is to hurling there is nothing quite like Cork-Tipp encounters. Other pairings may produce more exciting clashes and even better hurling on occasion, but the anticipation leading up to a Cork-Tipp championship meetings and the consistent quality of these encounters stand apart. Tipp bring the best out of Cork and vice versa and if there are occasional recriminations after a game, they are usually not of much consequence. There is a general acceptance that, in the normal course of things, if luck or a referee's lapse favours one side this year, the reverse may happen next time around.

When Cork travelled to Thurles to play Tipp on 12 July 1987 the two counties were meeting for the fourteenth time in a Munster final in forty years. If one were to add semi-final and first-round meetings, one would be talking of something like a million spectators who in that period alone saw the two counties clash.

The crowd of 60,000 which gathered at Semple Stadium on 12 July was not entirely unexpected and if Cork were represented in force, the great majority of those present were from Tipp. A measure of the enthusiasm in Tipperary was that training sessions by the Tipp squad for some time past had been watched by crowds as large as attended many club games. But even an infrastructure which had dealt efficiently with the All-Ireland final of 1984 was put under some strain by the volume of the attendance on this occasion. Before the game there was an incident in which a detective, confronted by a crowd attempting to break down a gate, drew a revolver and pointed it in their direction. That, it seems, ended the problem at that particular point.

What the huge crowd saw has regrettably been overshadowed in popular lore by the events at Killarney a week later. However, the contest that unfolded on 12 July does not deserve to be forgotten. It provided hurling of the highest standard usually to be expected from the two counties. The game might well have gone down as a classic had it not been followed so quickly by the epic Killarney contest.

But Tipp again nearly left it behind them, so that once more as their followers left the ground many of them were pleased enough that they were 'getting another day out of them'. When they had been drawn to meet Kerry in the first round at Killarney there were those who decided that, in the circumstances, undertaking the long journey was justified because it might be the only way that 'we'd get the second day out of them'. Thus, even with the feeling that they should have beaten Cork, there was an undoubted pleasure in having seen a display that was worthy of champions By the time affairs in Munster were concluded they would have got five days in all.

From the beginning it was evident that a classic was in the making, with Cork's craft and experience not quite matching the sheer enthusiasm with which Tipp went about reversing the trend of recent history. John Kennedy was at times majestic at centre-back and Donie O'Connell at centre-forward played the bustling game which so often proved upsetting against Cork backs. In the middle of the field Joe Hayes personified the commitment of the entire team, and Ken Hogan in goal was an inspiration to those outfield.

But enthusiasm is not always enough and by half-time Tipp, with a lead of 0-11 to 0-7, did not have nearly enough on the board to reflect their share of the ball — and they would be playing against a slight breeze in the second half. Soon after half-time Ken Hogan set Tipp hearts aglow with a wonderful and utterly vital save from Kieran Kingston, a feat he would later repeat when John Fitzgibbon tried his hand. But every lapse on the part of Tipp's backs was punished by

John Fenton's never-more-accurate stick. At the finish he would have raised no less than twelve white flags.

For many, a game may be lighted up by a single incident which, when all other details are forgotten, is remembered in its every movement. Such an incident occurred half-way through the second half and it would be played over and over that summer on television replays and on videos. Tipp were hanging on to a four point lead when Nicholas English, now at full-forward, suddenly appeared behind full-back Richard Browne, without a hurley and with the ball at his feet. He was in the habit of practising control of a sliotar with his feet and now all he had ever learned came to him in one magical moment. Ger Cunningham had only a second to assess the situation; perhaps if he had remained on his line, his chance of saving would have been considerably better. But having committed himself, he had to stay coming. English, too, had only a second to assess the situation and, with Cunningham on his way, he side-footed the ball past him to the net. It was a goal in a thousand; it was the stuff of Maradonna and Mikey Sheehy; and it confirmed English in his role of new superstar. It put Tipp seven points ahead.

They needed every one of those points. Three soft frees were sent over by John Fenton; Tony O'Sullivan and Teddy McCarthy had points; Kieran Kingston blazed to the net and John Fenton pointed again to put Cork two points ahead. Tipp heads were down and it seemed that the bad old days were back. How was it that in recent years Tipp seemed utterly incapable of holding a lead in the closing minutes? The ghosts of 1984 had all become real again.

But only the heads beyond the sidelines were down; on the field the battle still raged in all its fury. With a minute left and the Tipp crowd shouting at him to drop it in the square, Pat Fox calmly drove a free over the bar. A second later Nicholas English gained possession and in rounding Browne was fouled. Again Fox stood over the ball, and now the crowd were glad he had not taken their advice with the previous one. From a comfortable position he had no difficulty sending it over the bar, and the game was over. Tipp had brought their supporters from ecstasy to despair, to elation. They had not won but they had shown they could have and there would be another day. Not that having another day would be good enough anymore. By this time the expectations of Tipp's supporters were on a grand scale.

They would go to Killarney for the replay with Cork and when they did, things would never be the same again. This would be their fourth time within a few weeks playing in Fitzgerald Stadium. But after this next time, the very name of Killarney would have magical connotations. And they would be coloured in blue and gold.

Chapter Six

THE EUPHORIA REMAINED, 1987

It is difficult for anybody who did not share the Tipp triumphs of the 1960s and the despair of the famine years to understand the kind of excitement that was generated by the recovery of the Munster crown. Somebody said that in the weeks that followed it was difficult to find a field without a youngster hurling in it. For several weeks an entire county was on a high that is normally associated with the morning after an All-Ireland win by counties not used to winning them.

When the team stepped off the train at Nenagh station on Monday evening they were met by a huge crowd led by local political figures and they were played to Banba Square to hear speeches that would become more than a little familiar over the next few years. At Ballyroan Bridge outside Borrisoleigh, which locals liked to think one had to cross if in search of 'a horse, a dog or a man', the Sean Treacy pipe band and several thousand well-wishers had gathered to escort the conquering heroes into the village to hear further speeches. Bonfires blazed from the hills to mark the return of excitement to the lives of people who regarded hurling as more than just a game.

It took a while, understandably, for cold reason to reassert itself and for the mind to be concentrated on the All-Ireland semi-final against Galway. Even in the most enthusiastic moments of the post-Killarney euphoria, Babs, from early age no stranger to winning, had made an attempt to focus attention on what lay ahead. The first training session for the Galway game took place on the Wednesday evening following Killarney, while the stars were still in some players' eyes and certainly in lots of supporters'. The rest of the training sessions would be watched by hundreds who became experts on the current form of every member of the panel. It was just like old times.

As a result of Tipp's failure to perform in championships, the paths of Tipp and Galway had not crossed often over a long period of years and the knife-edged rivalry between them which was to give colour to hurling over the next few years was still in the future. In 1979 Tipp had demolished the westerners in the League final only to fail again at the first hurdle of the Munster championship. Babs was well acquainted with Galway's fortunes, since it was he who was brought in as Galway manager after that defeat in an attempt to put the western county back on the map. He met with some success in that they succeeded in beating Cork in the All-Ireland semi-final, only to fall to Kilkenny in the final. And Galway were now League champions.

It certainly was like old times in Croke Park on 9 August 1987 and commentators were moved to comment on the size of the crowd — a near record — and on the degree of excitement not normally associated with hurling semi-finals. There had been good-humoured traffic signs along the way in County Kilkenny pointing the way to Croke Park for a generation of Tipp youngsters who had not been there before and in a television interview immediately before the game Kieran Brennan, the Kilkenny star, reminded viewers of the daunting experience of stepping on to Croke Park for a team who were unused to such occasions. It was a factor which those on the stands and the terraces could hardly be expected to appreciate.

The proceedings commenced on an eminently happy note for Tipp supporters who were given a much-appreciated pipe-opener by their minors who pounded Galway into the ground in a 4-12 to 1-9 victory in the curtain-raiser. Less will do us in the senior game, said the wits. The seniors scored almost as much — only a point less — but it was not enough.

The game was less than a minute old when Tipp were given a stunning reminder of the kind of powerhouse they were up against. Nicholas English put over a left-handed point from out on the wing within nine seconds of the start, but the crowd had barely ceased cheering when Galway struck back, serving notice that the outcome of the game would be decided between the Galway forwards and the Tipp backs. From under Hill 16 Joe Cooney got a ball out to Brendan Lynskey who, head down, tried to burrow through. Richard Stakelum rushed to help John Kennedy cut off the danger and Lynskey parted out to Martin Naughton, now unmarked, champing at the bit and rarin' to go. With all the room in the world, he ran and blazed low into the corner of the Tipp net.

The pattern was to be repeated for much of the first half as the Tipp backs struggled to get a grip on a Galway forward line that refused to be held. Time and time again there were fine examples of perfect understanding and cohesion among the Galway forwards.

Martin Naughton raced goalwards and without looking passed to his right and continued running as Michael McGrath collected and drove over the bar. Bent low over everything that came his way, Lynskey, now charging ahead, now distributing to his wings, made life impossible for a Tipp backline that seemed always ill at ease. Thankfully, Ken Hogan was at his most brilliant best and on one occasion only his going down on the ball on his line — while more than one Galway stick waved threateningly over his ample hide — saved a certain goal. At midfield, too, Tipp were in trouble.

Yet Galway could never be happy as long as anything was coming upfield where Nicholas English had the decidedly upper hand over Conor Hayes. Donie O'Connell, industrious as ever, was narrowly wide with a shot at goal when Tipp were five points down and a moment later he burst through again, but the pass which he threw to an unmarked Martin McGrath was marginally off target for what would certainly have been a goal. There were points from Martin McGrath and Paul Delaney put over a free from his own 65, but Galway continued to drive upfield to reply to Tipp scores. Cooney's point immediately after Delaney's seemed to be the story of the game so far and after a fine save by Ken Hogan in the 27th minute, Cunningham pointed to stretch the lead to 1-10 to 0-6. English pointed again and then in an effort to steady the backline, Seamus Gibson was withdrawn and John McGrath came into the forward line, allowing Bobby Ryan to fall back to corner-back.

As if to show approval of the dugout decision, English was again galvanised into action. Leaving Conor Hayes wrongfooted and drawing John Commins out of goal, he drove for an empty net. But with the alertness of the experienced campaigner, Pete Finnerty was there to block English's shot and the situation was saved.

Bobby Ryan in defence was making a difference. Points were exchanged, Pat Fox pointed for his first score of the day and English, from an acute angle near goal, drove low over the bar. The umpire waved wide and English was seen, uncharacteristically, to argue until unceremoniously nudged aside by an attentive Sylvie Linnane.

On the 33rd minute Eanna Ryan pointed to make the score 1-12 to Tipp's 0-9 and a minute later came one of the high points of a pulsating game. Hit by Galway granite while in possession on the square, English was awarded a penalty. Fox, as yet hardly having a dream game, drove to the net. Suddenly Tipp were heading towards half-time only a goal behind.

But as had been the pattern in the first half, Galway surged upfield again. A minute and a half into injury time Steve Mahon pointed after Ken Hogan had again saved. By the time the whistle sounded all six Galway forwards had scored. Three of them, Eanna Ryan, Michael McGrath and Joe Cooney, had scored three points each.

Under the Hogan Stand at half-time an old-timer complained of the attitude of the younger generation of supporters. 'Will you listen to them complaining!' he said. ''Tis easy knowing they were never here before. They think All-Irelands grow on trees.' Later in the evening Babs Keating would console a grieving well-wisher. 'All-Ireland medals do not come in the post', he told him.

No sooner had the second half begun than Tipp showed the effects of a dressing room tongue-lashing. Within ten seconds Donie O'Connell had pointed. Then Aidan Ryan pointed and Delaney put over a 65 after Commins was lucky to save from English. Eanna Ryan replied with a point and English, having been held, put Tipp within a point of Galway in the 7th minute from the free. Now Tipp's supporters had something to shout about.

Martin McGrath made a great run in from the corner and from ten yards hit the post, much to John Commins's relief. Steve Mahon pointed for Galway and Joe Hayes replied for Tipperary. It was that kind of game. On the 14th minute the score stood Galway 1-15 Tipp 1-14. Now Michael Doyle, whose goals in Killarney had done so much to bring them to Croke Park, was on the field at full-forward. The full-forward line read Fox, Doyle and John McGrath. Nicholas English was in the half-forward line which must have been more than a little welcomed by Conor Hayes who had coped badly with the Lattin-Cullen man's phenomenal artistry.

The removal of Martin McGrath would be the subject of controversy for a long time afterwards and the story persisted that there had been a mistake in the issuing of the slip for the referee, with the result that the wrong McGrath was taken off. The truth is that had the introduction of Mick Doyle worked as magically as it had done in Killarney, nobody would have noticed who went off.

For a few minutes it was as if the effort to draw close had been too great for Tipp and the effort to resist the challenge had been too great for Galway. There was a series of wides, including one from Pat Fox from a free near the sideline. However, in the 20th minute there was a flash of the genius that made Fox one of the most dangerous forwards in hurling. Gathering a ball wide on the wing, he accelerated out of reach of the maroon jersey in pursuit and scored the best goal of the game. For the first time Tipp were ahead at 2-14 to 1-16. Nicholas English pointed a couple of minutes later and Tipp supporters might have been pardoned for thinking that they were about to see a repeat of Killarney. But Galway manager Cyril Farrell had his share of the inspiration which had been allotted to Galway for the day. It was at this moment that he brought Noel Lane, seasoned veteran of many a fray, on to the field. Joe Cooney from a free reduced the Galway deficit to a point and a moment later Aidan Ryan fluffed a ball near the sideline for Steve Mahon to bring his side level. Tipp's lead had been short lived.

Then came the incident, eight minutes from the end, that will be discussed as long as the might-have-beens of hurling are talked of in Tipperary. A shot from Donie O'Connell was blocked out to the corner by John Commins who cleared into the middle. Nicholas English gained possession and in a flash the ball was over the bar. But as the Tipp crowd roared, referee Gerry Kirwan was seen to stand on the spot from where English had struck the ball, pointing down the field — a free to Galway. John McGrath, it seemed, had tackled the goalkeeper after he had delivered the ball. The free was taken, the ball broke to Eanna Ryan who, despite the attentions of John Heffernan, handpassed to the Tipp net. Galway were back in the lead 2-18 to 2-15. It was now in the 28th minute.

Still the epic struggle went on. Pat Fox was wide from a free when Aidan Ryan was pulled down. Cunningham pointed for Galway and O'Connell and English pointed for Tipp. It was two minutes from time when, in headlong flight, Eanna Ryan parted to Noel Lane who slammed the ball past Ken Hogan. And while the Galway fans were still on their feet Joe Cooney put over the final point of the game to leave the score Galway 3-20 Tipp 2-17.

Ted Dillon, writing in the *Clonmel Nationalist* the following week commented on the aftermath:

> They were disappointed, dejected and some were close to tears after last Sunday's game — that marvellous young blue and gold horde who have given a new dimension to Tipperary hurling tradition. To many of this happy band of young people, the majority of whom never saw Tipperary seniors hurl in Croke Park before — this was the end of a dream, we were beaten by

Galway and nobody disputed the result . . . Those with the lined faces and the caps who have seen it all before shared their disappointment, but not their dejection. They know this is not the end of the road, not the end of the dream. They saw a team of young men who gave the game everything, who might have won but who went down to a better team on the day . . .

A few Sundays later Tipperary's minors bit the dust against Offaly in Croke Park before Galway bounded out to win their third senior All-Ireland title. Injuries, it seems, were not confined to seniors. In the weeks before the final two of the minors, by strange coincidence both Ryans — Brendan and Kevin — sustained broken legs in club games and saw the final on crutches.

But the euphoria which had hung over an entire county since Killarney remained.

Chapter Seven

JUST LIKE OLD TIMES, 1987–8

Young Tipp supporters could not wait for the League to begin to see their heroes again and when they did see them they vented their enthusiasm in a way that was not entirely welcomed by their elders. At Thurles against Limerick on 11 October they showed their lack of familiarity with the rubrics of hurling by greeting Limerick puckouts with derisive groans. 'They'll learn better when they get used to winning', somebody remarked. If the famine was over, it would still take time to get rid of the side effects. But it was nice to see enthusiasm for a winter League game, with youngsters sporting the blue and gold flags, headbands and paraphernalia which had become standard youngsters' gear since Killarney.

It was important for the maintenance of the new morale that Tipp should perform well in the League. They had begun life the previous year in Division 2 and by now, with most of them finished with club games, there was evidence among the players of a desire to get back playing together again. Understandably, they were basking in the newly bestowed public esteem.

The team which fielded was: Hogan; Heffernan, O'Donovan, Gibson; Kennedy, Stakelum, Delaney; Fitzelle, Colm Bonnar; Martin McGrath, O'Connell, Aidan Ryan; Fox, English and Bobby Ryan. Austin Buckley replaced the injured McGrath after a few minutes and in the second half Noel Sheehy replaced John Kennedy, while Joe Hayes replaced Delaney.

The game had barely started when Pat Fox blazed a goal from an acute angle and by the time Tipp had notched up 3-12 to Limerick's 1-4 Tipp could spare some sympathy for Eamon Cregan who was responsible for preparing Limerick for the championship. 'Watch Tipperary!' was his advice to a journalist after the game.

Yes indeed — watch Tipperary — and that turned out to be a painful exercise a fortnight later. The Indian sign which Wexford seemed to have put on Tipp during the famine years had persisted and the handful of Tipperary supporters who travelled to Enniscorthy retreated across the Barrow with their tails firmly tucked between their legs. Short only Donie O'Connell and Martin McGrath of their very best, Tipp went under to a Wexford side that was strong on both skill and grit.

Behind by only three points at half-time, after having played into a stiff wind, it looked good for Tipp as they set their backs to the wind for the second half. But by the half-way stage it was obvious that nothing was going to shake Wexford before the home crowd. Goals from Eamon Synnott, from substitute Mark Morrissey and in extra time from John McDonald sent Tipp away with a not very impressive 1-7 in answer to Wexford's 3-11.

It was a game which did little for some Tipperary reputations. Even Nicholas English was kept quiet when he found himself on Eamon Cleary and failed to register on the scoreboard. And when John Kennedy retired with a broken bone in his hand, it marked the beginning of an absence from the team that would last until the semi-final stages of the League. What looked so rosy a fortnight before wore a bleak enough tinge now — two points from two games and Galway to face next.

Galway had a record that was consistent with their current talent — in twelve months they had not been beaten in championship or League. They had a reputation to uphold and already there was a recognition that Tipp were the ones to be put down at every possible opportunity. How good Galway were was shown in that without Finnerty, Keady and Gerry McInerny, they managed to hold Tipp to a draw on Tipp's home ground.

For Tipp the Wexford defeat proved to be a blessing in disguise and it was used in the dressing room to concentrate the mind on what needed to be done. The unusually large attendance which braved the atrocious weather conditions saw a contest of Herculean commitment, with a standard of hurling which seemed incredible in the heavy downpour that persisted for much of the game. Perhaps it was the recognition by the players that all right-minded folk should be at home stoking the November fires and that stylish hurling was out of the question which resulted in a number of wonderful passages of ground hurling which produced a degree of excitement more usually associated with summer conditions.

As became the pattern of Tipp-Galway games over the next few years, the game had its controversial incident. Almost on half-time, with Galway leading by five points to four, English on the edge of the square received a ball from Pa O'Neill — one of the Cappawhite players who had won the county championship the previous Sunday — and handpassed to the net. But just as the Tipp crowd dropped their umbrellas in their excitement, the referee was seen to signal a penalty. He had already blown for a foul on English. Pat Fox sent the ball inches over the bar, leaving the sides level at the interval, as they had been three times before then.

They were level again at full-time with 0-7 each, the final score of the game coming from Conor Stakelum who had come on in place of his cousin Aidan Ryan. It was a fitting end to a game which augured well for the future of both teams as well as for future meetings between them.

On the Friday night before the League game against Galway, the Tipperary Association in Dublin conferred the 'Tipperary Person of the Year' award on Babs Keating. Four hundred guests listened to Tom Quigley, president of the association, laying a verbal wreath at Babs' feet:

> Whatever the rest of Ireland might say, we think of ourselves once again as the premier county where, but for a slight mishap, the McCarthy Cup would once again be residing. . . . To Babs was due that wonderful day in Killarney which turned back the clock to the days when the last few minutes of a game was a time to fear a Tipperary man . . . Babs was the one who put the fires blazing on the hillsides and the blue and gold flags waving in the towns and villages as Tipp folk made their way home carrying as trophies full hearts. He has given a confidence which all Tipperary people now have, that at last there is a captain on the bridge and that we are going somewhere, not drifting.

If anyone present or at home in Tipperary disagreed with those sentiments, he kept his opinion to himself.

For a Tipp hurler there is no joy like unto that of beating Cork. It is an experience that is best savoured in summer, but anytime will do, even in bleak November conditions. The effect of the 2-10 to Cork's 0-8 victory on the large Tipp following at Pairc Ui Chaoimh on 22 November was to move them to a standing ovation as the team left the field. It was a gesture that was well deserved.

On a sodden pitch Tipp had only succeeded by half-time in putting themselves three points ahead despite a wind advantage. But seven minutes into the second half Aidan Ryan dodged past three defenders to part to Fox who gave it to Donie O'Connell to finish to the net. Eight minutes later, to a huge ovation, Nicholas English — benched through illness — ran on to the field as a substitute for Conor Ryan, the Cappawhite representative on the team. He had barely arrived when he made the journey to Cork worthwhile for his admirers. From a bursting run through by O'Connell he took a pass and, only pausing to send Ger Cunningham the wrong way, he crashed the ball to the net for a score from which Tipp never looked back.

It wasn't a championship game, reflected many Tipp supporters as they made their way home in the November twilight, but it was the next best thing. There had been none of the shilly-shallying that had been seen against Wexford. And the introduction of big, red-haired, young Declan Ryan in the forward line looked like the start of something, which indeed it proved to be. Only a year out of minor grade, he had proved a handful for Jim Cashman. 'The beet was pulled and Cork bet!'

A week later Tipp turned a half-time point deficit against a tenacious Waterford team into a seven point lead at full-time. Pat Fox scored nine points from frees and English four from play. Once again Declan Ryan looked good, scoring two points. Waterford had been joint table-toppers, but now going into Christmas Wexford were at the top, with Tipp and Galway sharing joint second.

Soldiers, rest . . .

On a bitingly cold afternoon — the first Sunday of 1988 — Tipp began the process of shaking out the Christmas cobwebs with a strenuous practice session in Thurles. If any of the players felt this was taking things a bit far, there was some consolation. A week later they were flying to the Canaries for a fortnight's rest. They travelled on the same flight as the Galway team and this led to much good-humoured banter as players seated themselves beside travel companions whom they would have wished further from them some months before. The Tipp lads were carrying hurleys which moved Galway corner-back Sylvie Linnane — no wit when the ball has been thrown in — to joke, 'We're going to rest, ye're going to get fit.' There was more than long restful hours of sun soaking in store for the weary warriors as Babs would ensure that there were some strenuous, if enjoyable, workouts on the beach.

The holiday cost the County Board nothing, the expenses having been borne by the Tipperary Supporters Club, but that did not leave the entire operation immune from criticism. At the mid Tipp convention a speaker suggested that 'the sunny sands of the Canaries' was not the place to prepare for the remaining games of the League. Amateurs they might be, but they were expected to be on the job 365 days of the year.

In the meantime the new status of the county was recognised in the selection of four players — Ken Hogan, Aidan Ryan, Pat Fox and Nicholas English — to the Bank of Ireland All-Stars. Not since 1971 when Tadhg O'Connor, Francis Loughnane, Mick Roche and Babs Keating were picked did the county have so many on the selection. The All-Stars selection was: Ken Hogan (Tipp), Joe Hennessy (Kilkenny), Conor Hayes (Galway), Ollie Kilkenny (Galway), Peter Finnerty (Galway), Ger Henderson (Kilkenny), John Conran (Wexford), Steve Mahon (Galway), John Fenton (Cork), Michael McGrath (Galway), Joe Cooney (Galway), Aidan Ryan (Tipp), Pat Fox (Tipp), Nicholas English (Tipp) and Liam Fennelly (Kilkenny). Later Conor O'Donovan, Paul Delaney and Donie O'Connell would be added to the panel as subs for the US tour.

A beautifully mild late February day saw a sizeable Tipp crowd in Ennis for the first game of the new year. Clare had had internal problems and had been performing badly thus far. With a weakened backline they could do little to prevent the Tipp forwards from running riot. Pat Fox scored 2-7, Nicholas English 1-3, Colm Bonnar 1-1, Donie O'Connell and Declan Ryan 1-1 each, leaving wise old heads remarking that a bit of sunshine never did anybody any harm and can even do a lot of good. There were smiles all round — except on Clare faces — and it occurred to few that it might have been Clare's weakness that made Tipp look so good. They learned better a fortnight later.

Under the new stewardship of Eddie Keher, Kilkenny had something to prove. In six games they had gleaned only six points and had been subjected to much criticism at home. If they didn't beat Tipp, they could be involved in a relegation play-off, a consideration profoundly offensive to the sensitivities of the Leinster champions. Besides, it would be the first time in a number of years that they had met Tipp before a Nowlan Park crowd.

The proceedings at Nowlan Park, where they were hammered 2-12 to 0-4, was a matter most of the Tipp players would like to forget. Short only John Kennedy, Aidan Ryan, Richard Stakelum and Martin McGrath and with replacements who were just as likely to figure in a first fifteen, they provided a closely contested game for three-quarters of an hour. And that was it. Four points was the result of their endeavours — two in each half!

It all started reasonably well except for some poor free-taking by Fox and Delaney. At first Pa Fitzelle and Joe Hayes were holding their own at centre-field and generally there was nothing to panic about, though they were behind by 0-7 to 0-2 at half-time. Conor Stakelum came in to replace Joe Hayes, but by the seventh minute of the second half Tipp had scored all they were going to score. English tried to create opportunities by darting outfield, but Joe Hennessy was able to keep pace with him — to the inspiration of the whole team and the delight of the Kilkenny following. John Henderson was keeping a tight rein on Pat Fox. Conor O'Donovan, who had started well, found Christy Heffernan an increasingly troublesome handful, while Paul Delaney and Seamus Gibson were repeatedly in trouble.

All Kilkenny's craft was concentrated on giving Tipp a humiliating drubbing and as they tightened their hold on the game their supporters grew more vocal. Ten minutes from the end, with Kilkenny now six points in front, Michael Phelan sent a pass from Christy Heffernan to the net and that, effectively, ended Tipp's challenge. Two minutes from the end he repeated the trick. It wasn't so much the defeat, Tipp supporters told one another as they left the field, but the manner of it. 'Back to the drawing board!' rang in their ears from Kilkenny men, who were all too pleased at the chance of rubbing it in, until they reached the blessed sanctuary of their cars.

But for Kilkenny the victory was the possible difference between being relegated and not being relegated. For Tipp there was no similar incentive. In early March, such considerations can make all the difference.

At Croke Park a fortnight later Tipp retrieved some of their damaged self-esteem with a resounding win over Antrim, though the 2-20 to 2-9 margin was not quite as wide as that which had divided them from Kilkenny. 'English Lesson for Antrim' headlined one report of a game whose highlight was the dazzling performance of the Tipp forward whose 2-7 almost totalled Antrim's score. He had, however, taken over the free-taking from Pat Fox and six of his points were the result of Antrim fouls, some of them against himself. All of Tipp's starting fifteen played well and once again Declan Ryan impressed, contributing to the scoreboard four times. John Leahy's senior debut was watched with special interest and it was noted that, though he did not figure among the scorers, his faults were of over-eagerness. Bobby Ryan was back at wing-back and there was a growing feeling that he should remain there where his boundless energy allowed him to make those sallies upfield which made life so troublesome for an opposing half-back line. And yet, Antrim's display had served notice that they truly belonged in the 1st Division. Many a game had been won with a score of 2-9, ensuring that when they met again Tipp would not take them too lightly.

Before Tipp proceeded to the next round of the League there was a tussle with Wexford in the Oireachtas. Conscious of things to come and still smarting from the slapping at Enniscorthy, Tipp fielded only five of their best side, though all the team had inter-county experience. Wexford fielded ten of theirs. It was a fine, spirited game — so spirited that John Heffernan was sent to the line after only four minutes of play, leaving Tipp for the rest of the hour with only fourteen men. But the fourteen rose to the occasion in fine style and Wexford were lucky enough to win by a point from a 75 yard free from James Houlihan in the last couple of minutes. Joe Hayes was the best of the Tipp side and Pa O'Neill scored 1-3 from play, but the most significant feature of Tipp's game was the energy and commitment shown by the fourteen. They would be without John Heffernan for the next League game which would be the semi-final. The Nenagh man's sending off was a unique event in that he was the only Tipperary player during the Keating years to be dismissed. When one takes into account the number of opponents who were sent off, the clean slate of Tipperary during those years is perhaps a consideration for which neither Tipp nor their mentors have received sufficient credit.

As it happened, they did not need John Heffernan for the semi-final. The GAA administration in its wisdom brought Tipp and Waterford — who had met in an earlier round in Thurles — to play in Croke Park as a curtain-raiser to the other semi-final between Wexford and Offaly. For those who had thought that the Antrim game might have flattered Tipp, this game proved an utter damp squib. Tipp were ahead by 1-11 to 0-6 at half-time and in the second half merely piled on the punishment. Again, the proceedings were remarkable principally for the wonderful display of Nicholas English who made a poor game interesting by the sheer magic of his command of hurley and ball. Though subjected to the most uncompromising tackling, he delighted the crowd with impeccable anticipation and dazzling, jinking runs which earned him a total of 2-4 from play and a further 0-7 from frees. Pat Fox scored 2-4 and in those two goals English also had a hand. Between them, English and Fox amassed the colossal total of 4-15, a performance which alone made the long journey worthwhile for Tipp supporters.

But there was a moral that was obvious to many of these supporters as they settled down to watch Offaly and Wexford slug it out for the right to meet Tipp in the final. Even though they had already beaten Waterford in an earlier round, they had refused to take victory for granted and they had treated them with the greatest caution. 'Waterford will be a handful', the *Tipperary Star* had bannered the previous day. They had expected the worst and they had produced the best. Now Offaly were the next obstacle to the League crown.

There was no tradition of Tipp-Offaly rivalry, since in the days when Tipp were lording it, Offaly did not exist as a hurling power. Offaly's rise had coincided with the famine so that in Tipp there was a kind of friendly welcome for the new star in the hurling firmament. At the same time there was a healthy respect for the incredible never-say-die quality which seemed to be a feature of both hurling and football teams from Offaly. With the absence of the kind of cut-throat rivalry which so often dominates the approach to a match and the game itself, there was keen anticipation of a game of hurling which Tipp wanted to win for all the right reasons. A League title was not an All-Ireland, but if the All-Ireland was not available, it was the best of all substitutes. Tipp had not won a League title since 1979, when they had beaten Galway in the final, and it was felt that if they were to be serious contenders for the championship, now was the time to prove it.

The main subject of conversation during the period before the League final was as much where it was going to be played as who was going to win. It was at first fixed for Croke Park which at the time had the Hill 16 alterations under way. Then it was learned that, instead, Dublin and Meath footballers would replay an earlier drawn game there and an alternative venue would be found for the hurling game.

Finally, it was changed back to Croke Park and of the 33,000 who saw a wonderfully sporting exhibition of skilful hurling the substantial majority seemed to be from Tipperary. This was a big change in that Tipp folk were now getting excited at being in a League final. There was a brief flutter when it was suggested that John Kennedy because of an eye problem would be unable to start, but everything came right and the Tipp team which started was: K. Hogan; C. O'Donovan, N. Sheehy, S. Gibson; B. Ryan, J. Kennedy, P. Delaney; J. Hayes, Colm Bonnar; D. Ryan, D. O'Connell, P. O'Neill (capt.); P. Fox, N. English and A. Ryan. Three substitutes would be introduced during the game: Conor Stakelum for O'Connell in the 46th minute, John Leahy for Aidan Ryan in the 59th minute and Michael Corcoran for Gibson in the 60th minute.

Richard Stakelum had slipped from the first fifteen and his inclusion from now on would depend on injuries. He had been substituted against Waterford and it was felt that he had never quite regained the consistent form of the previous year, a matter of great regret to the entire county. He was an ideal front-figure and he would continue to be regarded with affection by the younger followers for whom he had spoken on and off the field on the day in Killarney when Tipp had risen from its knees. His place in Tipperary hurling lore was entirely secure.

The Offaly team was J. Troy; J. Miller, A. Fogarty (capt.), M. Hanamy; B. Keeshan, M. Coughlan, G. Coughlan; J. Kelly, J. Dooley; P. O'Connor, D. Fogarty, M. Corrigan; P. Cleary, E. Coughlan and P. Corrigan. Three subs would be introduced: M. Duignan, G. Cahill and J. Martin.

Lacking the almost personal spleen that can arise between counties, the game was an example of what one would like exhibition hurling to be. Sunshine, without the heat of summer, lent a carnival air and made for ideal hurling conditions. Buoyed by the curtain-raiser victory of their youngsters over Kilkenny in the All-Ireland Vocational Schools final, Tipp were on top in the opening quarter but were having difficulties piercing a rock-hard Offaly backline. Both goalies made excellent saves and Offaly were twice foiled by the brilliance and courage of Ken Hogan, once when Pat Cleary had left the Tipp backs wrongfooted and had only the big Lorrha man to beat. A moment later Hogan deflected a low shot over the line for a 65. At the other end Jim Troy was equally inspired and there were similar escapes, once when Pa O'Neill, with only the goalie to beat, sent the ball whizzing inches over the bar. At half-time it was nine points to five and neither side showed any signs of wilting.

If the half-back line, magnificently led by John Kennedy, was the key to Tipperary's success in the second half, it fell to Pa O'Neill to surpass the closely policed English in providing the goals which were to end Offaly's hopes. Tipp's eleven points lead had been whittled back to four and Offaly were looking good when a low shot from sub Conor Stakelum was blocked by goalkeeper Troy. O'Neill was in like a flash to tap the rebound to the net for his second goal (he had already first-timed a crossing ball past Troy). Points followed and the margin had again reached nine points when the full-time whistle left the score: Tipp 3-15 Offaly 2-9.

For Pa O'Neill it was a personal triumph. He had been the leading scorer in his county's 15th National League triumph, deriving maximum advantage from the close attention that was being lavished by the Offaly defence on English and Fox. Less than six months before, he had been part of his club's first ever county title victory and now he had ably led his county to a historic victory. When the statistics of the League had been sorted they would show that Tipp had played ten games and won eight. They had scored in the campaign 21-123 and they had conceded 13-87. Pat Fox had scored the huge total of 6 goals and 40 points and Nicholas English had scored 7-31.

But the statistics were for later. As the thousands of Tipperary followers made their way home into the sunset they could only foresee success following success. A glorious summer stretched before them marked by tussles with Limerick and Cork and at the end an opportunity to show that the outcome of last year's semi-final against Galway was all a mistake. It was just like old times and it was great to be alive.

Chapter Eight

SWEET BUT NOT INTOXICATING, 1988

It wasn't so much the winning of a League title as the confirmation of Tipp's All-Ireland potential that made the victory over Offaly so pleasing to Tipp followers. It meant that the county would be facing into the championship as winners rather than as the team that had failed to beat Galway the previous year. Psychologically, that was of immense importance to a county that had lost faith in itself for so long.

If a low-flying aircraft — or even a high-flying one — passing over Tipperary in early May heard a loud unexplained sound from the ground, it was probably the chorus of curses which greeted the news from across the Atlantic that Nicholas English had sustained a hamstring injury while playing with the All-Stars. In the remaining weeks before the Tipp-Limerick championship game his condition dominated all pre-match speculation and there was a cold realisation that Tipp's prospects as a team were closely related to English's physical fitness.

There were other injuries as well and it looked like Tipp would be short a number of players when the time came. Apart from English, Noel Sheehy, Fox, Donie O'Connell, Pa Fitzell, Seamus Gibson, and sub Peter Hayes were also nursing injuries of one degree or another. John Heffernan, meanwhile, was still serving the three month suspension which had been handed down to him for his Oireachtas game misdemeanour when he became the only Tipp player to be sent off during the entire Babs era.

Nevertheless, confidence was high among the crowds which flocked to the twice-weekly training sessions. Injuries notwithstanding, there was a feeling in Tipp that, even without English, the biggest single danger could be over-confidence and this was a matter repeatedly stressed by Babs and the other selectors and in local papers. It was even suggested that all the reports of troubles in the Limerick camp were part of a sustained strategy on the part of Eamon Cregan. For Cregan, formerly as a hurler and now as coach, there was a healthy respect in Tipp.

The team which fielded at Pairc Ui Chaoimh on 5 June 1988 reflected the injury problem. Back came Paul Delaney instead of Gibson; on came Richard Stakelum in Paul Delaney's place; and into the attack came the young John Leahy. English was described as 80 per cent fit, available, presumably, to be used if the worst came to the worst. The starting team was: Ken Hogan; Conor O'Donovan, Noel Sheehy, Paul Delaney; Richard Stakelum, John Kennedy, Bobby Ryan; Colm Bonnar, Joe Hayes; John Leahy, Donie O'Connell, Pa O'Neill; Pat Fox, Declan Ryan and Aidan Ryan.

The day began well for Tipp, with their juniors lording it over Limerick to beat them by 4-11 to 1-4. The margin in the senior game was nothing so comprehensive, though it was in its way decisive enough. Without English, nobody expected fireworks from the Tipp forward line, but the failure to produce even one green flag was a consideration which sent many a Tipp supporter home in pensive mood. The absence of goals on both sides was not due, it was pointed out, to any great feats of goalkeeping but to shortcomings among the forwards.

It was a good job for Tipp that at midfield Joe Hayes and Colm Bonnar — with tremendous support from Bobby Ryan, happily settled at wing-back — quickly established dominance over Ger Hegarty and Jimmy Carroll and maintained the upper hand through the seventy minutes. Yet, despite this midfield superiority, Tipp could only manage a 0-9 to 0-5 lead at half-time. Balls sailed wide at either side of the posts and there were few occasions when goalie Tom Quaid was worried by what came his way.

With the wind at their backs in the second half, Tipp almost camped in the Limerick end of the field and again proceeded to shoot wide after wide. Brian Finn had pointed a 65 for Limerick, reducing the margin to three points, when Joe Hayes finally broke the Tipp log-jam with a point from far out. A few minutes later Pat Fox took a point and then sent two frees over the bar, following with a further point from play. Eight points behind with ten minutes to go, Limerick never really looked like catching up. The final whistle saw the scoreboard reading 0-15 to 0-8, of which Culbaire in the *Tipperary Star* would say: 'Seven up was the margin; like the drink itself, sweet but not intoxicating.' On the one hand Tipp had won, but on the other they had not done so in a style that would inspire much confidence. Nevertheless, they had survived without English, who had been togged out ready to go in should a crisis situation have arisen, and each week was bringing Fox closer to complete fitness.

Cork were not tested against Clare, who after the first quarter of an hour never looked like raising a real gallop, but still Tipp treated them with considerable respect. They might have performed badly in the League and they might not have impressed so far in the championship, but Cork is Cork was the attitude of the mentors who were fully aware that their opponents were capable of turning their very weakness to their advantage. Tipp had not played Cork in Limerick since 1973 and the associations of Tipp championship victories there over Cork had long since faded. Cork, too, had recently given a hammering to Tipp's under-21's. All this was repeated over and over, so that by the time training ended in Thurles before a thousand onlookers on the Tuesday night before the game, the team were psychologically ready for the worst that Cork could do to them.

With fine insensitivity and disregard for supporters, the Tipp-Kilkenny All-Ireland Junior final had been fixed for Portlaoise on the Friday night before the senior game. Thus, the unfortunate juniors felt they were getting a raw deal in being obliged to play their big game when the attention of the entire county was focused elsewhere. Nevertheless, a big crowd travelled to the game and refused to be disheartened when Kilkenny snatched a win in the last quarter. Spiritually, the supporters were already in Limerick.

Fifty thousand travelled to Limerick two days later and, if what they got was no repetition of Killarney in terms of quality or of drama, it certainly had its moments. The team which Tipp fielded once again showed English at full-forward, sending John Leahy back to the subs bench. Back, too, to the subs went Richard Stakelum, now that Seamus Gibson had got over his leg injury. Conor O'Donovan moved to full-back, Noel Sheehy to right-corner and Paul Delaney and Bobby Ryan to the wings. Aidan Ryan and Pa O'Neill swapped positions and Cormac Bonnar, who had figured on the team some years previously, returned to the substitutes. The team was: Ken Hogan; Noel Sheehy, Conor O'Donovan, Seamus Gibson; Bobby Ryan, John Kennedy, Paul Delaney; Joe Hayes, Colm Bonnar; Declan Ryan, Donie O'Connell, Aidan Ryan; Pat Fox, Nicholas English and Pa O'Neill (captain).

Cork fielded: Ger Cunningham; Denis Mulcahy, Richard Browne, Denis Walsh; Pat Hartnett, Tom Cashman, Jim Cashman; Teddy

McCarthy, Paul O'Connor; Pat Horgan, Kevin Hennessy, Michael Mullins; Tom Mulcahy, Ger Fitzgerald and Tony O'Sullivan.

For the first quarter of an hour Tipp were on top, but just about. Then Bobby Ryan and the Tipp half-backs began to assert themselves, Joe Hayes and Colm Bonnar started to control midfield and, though the inside Tipp line was still tied up, the half-forwards started to make an impression. Between the 20th and the 30th minute they put over six points without reply. A couple of minutes from the interval, Declan Ryan took a hand-me-on from English to blaze to the net. The game as a spectacle was doomed. A half-time margin of 1-13 to 0-5 would silence most crowds. But not this one.

The second half saw Nicholas English stretching the lead a point further. Then Cork got off their knees. Pat Horgan pointed a free and Teddy McCarthy sent over a point from some fifty yards. Boxed in by blue and gold jerseys, Tony O'Sullivan nevertheless managed to put over another and Teddy McCarthy, jumping high and catching, put Cork into the attack again. John Kennedy's clearance dribbled over the sideline and Paul O'Connor, as if it was no trouble in the world, cut the sideline puck over the bar. Another ball over the sideline, and again O'Connor prepared to take it. Before he did so, Charlie McCarthy had a word in his ear and, as if to prove that the first one was no fluke, he repeated the wonderful feat. Now the score stood at 1-14 to 0-10.

Worse was to come for Tipp. Nothing could go wrong for Cork. Tomas Mulcahy burst through and Ger Fitzgerald, pucking the ball back over his head, sent it over for a point. An uncharacteristic but mild flare-up near midfield gave Donie O'Connell a booking and Tom Cashman a free. The ball sailed all the way over jostling players to brush off Noel Sheehy's fingers to the Tipp net, with Ken Hogan wondering where it had come from. Now only three points separated them. Cork tails were up and Tipp confidence was tottering. Visions arose of the bad years when they could not be depended upon to hold a lead, no matter how substantial. Ger Fitzgerald and Pat Horgan nearly rushed another goal, only to be foiled by the bulk of Ken Hogan on the ground.

It was at this point that inspiration struck the Three Wise Men in the Tipp dugout. John Leahy, who had come on at half-time in place of Pa O'Neill, moved to centre-field instead of the injured Joe Hayes. In came big Cormac Bonnar at full forward and Nicholas English went out on the wing. It was the big bearded Bonnar — almost unknown to many supporters, since he had not figured with the county for several years — who restored Tipp's confidence, as he would so often do over the next few years, and put them hurling as an efficient combination again. Tony O'Sullivan from centre-field had just sent over a point to leave only two points between them. A long-range free against Paul O'Connor, its fairness later disputed by Cork men, was taken by Paul Delaney. As the ball sailed in, it was met behind the Cork lines and turned deftly to the net with a one-handed flick by Bonnar in such circumstances as left most spectators wondering who exactly had got the vital touch to it. But Tipp supporters didn't care who touched it. The team was in gear again. Declan Ryan, working like a beaver, passed to English who, out near the sideline, wrongfooted a defender, turned and from his left side drove unerringly over the bar. For the remaining ten minutes of the game Tipp were again in control and they never relinquished their hold. The final score read Tipp 2-19 Cork 1-13.

The day had begun badly for Tipp with their minors getting a severe drubbing from Cork, but the minors' defeat did nothing to dim the colour of the day. This in itself was a reminder of the importance of the senior title. When it came to it, nothing else mattered. During the bad years Tipp had won other titles, but they were still the years of famine. Without senior success there is hunger; nothing else satisfies. It was nice to be taking home the Munster cup for the second year running. Even though anybody who knew the game of hurling knew they still had problems, Tipp had proved that Killarney was no fluke. Coming out of Munster once may in some circumstances be considered lucky, but coming out in two successive years points to something else. It was nice to be setting out for Croke Park again.

John Heffernan came back into the full-back line instead of Seamus Gibson for the All-Ireland semi-final against Antrim. And despite the big contribution of Cormac Bonnar to the defeat of Cork, he too remained on the subs bench, as did John Leahy. The line-out for the game, which was to be the curtain-raiser to the Galway-Offaly semi-final, was: Hogan; O'Donovan, Sheehy and Heffernan; Bobby Ryan, Kennedy and Delaney; Joe Hayes and Colm Bonnar; Declan Ryan, O'Connell and Aidan Ryan; Fox, English and Pa O'Neill.

Despite the best efforts of the Tipperary mentors to play up the positive attributes of Antrim, it is always difficult to consider the possibility of being defeated by a team that you have comprehensively beaten a few months before. Notwithstanding all the emphasis on the danger of over-confidence, the fact remained that Tipp hardly took into consideration the possibility of defeat. It was a difficult situation for any team. If they won, they would hardly be thanked. And yet, in the tension of the dressing room before the game on a day that was much too warm for players, though ideal for spectators, they were tortured by the possibility of a sensational upset by Antrim. Such things had happened before.

The nightmare nearly became a reality, much to the delight of those who wanted to see Tipp's expectations humbled. Not everyone had shared Christy Ring's opinion that the GAA without Tipp is only half dressed. There were those who took exception to Tipp's resentment of its decline and who took umbrage at the feeling in Tipp that the county should never be far from the shake-up for an All-Ireland title. So when Antrim made it clear that this was going to be no pushover for Tipp, there was a certain amount of glee at Tipp's discomfiture.

Referee John Denton had barely set the game in motion when Olcan McFettridge was narrowly wide. Nicholas English, having got inside the Antrim backs, was pushed from behind and ended by winning only a 65 — an omen of the tough handling he could expect from a backline which, from experience, was keenly aware of what he could do if not closely attended. A moment later English hit the crossbar, but a penalty was awarded which Fox drove neatly a foot above the ground just inside the post. It was a cruel blow to Antrim, since the shot was saved but somehow crossed the line giving Tipp a goal they badly needed. Once again English was crowded off the ball and Terence McNaughton drove a long clearance which dropped behind the Tipp backs and in a twinkling McFettridge had eluded Conor O'Donovan to hammer it to the net.

In the 19th minute Ken Hogan was on his toes to save a rasper, but Fergus McAllister was about 15 yards away to take the rebound with a full-blooded first-time connection. This time there was no save. Now the teams were level and it was almost half-time. But before half-time there was a classic piece of Fox-English virtuosity. From near the sideline Pa O'Neill sent a cross to Fox who delayed long enough to attract the backs, leaving English free in the corner. Out came the pass, English picked his spot and the ball hit the net under the crossbar in a way that left goalie Patterson totally helpless. At half-time the score stood: Tipp 2-6 Antrim 2-4. The eleven wides which Tipp had registered as against five for the Ulstermen were an indication of the success of Antrim's forward line with only a limited supply of ball and pointed to a weakness in the Tipp backline which would cost them dearly against Galway.

Tipp had two points from Paul Delaney and two from English before McFettridge got Antrim's first second-half score in the 10th minute. Now Tipp's forwards were at their sharpest while Antrim's shooting was loose. Ciaran Barr palmed wide and later he blazed the ball over off the crossbar. But Tipp responded immediately and it was at this point that Pat Fox scored what proved to be the vital goal. Taking a ground ball from O'Neill, he set off for the corner of the square, with McNaughton in hot pursuit, to handpass to the net. It was a killer blow to Antrim and Tipp never looked back. The full-time whistle left the score reading: Tipp 3-15 Antrim 2-10.

Though the victory had gone to Tipp, the admiration had gone to Antrim, and as the northerners settled down to watch the Offaly-Galway game they did so in the knowledge that they were not least among equals in the exclusive club of hurling counties. They had turned in three excellent championship performances, they were in Division 1 of the League and there was a real feeling that theirs was a case of tiochfaidh ar la.

A Tipperary official to whom somebody remarked later that evening that the real winners in the entire day's proceedings had been Antrim, simply replied, 'Yes, but it's ourselves and Galway who were the winners on the scoreboard.' The years in the wilderness had taught Tipp a lot about the unsatisfactory nature of moral victories.

WE LOST TWO BEFORE WE WON ONE, 1988

When Tipperary raced on to the field on the first Sunday in September of 1988 it seemed that Slievenamon and the Rock of Cashel and everyplace else that lies between Shannon and the mouth of the Suir had come to Croke Park. The roar that went up could only have come from followers who believed that their hour had come. There were those who later spoke unashamedly of having thought of family members who had gone ar sli na firinne — if only they could have seen this! For many it was like the turning back of a clock to a time when their world was young.

In Tipperary there was a traditional regard for Galway hurling which went back to the 1920s with Mick King, Mick Gill, Ignatius Harney and the rest — and way beyond. There were memories of Galway taking on the cream of Munster and Leinster in Railway Cup games, and to a generation which grew up in the days of Seanie Duggan, Josie Gallagher, 'Inky' Flaherty, John Killeen and their like, there could never be anything other than the most profound respect for Galway hurling.

It had been thirty years since the two counties had last met in an All-Ireland final and on that occasion Tipp had had an easy win. Of those who had worn the blue and gold that day many had passed into legend. They were: John O'Grady; Mickey Byrne, Michael Maher, Kieran Carey; Jimmy Finn, Tony Wall (capt.), John Doyle; John Hough, Theo English; Donie Nealon, Tom Larkin, Jimmy Doyle; Larry Keane, Liam Devaney and Liam Connolly.

But the bulk of the Tipperary followers who shouted themselves hoarse at the sight of a Tipp team marching behind the Artane Boys Band were not born in 1958 and they had seen more Galway than Tipperary triumphs. Like it or not, Galway were the All-Ireland champions, and deservedly so.

It was Nicholas English who led Tipp in the parade. Pa O'Neill, the captain who had played such a distinctive part in the League final, had been dropped. It was a move which had sparked much controversy and ulterior motives were attributed to the selectors. Cappawhite were county champions for their first-ever time and it was a blow to local pride that their man was replaced. But having made their decision, the selectors were then faced with the problem of appointing a replacement captain. Like Pa O'Neill, English was from west Tipperary. Partly in the belief that the honour would draw extra motivation from him, partly because he had come to be regarded as the key figure of the team, English was appointed. It was a decision that was resented by some, but luckily it did not have the awkward repercussions it might have had in the dressing room. Unfortunately, the wearing of the mantle of captain did nothing for English's game and Pa O'Neill might well have done at least as well as, if not better than, others on the day. But it is easy to be wise after the event. The only thing that is certain is that the selectors acted in good faith. The game was lost on the field and not in the dugout.

Given the peculiar situation in which they found themselves in being the first team from the county to appear in an All-Ireland for so long, Tipp's preparations for the game had been conducted under the greatest difficulties. As the crowds of spectators who made an evening of watching the team training continued to grow, parents arriving with children who wanted to meet their heroes and get their autographs became an impediment to the training. For their part, the players did not want to be less than accessible to their admirers, but when it came to the point that youngsters were tumbling on to the pitch and running across to players during training, the selectors took the decision to exclude the general public. It was better to have spectators excluded altogether than to have training disrupted or even for a single player to give the impression that he was not willing to be nice to a youngster. What should have been a good public relations exercise might not alone prove a distraction from training but could have turned out to be a public relations fiasco. It was as simple as that. There was no question of working out secret moves to hoodwink Galway.

The story was given wide currency that each night an opposition team in these 'secret' training sessions wore Galway jerseys in order to familiarise the Tipp squad with the appearance of the 'enemy'. This too was total bunkum. Babs Keating, Theo English and Donie Nealon had won All-Ireland medals themselves in the days when less was talked of dugout strategy than is the case today. They knew from experience that All-Irelands are won on the field and on the day. If you're not good enough, you don't win. A Tipp mentor of former years, who himself had won All-Irelands, said, 'You can't win an All-Ireland by accident.' He might have said you can't win one in the dugout either.

The team which English led out showed Conor O'Donovan back in the full-back slot in which he was most comfortable and Noel Sheehy in the centre-back position in which John Kennedy had not been too happy of late. Paul Delaney was moved back into the corner, John Leahy was at left half-forward and Aidan Ryan was moved to left corner-forward. The team was: Ken Hogan in goal; Paul Delaney, Conor O'Donovan and John Heffernan; Bobby Ryan, Noel Sheehy and John Kennedy; Colm Bonnar and Joe Hayes; Declan Ryan, Donie O'Connell and John Leahy; Pat Fox, Nicholas English and Aidan Ryan.

The Galway team was: John Commins in goal; Sylvie Linnane, Conor Hayes and Ollie Kilkenny; Peter Finnerty, Tony Keady and Gerry McInerney; Michael Coleman and Pat Malone; Anthony Cunningham, Joe Cooney and Martin Naughton; Michael McGrath, Brendan Lynskey and Eanna Ryan. On paper it was a formidable Galway team. On the field it was even more so. And just as Tipp had every incentive to win, so had their opponents. Hurling has been every bit as much part of rural tradition in Galway as in Tipp. The GAA itself had almost been founded in Galway. Loughrea might well have been the cradle of the GAA just as easily as Thurles. And yet, despite a richness of hurlers over the decades, they had won only three All-Irelands. This was the first time they were defending their crown in an All-Ireland final since 1981.

Tipp, having won the toss, elected to play into a lively breeze in the first half and it quickly became obvious that this was going to be one of those games in which the marking is too tight to allow for any outstanding individual displays. As they lined out, Joe Cooney slipped into the full-forward position and Brendan Lynskey took up his position on the 40. Each side was concentrating on containing the other, each side highly nervous of the potential of the opposing forward line. Galway were keenly aware of the scoring power of Fox and English when given sufficient room. Tipp were likewise conscious that in Galway's semi-final game against Offaly, each of their forwards had scored. Noel Lane, now on the subs bench, somebody calculated, had scored 52 goals for his county. Before the day was over, that figure would be increased.

Tipp's decision to play against the wind in the first half would later be the subject of much criticism. The argument went that they forfeited the opportunity to put Galway under immediate pressure; that they might have succeeded in building up an unassailable lead if they had taken the wind; that a team new to the occasion needed just such a lead. This may be so; but in view of the difficulty in cutting back a lead of four points when they did get the wind, it is somewhat questionable.

The half-time deficit of four points was probably due more to Tipp's failure to control centre-field than to any other single factor. And the ball was running for Galway. A needless centre-field foul saw Conor Hayes pointing an easy free. A moment later Tony Keady pointed after another Tipp foul in the same area and after dissent had brought the ball forward ten metres. Tipp seemed to be working harder for their scores and by half-time had only six flags to show against Galway's ten.

A Declan Ryan point after the resumption cut back the Galway lead, but Michael McGrath quickly re-established it. Lynskey was again at full-forward and Cooney at centre-forward, but there was as yet no real difficulty among the Tipp backs. Declan Ryan again pointed from long range and as, from a cross by Cooney, McGrath's shot just screamed wide, Noel Lane was seen warming up. Another Declan Ryan point followed from near the sideline and by the time Paul Delaney had driven over a free from near midfield — the result of a late tackle — cutting the margin down to a single point, Noel Lane was on the field substituting for Cunningham.

The psychological lift given to the Galway team by the appearance of Lane (of the many goals) can hardly be calculated. Its effect on their followers was evidenced by the ear-shattering roar as he ran to take up his position. A point from Michael McGrath had Galway moving once more, as the lead again stretched to two points.

Then came the incident which was to have a crucial effect on the game and which may well have decided its outcome. Donie O'Connell, barging through directly in front of the goal, released the ball to John Leahy who pounced cat-like to bat it neatly past John Commins. Supporters went wild as Tipp forged ahead for the first time. Or so they thought. But their jubilation turned to bewilderment as they realised that referee Gerry Kirwan was calling the play back and awarding a free to Donie O'Connell who had been well and truly fouled. The whistle had been blown, it seemed, a split second before Leahy connected, but it was hard to expect Tipp supporters at this point to be philosophical or even reasonable. The advantage rule had already been applied a few times during the game and it was a cruel irony that on this occasion it should have been ignored. English pointed the free, but it was poor consolation in a game in which goals were hard to come by. Besides, a goal at that juncture would have put Tipp 1-10 to 0-12 ahead and the importance of taking the lead just then — it was twelve minutes into the second half — to a team that was still learning, can hardly be exaggerated. Instead, punished for a Galway foul, they were still a point behind. It was going to be even harder work than it might have been.

Galway took the next score in a manner which underlined the sheer fluency which their forward line had achieved. McGrath tossed it to Lane who parted to Cooney who put it over. Each had been tackled in turn before the opportunity to shoot was found. Now it was nineteen minutes into the half and Lane was increasingly noticeable. A Paul Delaney free found John Commins at his best and then Declan Ryan pointed to leave only a point between them. Ominously, except for the disallowed goal, that margin was always there. From centre-field Pat Malone stretched it to two and Gerry McInerney, heroic in defence, with a long drive made it three.

But Tipp were a long way from lying down. A superb long shot by Leahy dropped into Commins's hand and Conor Hayes cleared. With four minutes left, Donie O'Connell reduced the margin to two points and Tipp were showing such fire that supporters were having visions of another Killarney, with a final stroke of luck overturning the entire trend of the game. Cormac Bonnar was in and by a whisker failed to catch the rebound from a wonderful Commins save from Fox. A further stroke of bad luck followed when the 65 which everyone expected Paul Delaney to drop into the square went sailing wide.

And then the sky fell in. Almost into injury time the ball broke down the middle of the field leaving only Lane and O'Donovan to contest it. They tussled. Lane turned and was past with the ball rolling in front of him.

Many years ago I was trying to ascertain from a Tipp centre-forward of the 1920s, Paddy Dwyer, what it was that made the Tipp forward line of that time such a formidable combination. Not a man for pretence, Paddy replied, 'Arrah nothing. We just ran like hell and flaked the ball along the ground in front of us.'

Noel Lane ran like hell and flaked the ball before him. He connected well and only an extraordinary fluke could have saved it for Ken Hogan. It was effectively the end of the titanic struggle — the scoreboard now read 1-15 to 0-13 — but it says much for the stern stuff of Tipp that, five points behind and in injury time, they managed to provide additional drama.

As if to make up for the catastrophe of 65 minutes before, Paul Delany ranged upfield and from under the Cusack Stand dropped the ball on to the edge of the square. Never one to be put off by swishing ash, Cormac Bonnar's hand went high and with Galway men pulling him back he tried to burst his way through towards goal. This time the whistle blew before the ball was released. Penalty to Tipp.

There are times in sport when the impossible happens. It happened in Killarney when Nicholas English handpassed over the bar to draw a game that was all but lost. It happened in 1994 when Offaly's Johnny Dooley began an avalanche with a goal against Limerick. But it does not happen often.

The Tipp supporters who roared themselves hoarse as the referee waved all but three defenders out of the Galway goal were oblivious of the fact that time was up and, penalty-goal or no penalty-goal, they were five points behind. They saw only Nicholas English having a word with Pat Fox and standing over the ball. Then he lifted and drove it — over the bar.

Seldom has a great game ended on such a note of anticlimax. A goal would have left Tipp still two points behind, but to point a penalty with the last puck of the game left it bordering on the farcical. And English, never one to make theatrical signals when he had failed to do what he had intended, simply left it to the intelligence of Tipp followers to recognise that he certainly had not intended taking a point.

For Tipp it was the final calamity. As the Galway crowd surged on to the pitch there were few Tipp followers who would deny that they were well entitled to take home the McCarthy Cup across the Shannon. But there was a feeling of dissatisfaction with the way fortune had mistreated the blue and gold. The Leahy goal that was deducted and the failure to put away the final penalty made some, in the first moments of defeat, overlook the fine qualities of the game. The negative reaction, however, was short lived and the most begrudging soon conceded the splendour of the Tipp challenge to a

Galway team that time will prove to have been one of the best hurling teams of the last few decades.

Galway manager Cyril Farrell lost no time in getting to the Tipp dressing room where he saw the kind of dejection with which he had every reason to be familiar. 'Lads, remember we lost two finals before we won one', he told them.

Within the hour wounds were less painful and that night when the team was piped into a function hosted by the Dublin Tipperarymen's Association they were accorded a reception reminiscent of their appearance on the field in Croke Park. And when one of the speakers touched emotionally on Babs Keating's contribution to the day's events, the whole assembly rose for a prolonged standing ovation.

When the team returned to Thurles the following evening the supporters surpassed themselves. Over twenty thousand of them packed into Liberty Square and the streets around and there were scenes of wild excitement when the team made their appearance. They didn't have the All-Ireland cup, but they made their way just the same to the cathedral where Archbishop Tom Morris, surveying the immense throng, wondered aloud what it would have been like had they won. The McCarthy Cup was absent, but it was a defeat with a difference. The atmosphere was all of carnival. And next time, the cup would be there.

Chapter Ten

A TINY BIT CLOSER, 1988–9

It is indicative of the level to which Tipp morale had sunk during the famine years that the euphoria which had hung over the county since Killarney in 1987 survived both the semi-final defeat by Galway of that year and the All-Ireland defeat by Galway in the following year. It was all concerned in a peculiar way with the recovery of self-respect, with fathers being able to look their children in the eye when 'The Sunday Game' came on the screen, with the feeling that, whatever else, the time for jokes at the expense of Tipp hurling had passed. 'Just think', a mourner was heard to say at the funeral of an old Tipperary hurler, 'how many went to the graves in the years past not knowing how long 'twould be before we were back — or if we'd ever be back.' It was now clearly demonstrated that the gloom of the famine years was not so much the result of not winning All-Irelands, but of the feeling that Tipp simply did not count.

And so the flags continued to fly, the blue and gold plaits to dangle from car mirrors and the stickers to proclaim that Tipp are magic. And most of all, confidence remained firm that Tipp would cut a fine dash in the League and that it was only a matter of time before they made the breakthrough that would lead to, not just one, but a succession of All-Irelands. Famine years apart, Tipp followers are never far removed from optimism.

The early stages of the League confirmed that optimism. Before the social whirl that was the inevitable accompaniment of the All-Ireland aftermath had run its course, Tipp travelled to Dungarvan on a bitterly cold October day to defeat Waterford 1-12 to 0-11. Without seven of the team that had fielded in Croke Park, they won the game in a manner that led older supporters to think that perhaps they were developing the ability to finish strongly which had been a traditional feature of their county's hurling.

Waterford, also short many of their regular side, chased everything from the beginning and were leading by 0-9 to 1-3 at half-time. When Colm Bonnar took over at centre-back things began to look up for

Tipp and the introduction of his younger brother Conal was an augury of things to come — as was that of Declan Carr. It was a perfectly placed pass from the third Bonnar, Cormac, that gave Pat Fox the only goal of the game but, nevertheless, supporters came away pleased enough with what they had seen. The next meeting of the counties would not end with such a narrow margin, but it would be remembered more for other reasons.

Only a week later at Semple Stadium Tipp withstood a less formidable challenge, from Offaly, though the margin of 1-19 to 0-10 was flattering. This time the only goal was scored by newcomer Michael Cleary. For nearly fifty minutes there was little between the sides and Offaly only dropped their heads and conceded a flurry of points after a Mark Corrigan penalty had been stopped and immediately afterwards the same player missed a scoreable free from fifty yards. A local sportswriter, while admitting that Tipp might have been more decisive in both games, however, remarked, 'It's not so long ago since we were afraid of everybody.'

When Wexford came to Semple Stadium for their third game they had more problems than they could cope with and Tipp, fielding for the third consecutive Sunday, gave them a drubbing that did little for either side. It had been many a long year since they had beaten Wexford in a League game and as supporters made their way back to their cars in the November gloom they shook their heads in remembrance of great Wexford teams of the past. Between the two counties there was a traditional respect and trouncing Wexford by 2-20 to 1-4 was an experience that gave Tipp no great pleasure.

For their last match before the Christmas lay-off Tipp travelled to Limerick on a day when visibility was such as to make it difficult at times to see the ball from the Mackey stand. It was a game that sent both sets of supporters home in a happy frame of mind — Tipp's for having seen their team come back after having lost an early ten point lead and Limerick's for having seen their team make an astonishing recovery. Perhaps it was the apparent ease with which Tipp found themselves with that ten point lead after only twenty minutes of play that induced the lethargy which nearly brought about their downfall. Eleven minutes from the end the teams were level; then came two Tipp points from frees by Pat McGrath, to be quickly followed by a mighty roar which signalled the arrival on the field of Nicholas English. It was English who once again stole the limelight and it was he who provided the most memorable score of the match when, only three minutes from the end, with a deft kick he placed the sliotar into the path of the oncoming Cormac Bonnar with such precision that the Cashel man had only to connect to send it rocket-like past goalkeeper Tommy Quaid. It was a pass and a score such as dreams are made of and, fittingly, the last score of the game was a point that only English at his best could provide.

With a happy turn of phrase Babs himself later summed up the general attitude to the team that was now entering the Christmas recess, having played four and won four and sharing the top of the League with Galway. They could, he said, enjoy their goose.

Before the League resumed in the spring there was a rumble at the Tipperary county convention of an issue which, while it had been tossed around in idle chat, had not been publicly discussed until it was raised as a result of an article by Raymond Smith in the *Sunday Independent*. Tipp hurling, it was being whispered, had become slightly less physical than tradition demanded and perhaps the departure from the traditional style had cost the county the All-Ireland. Babs, it seemed, had complained of the physical quality of Galway's approach to the All-Ireland and in his report to the convention the county secretary raised the question of whether more 'drive' was desirable in the team. While the matter was under discussion in the convention hall, Babs was in the adjacent field at a training session, but he came into the hall to play down the controversy and to plead that he had been misrepresented in the reporting of his remarks. The matter of Tipp's 'new' style, however, and Babs' tendency to speak his mind at all times would provide discussion points in and out of the press for some considerable time to come.

As the two teams pucked around prior to the Tipp-Antrim game at Semple Stadium in mid-February the heavens opened and they were lashed with rain, hail and sleet. Referee Terence Murray, understandably, threw in the ball a few minutes before the official starting-time and spectators, still huddling from the blast, missed Nicholas English's spectacular opening point against the wind. That score was indicative of things to come and Antrim enthusiasm proved no answer to Tipp efficiency. The final score was Tipp 2-15 to Antrim's 0-7 and once again it was felt that the game did little for either team. But Tipp were now in the position of needing only one more point to go directly into the League semi-finals.

Events would show that necessary point being earned with apparent difficulty, but the difficulty may have been more apparent than real. Assured of a place in the quarter-finals, Tipp opted to defuse much of the excitement that was building up for a Tipp-Galway meeting by sending to Ballinasloe a team which started with only six of the All-Ireland side. There was no point in risking injury and, anyway, they wanted to give a game to some players who had been on the bench for the past few games, explained selector Donie Nealon. But whatever the real reason, it was widely believed that Tipp were merely putting the showdown with Galway on the long finger. Sooner or later they would meet in a vital decider and there was no point in fully showing one's hand before it was necessary to do so.

Thus, while the *Tipperary Star* would report, 'Ultimately last Sunday's result (Galway 0-12 Tipperary 1-7) reaffirmed Galway's superiority over Tipperary at the present time, bringing to three the number of victories by the All-Ireland champions over the current league holders, in competitive meetings since 1987', it was not the entire truth. The game was played with the fierce competitiveness which followers had come to anticipate and Tipp might well have won. The sudden realisation of what it would do for morale to win with such an under-strength side was underlined by the introduction of Nicholas English near the end of the game. Galway, too, seem to have realised towards the end the shock to morale such an outcome would be and they introduced Noel Lane who had so effectively sunk the Tipperary ship at Croke Park. But in the restricted time at their disposal neither Lane nor English was permitted to shine.

The selectors were subjected to a considerable amount of criticism in the days that followed and perhaps it was this which dictated that all hands should be called on deck for the game against Kilkenny only a week later at Thurles. There is an ingrained habit in Tipperary of regarding performance against Kilkenny as much as against Cork as a kind of indicator of the state of hurling at any given time. Thus the word was out that this would be 'serious stuff' and on a day which saw a cool, blustery wind making a last-ditch stand against the advancing spring 16,000 spectators turned out. The volume of the cheering which greeted Kilkenny scores indicated that Tipperary were not the only ones taking the game seriously.

Both sides had much to cheer about. Five times they were level in the first half when Tipp, playing with the swirling wind, encountered

71

a tenacity in the opposition which one associates more with the championship. There were passages of first-class hurling and Tipp made most of the running in the second half, but they were unable to overcome the determination of the Kilkenny backs. With only three minutes to go they were three points ahead when, in dramatic fashion, Liam Fennelly connected with a long-range free from John Power to crash the ball to the net. For the last couple of minutes defeat stared Tipp in the face, with the result that when the final whistle sounded disappointment was tempered with relief.

The two counties were to meet again in the League semi-final in mid-April. With more reluctance than enthusiasm Tipp agreed to support the Kilkenny request that the game be played in Nowlan Park. Conscious, however, of the importance of giving away no ground advantage, they gave a sigh of relief when it was announced by the GAA press officer that the game would have to be played in Croke Park. This time there was no doubting from the Tipp side that failure to win would constitute a major defeat. In recent times Tipp seemed to bring the best out of Kilkenny, who had long forgotten the decades when they had to be twice as good as Tipp to beat them.

There was a new ingredient to Tipp's preparation in the presence of fitness coach Phil Conway, ex-Olympic weight-thrower, who brought to the camp a new concept of match fitness. Travelling from Dublin a few times a week, he demanded of each individual player a higher level of personal fitness than many of them had ever thought possible and he would be an important factor in the county's match preparations for the following months. With Heffernan, Fox and John Kennedy out of the reckoning through injuries, nothing was being left to chance.

The surprising part of the game, which was second on a double bill, the first part of which saw Galway demolish Dublin, was that it remained tame for so long. For forty minutes it strolled along with many of the characteristics of an evening tournament. Then, when Kilkenny went in front with a goal from Adrian Ronan, Tipp fought back and the game burst into flame. For the first time the policy of containment adopted by both teams was abandoned, substitute Michael Cleary figured prominently in the proceedings and in a frenzy of excitement the game ended with Tipp a single point ahead. There had been many games in which there had been a higher standard of hurling, but Tipp had won and that for the moment was the main thing. In the meantime there was another important matter to consider. Conor O'Donovan had to retire injured in the first half and for the greater part of the second half English was in obvious pain. Joe Hayes and John Cormack were also on the injured list. Injuries were becoming a problem that would dog Tipp for the rest of the year.

Over the next couple of weeks it was obvious that Tipp would have nothing like a full-strength team to line out against Galway in the League final. Babs, with his penchant for public relations, spoke to pressmen of how the championship was his priority but that, nevertheless, Tipp would be pulling out all the stops to hold on to their League title. In training, however, there was less talk of the championship and a very great deal about beating Galway. One way or another Tipp's face would be saved and no matter what happened they would go into the championship with buoyant expectations. In the meantime Phil Conway stressed that his target for the squad was peak fitness for the summer games. Win or lose, Tipp were ready for the outcome of the League final — players and supporters alike.

Galway too, however, had problems with injuries and when they lined out at Croke Park on 30 April 1989 before a crowd of 34,500 they were short McInerney, Cunningham and Steve Mahon. But from the moment of the throw-in it was clear that the crowd was watching a classic. Bodies crashed with reckless abandon as every ball was contested with ferocious determination and through it all there was a standard of hurling that from a partisan or non-partisan point of view was a delight to watch.

From both sides there were memorable scores. There was a whole bag of beautifully taken points by Galway that kept them ahead of Tipperary's four goals. And from Tipp there were those memorable goals, the result of a mixture of skill and tearaway aggression — one the result of a perfectly placed pass from captain Pat McGrath to lurking Michael Cleary and one when Cormac Bonnar appeared to take on the entire western backline to palm the ball past goalkeeper Commins. There was, too, the finely taken penalty by Pat McGrath on which Tipp failed to follow up and there was the persistence which ensured that until the final whistle left the score at Galway 2-16 Tipp 4-8 the outcome was in doubt.

In the dressing room afterwards there was the generous recognition of giant for giant. After the titanic tussles of the past two years there was still only a puck of a ball between the two sides. Phelim Murphy of the Galway Board made this point strongly while the Tipp players were still sitting with heads bowed, reluctant to face their supporters, and he generously assured them that the All-Ireland title was not far away. Theo English put it slightly differently. If you want to win a championship, he said, Galway are the team to beat; Tipp are within a puck of a ball of them, but are still that bit behind.

But defeat apart, there was the feeling among Tipp supporters that they had inched a tiny bit closer to beating Galway. English and the others would be there next time, and next time they would do it. Then came the reflection that in order to get at Galway again they would have to come out of Munster. They had too much respect for Cork to count those particular chickens before they were hatched. What didn't occur to them was that someone other than Cork would face them in the Munster final.

Chapter Eleven

THE IMPORTANCE IS ALMOST FRIGHTENING, 1989

As their first round championship game against Limerick drew closer it became obvious that the years of the famine had taken a heavy toll on Tipp self-confidence. Before the hungry years they were generally able to assess themselves fairly accurately and to know who was likely to beat them and who was not. But now there was a residue of the time when 'we were afraid of everybody', so that the nearer the Limerick game came, the more the confidence of the previous few weeks ebbed. There was a new psychological barrier to be faced too — the elusive three-in-a-row Munster titles which had been achieved by the county only three times in the past. On the other hand, the few weeks since the League final had done wonders on the injury front and the biggest problem facing the selectors was not how to plug gaps, but who was to be dropped to accommodate those who had been previously unavailable.

The problem of who to drop was simplified somewhat when a fresh injury during training left Michael Cleary in doubt and only at the last minute was Pat Fox included in his place. The team that lined out at Pairc Ui Chaoimh against a Limerick team which was yet in the making was: Ken Hogan; John Heffernan, Conor O'Donovan, Noel Sheehy; Conal Bonnar, Bobby Ryan, Paul Delaney; Declan Carr, Colm Bonnar; Declan Ryan, Joe Hayes, John Leahy; Pat Fox, Nicholas English and Pat McGrath.

There is always danger in meeting a reasonably good team that has nothing to lose, and in view of bookies' odds and media hype, Limerick fitted into this category. They proceeded then to tear into everything and to show some fine touches of stickmanship so that by half-time, having played against the wind, they stood level (1-7 each) with the much vaunted champions whose supporters were beginning to feel again the chill that had become so familiar in the past.

But if there was apprehension among Tipp supporters in the tunnels at half-time, in the dressing room there was quite something else. There was blistering criticism from the selectors. Cormac Bonnar replaced Pat McGrath, with English now moving to corner-forward to fill McGrath's place. Within ten minutes of the resumption the game had been won.

It was a bustling, aggressive run from the corner by Bonnar which began the trend that left Limerick floundering and made most of the remainder of the game interesting principally for the wonderful combination of the Tipp forwards. Collecting a ball near the corner flag, he made towards goal, managing to retain possession despite the attentions of three Limerick backs. But in giving him their attention, they had neglected English and it was too late to recover when the big, bearded Cashel man sent a handpass with pinpoint accuracy to the superstar who was momentarily alone on the edge of the parallelogram. One mighty connection, the net billowed and Limerick's hopes, so briefly raised, were effectively dead. With Bobby Ryan increasingly in command at centre-back, the forwards who had shot a disastrous eleven wides to Limerick's four in the first half turned on such a display of skill and accuracy as left their supporters wondering what exactly it was that had worked the transformation.

As point after point effectively nailed down Limerick's coffin, Pat Fox, displaying none of the after-effects of his recent injury, turned in such a performance as earned him the RTE 'Man of the match' award. And Joe Hayes, bubbling with the confidence which Tipp were now showing, blustered towards goal and passed Tommy Quaid with a one-handed stroke which he thereby celebrated by turning a somersault — much to everyone's amusement except the hapless Limerick followers.

The final score of Tipp 4-18 Limerick 2-11 was, incredibly, a fair reflection of Tipp's eventual superiority in a game that had looked to be in the balance for forty minutes. It did much to bolster confidence in Tipp's dugout capability, which had recently been the target of some criticism, and it was generally regarded as a victory as much for the mentors as for the players. The changes they had made — the introduction of Bonnar and the switching of Declan Ryan to midfield — had worked like a dream and now they could sit back and wait for Cork to overcome Waterford.

There was a snag, of course. On a day when the crowd was depleted by the attraction of an Ireland v Hungary soccer game, Waterford had succeeded in drawing with Cork, or to put it more correctly, Cork had succeeded in drawing with Waterford. There were many who saw

Waterford's failure to hold on to a six point lead as evidence of the absence of a basic will to win and, accordingly, counted them out for the replay. But in a wonderfully exciting sun-drenched game that saw nine goals scored, Cork were sent packing from the 1989 championship and now it remained for Tipp and Waterford to slug it out.

While it took everyone else as much as Tipp supporters a while to adjust to the novel pairing for the Munster final, there was good reason among those who mattered in Tipp to treat Waterford with a long spoon. It had been Waterford who had in 1963 interrupted the Tipp steamroller which would otherwise have achieved a magical six-in-a-row of Munster championships and all three of the Tipp mentors had belonged to that famous panel. And in recent times there had been a physical quality to clashes between the counties which had not always produced the open hurling that suited Tipp best. Thus, while there was a decided air of confidence in the Tipp camp which moved to Pairc Ui Chaoimh on 2 July, Waterford's crashing five goals against Cork in the replay — and other factors besides — left not too much room for complacency.

Somebody said after the Tipp-Waterford game that it was as well that Phil Conway had done his job as magnificently as he did. Perhaps Waterford felt that, being made rank outsiders by the press, they had nothing to lose. Whatever the reason, a few Waterford players from the beginning opted for a physical approach that paid no dividends either in scores or in popularity. At the end the scoreboard read: Tipp 0-26 Waterford 2-8. Out of an impressive thirteen points which Nicholas English chalked up, no less than eight were from frees and it was an assault on him which sent the second of two Waterford players to the line towards the conclusion of the game.

It was a bad-tempered business throughout and when Bobby Ryan took the cup — in place of Pat McGrath, whose club Loughmore-Castleiney nominated him to fill Pat's position — the usual pious platitudes about a fine sporting game were left unsaid. Live television coverage ensured that there could be no whitewashing the real flavour of the proceedings, though in the dressing room interviews afterwards care was taken that nothing was said to create future friction between the counties.

A week later a statement was issued by the Waterford County Board expressing regret 'for the actions of a small minority of our team for their indiscipline during the game'. At the same time the

Board rejected 'allegations levelled against our team manager and mentors that it was official policy to use strong-arm tactics against Tipperary'. That, it seemed, ended that, and now the decks were cleared for the much-awaited Tipp-Galway All-Ireland semi-final. But not quite.

The intervention of what came to be known as the 'Keady affair' was a godsend to journalists, but it introduced into the run-up to the game a degree of acrimony that would destroy the flavour of what might otherwise have been an epic. When Tony Keady, the lion-hearted and wonderfully talented Galway centre-back, played for a Laois club against a Tipperary club in New York, allegedly without proper clearance from Croke Park, the Tipperary New York club objected and the New York GAA suspended him for two games. The GAA authorities at home, unfortunately for Galway and for hurling itself, then took a hand and suspended him for twelve months. The manager of the Laois club in New York peevishly suggested that the entire business had been the result of intrigue on the part of Tipperary people back in Ireland, a mischievous allegation which in itself did a great deal to stir up trouble.

There can be no doubt whatsoever that public opinion in Tipperary, as elsewhere, was sympathetic towards Keady and towards Galway. Babs Keating issued a statement which distanced Tipperary from the matter, and while Galway's appeal to the Central Council was pending it was discussed by the Tipperary County Board. A number of speakers came out strongly in favour of Keady's reinstatement in time for the game, one of them saying, to applause, that they wanted to beat Galway with Tony Keady. The county's representative was instructed to vote in favour of reinstatement and county secretary Tommy Barrett not alone voted for the reinstatement, but urged it with such force that he was publicly thanked by the Galway Hurling Board secretary and team selector Phelim Murphy. Tipp had done all it could.

Nevertheless, it seemed that no matter what was done, it was going to be believed in some circles in Galway that Tipp was using all its influence to deprive them of the services of Keady on the vital day. So when, despite Tipp's support and despite reports that they would not field without Keady, Galway lost the appeal, a new ingredient was added to the razor-sharp rivalry of a few years standing. The ironic aspect of a bizarre situation was that while Galway would undoubtedly suffer greatly from the loss of their star player, his loss would be in a peculiar way a psychological disadvantage to Tipp. No team can afford to have the quality of a victory debased before it is even won.

Galway came to Croke Park, then, minus Tony Keady, but with a strong sense of grievance against Tipp — a situation which was not improved by Tipp's juniors having only two weeks before narrowly beaten a strongly fancied Galway team in the All-Ireland Junior final. Tipp came with exhortations to have confidence in themselves ringing in their ears. If they needed to be told to take nothing for granted against Limerick and Waterford, what they needed facing Galway was an appreciation of their own worth as a team. Culbaire of the *Tipperary Star* put it plainly: 'The importance of the game is almost frightening. A victory would take much of the sting away from the previous losses and put us well in line of the national title; a defeat would positively stamp us irretrievably inferior and prove that closeness is our utmost in this particular confrontation' — a sobering reflection for the young men concerned, and their mentors.

For an organisation which necessarily is keenly conscious of the importance of arranging fixtures to its maximum financial advantage, the GAA made an extraordinary decision in billing the two semi-finals for the same venue on the same day. Antrim and Offaly would have filled Croke Park without any assistance from Tipperary or Galway, and the latter pair would have filled it twice over. Yet, to all the controversy already surrounding the fixture was added the difficulty of satisfying the demand for tickets. Galway supporters had reason to be dissatisfied on more than one score.

If Galway and Tipp were regarded as the bigger draw of the two, it was Antrim and Offaly who provided the most sparkling entertainment of the day. Any hurling team from the North is at any time guaranteed on an appearance in Croke Park not alone the support of their own county but that of thirty others. Understandably, when a late Antrim flurry of goals put paid to Offaly's chances of an All-Ireland appearance, a forest of Tipp and Galway flags waved with those of the northerners. But Offaly, despite the shock of an unexpected defeat, did not forget themselves as sportsmen. As the Antrim players, delirious with excitement, left the field they entered the tunnel through a guard of honour of the Offaly team they had just defeated. It was a gesture which left many spectators and television viewers with the opinion that Offaly had won something much more valuable than mere victory on the scoreboard — they had won the respect and affection of the hurling public and of neutral observers everywhere.

No such chivalrous gesture marked the ending of the Tipp-Galway game. The meeting of the two finest hurling teams of their time — mighty Galway going for their third-in-a-row and up-and-coming Tipperary trying to satisfy the hunger of eighteen years — had all the ingredients of a memorable game. But the negative attitude which marked the weeks before the game was carried on to the field. Two Galway players were sent off and the huge crowd left Croke Park feeling that what they had seen was a far cry from what they had expected.

For Galway there was the frustration of fielding without not just Tony Keady but star forward Martin Naughton who had been injured. At the end of the game there was the additional frustration of knowing that even after two of their number had been sent to the line, the game was still there for the taking if only they had kept their heads as might reasonably be expected of twice-champions.

For Tipperary there was the knowledge that they had not played at all as well as they might. They had narrowly averted the catastrophe of losing to thirteen men which, if it had happened, would have made the county a laughing stock. And there was, too, a feeling that perhaps a couple of the Tipp players, while not meriting marching orders, might have on the day contributed towards the bad feeling which destroyed the game.

Once again Tipp's full-forward line of Fox, Bonnar and English was the key ingredient in the success, though of the actual play it was Eanna Ryan's two goals for Galway which would be remembered best. Pat Fox's goal should have lifted the entire Tipp team but failed to do so and later it would be a cause of much discussion how Tipp failed to capitalise on their having two extra players.

The match was full of incidents which would later be blown out of proportion and at the end referee John Denton of Wexford became the chief whipping boy for the Galway defeat. Typical of the incidents cited was when a penalty by John Leahy was stopped by goalkeeper Commins. On the grounds that there had been a defensive infringement, the referee brought back the ball and allowed Leahy another shot. This time the ball was safely cleared away, but the torrent of boos made it clear that the referee was not the most popular person in Croke Park, at least among the Galway supporters.

80

When the final whistle sounded Tipp were only three points ahead of the thirteen Galway men (1-17 to 2-11) and this time there was no guard of honour for the victors. There was instead a detail of Gardaí to escort the referee from the pitch.

In the Galway dressing room there was silence and all pressmen, including those from Galway, were excluded. From the showers in the Tipp dressing room came the raucous strains of 'Slievenamon', but some of the players simply sat silently, totally drained of emotion and energy. It was nice to have qualified for an All-Ireland final, but there was something missing.

When a well-wisher was identified as the chairman of the New York Tipperary club who had raised the initial objection to Tony Keady in the United States, he was approached by County Chairman Noel Morris and told he was not welcome. It was understandable, explained Morris, that Galway people should point the finger at us over the New York business and it must be clearly seen that we had nothing whatsoever to do with it.

Only a week later Tipp and Galway met in the All-Ireland Under-21 semi-final. It was a tough, tight but wonderfully sporting game which Tipp won by seven points and there was no bad blood at the end. Hurling games and hurlers are sometimes, it seems, best served by a minimum of media attention.

THE SUMMIT, 1989

A couple of days after the Croke Park game Phelim Murphy of the Galway Board was asked if there was any truth in the rumour that Galway would be objecting to Tipp on the grounds that some of the team had played, like Tony Keady, in America. He replied that the Galway beef was with referee Denton's handling of the game. Indeed they did have information regarding Tipp players in America, but as far as Galway was concerned the matter was closed. Games should be won on the field and not in the board room and they wished Tipp well in their quest for an All-Ireland, he added.

But the rumour refused to go away and increasingly Paul Delaney, the Roscrea half-back, was mentioned as being the possible target of an objection. There were some anxious days for Tipp officials until the deadline for an objection had passed, and when midnight of the following Saturday arrived and there was still no objection lodged at Croke Park there was a collective sigh of relief. There was, too, an appreciative admission that Galway had done the decent thing and there were those who saw this as Galway's *quid pro quo* for Tipp's casting their vote in favour of Tony Keady's reinstatement. Despite Delaney's insistence that he had played a couple of games in London with the proper clearance, an investigation into his precise situation was the last thing that was wanted. The years of famine had taken their toll and Tipp had been made dizzy by having arrived at the summit of all their endeavours. Nothing must be allowed to go wrong now.

So, as crowds turned up each night to see Tipp training, recalling the glory days when watching the county team working out was almost a regular part of summer's routine, rumours continued to fly and more and more County Board officers felt the compulsion to leave nothing to chance. Consultation with London officials appeared to indicate that, in view of the press coverage of the situation, it would be unwise in the extreme to play Paul Delaney. Besides, it would put Antrim in an unfair predicament and, anyway, with players by now jostling for positions, it did not make sense to include anyone about whose legality there was the slightest shadow of doubt. Nobody would thank the selectors for putting out a team that might subsequently be deemed illegal.

There was much consultation between Board officers and selectors and on the Sunday morning before the game County Chairman Noel Morris and North Tipperary Board Chairman John Tierney went to Roscrea to break the bad news to Delaney. For a young man being deprived of the chance of realising his life's ambition, Delaney received the news with remarkable self-possession, a factor which deeply impressed his two visitors and which they remembered with gratitude afterwards. When the team was announced later in the day there was issued simultaneously a statement from the Board to the effect that it had instructed the selectors not to consider Delaney 'so that no hint of controversy will attach itself to Tipperary'. John Kennedy, who had been injured and who had come on as a sub late in the semi-final, returned to fill Delaney's position at left half-back and the irrepressible Joe Hayes was replaced by his Clonoulty club mate, Declan Ryan, who was moved from centre-field to make way for the return of Colm Bonnar to the side. Then, the decks cleared, team and supporters had a week to prepare psychologically for the big test.

The team was: Ken Hogan; John Heffernan, Conor O'Donovan, Noel Sheehy; Conal Bonnar, Bobby Ryan, John Kennedy; Colm Bonnar, Declan Carr; John Leahy, Declan Ryan, Michael Cleary; Pat Fox, Cormac Bonnar and Nicholas English.

In a hurling context, preparing psychologically to beat Antrim is not at all as easy as it may sound. There is among the hurling fraternity a consciousness that the game is taken seriously only in a limited number of counties and that it has to be encouraged wherever possible. Hence there is always a welcome for any newcomer who shows the least sign of breaking into the select circle.

For Antrim hurlers there has always been in Tipperary a particular regard that is not entirely unrelated to an admiration for the nationalist tradition in the northern counties. When Cork beat Antrim in the 1943 All-Ireland by a whacking 5-16 to 0-4, they made themselves the target of much criticism for overdoing it. That Cork had to make sure they did not make the mistake of underrating Antrim as Kilkenny had just done in the semi-final was hardly taken into consideration. Tipp, on the other hand, never having had the experience of confronting Antrim at the final hurdle, could afford the luxury of feeling benevolent towards them. There was much raking up of evidence of Tipp-Antrim friendship over many years. As far back as 1929 a Tipp team had travelled to Belfast and speeches at the time had expressed the pleasure of Tipperary men in visiting the birthplace of the Society of United Irishmen. Years afterwards, when Casement Park was being opened in 1953, a casket of earth was carried from Semple Stadium and also from Croke Park to be mixed with that of the playing area of the new stadium. It was a big event in Thurles and among the relay of runners who carried the earth to its home in Antrim were Tipperary hurlers of the time, Mickey Byrne and Tommy Doyle. The first runner in the relay from Thurles was athlete Fr Jim Semple, son of the legendary Tom Semple after whom the Thurles stadium is named.

But now it was Antrim that stood between Tipp and the disgrace of a generation of Tipp men in being the first since the foundation of the GAA to let a decade pass without having won an All-Ireland. Next year would be 1990 and the disgrace would be intolerable if the entire 1980s remained blank. The situation allowed for no sentiment. The manner in which Paul Delaney was dropped was indicative of the frame of mind with which the game was approached by the selectors and the County Board. It now remained only for the team to show what their frame of mind was. In the event, they left no doubt — and it seemed as if the Croke Park administration unwittingly helped them along.

If any team of the past had become part of the folk memory in Tipp during the years of famine, it was the three-in-a-row squad of 1949–51. They had appeared at a bleak time in Tipperary hurling and for some reason had acquired a glamour which Tipp teams of the past had not always enjoyed. They had for only the second time in the county's history won the elusive three-in-a-row and they had provided tussles with Cork which will live as long as hurling is talked of. It was the heyday of Christy Ring and a generation of Tipp supporters had lived with the problem from year to year of how to contain the wizard of Cloyne. These were the men who for three successive years had contained him — in so far as he was ever contained. The Tipp team of the early 1960s had won four All-Irelands in five years, but they were still part of the recent past and they had not yet assumed the legendary quality that was associated with the older group.

This, then, by a miracle of Croke Park and Irish Nationwide

arrangement, was the team chosen to be honoured on All-Ireland final day in 1989 — chosen at a time when it was not at all clear who would be contesting the title. And as the heroes of old — the rock-like backs John Doyle, Pat Stakelum, Jimmy Finn and Mickey Byrne and the colourful forwards, Sean and Paddy Kenny, the wonderful Jimmy Kennedy and the ever so versatile Seamus Bannon marched on to the field somebody was heard to comment, 'If these young fellows are any good at all they'll have to play well in front of these old fellows.' And to mark the continuity that has always been a feature of Tipp teams, the veterans included the Ryans of Borrisoleigh, Tim and Ned, father and uncle of Bobby and Aidan and uncles of Richard Stakelum. For Tipp followers of a definite vintage, it was an emotional appearance which could not but have a salutary effect on the young fellows who would shortly emerge from the tunnel before a forest of blue and gold.

As a game of hurling the 1989 All-Ireland will never rate among the classics, although any game that produces seven goals will be conceded to have had its moments. But the final score of 4-24 to 3-9 suggests a margin of superiority which removed the element of unpredictability. It did not look so for the first quarter, but Antrim sent a number of wides which they would bitterly regret, and from the moment when Declan Ryan drove a fifty yard shot to the Antrim net, seemingly as much to his own surprise as anyone else's, the pattern of the game was sealed. By half-time Tipp led by 1-13 to 0-5.

There were times, however, when Antrim showed some of the qualities which had enabled them to sink Offaly, though one of them was not when a penalty by Aidan McCarry at a vital early stage was cleared away by John Kennedy. McCarry and Brian Donnelly had excellent goals and the latter might have had another had he not opted to take a point with only Ken Hogan to beat at close range. And in the last few moments of the game, after Hogan had stopped a 65 from Dessie Donnelly, Donal Armstrong took a fine opportunistic goal which left the northerners with what would have been in other circumstances a respectable tally on the scoreboard. A number of All-Irelands had been won with a smaller score.

But the day belonged to the Tipp forwards. With midfield dominance ensuring a plentiful supply of ball, they had every opportunity of showing the skills and marksmanship which their chequered early passage to Croke Park had made so difficult. English had a cracking personal tally of 2-12 and his final goal, almost on the call of time when he connected with a first-time drop-shot on a cross from Aidan Ryan, was one of the goals of the year. Both full and half lines combined superbly and one of the goals demonstrated the cohesion that made them such a lethal combination: Michael Cleary placed Nicholas English who placed Cormac Bonnar who hit the post only to have the rebound met by the advancing English to finally finish to the net.

In the end there was room for sentiment from the Tipp dugout. Before the final whistle three Tipp subs had been introduced — Joe Hayes, Aidan Ryan and Donie O'Connell. It was the last of these who got the biggest ovation as he came on. He had slipped from the fifteen during the year when work commitments abroad had interfered with training, but there was no doubt that his contribution over the years was much appreciated. Games against Cork had always brought out the best in him and there were many who would carry an abiding memory of a day in Killarney when Donie went on his knees in the Cork net and tens of thousands of Tipp supporters felt like kneeling with him.

There was further room for sentiment when Bobby Ryan lifted the McCarthy Cup and assured the Antrim team that their day was not far off. Suddenly it was as if Tipp realised that now they could afford to be generous and through the delirious singing of 'Slievenamon' there was now discernible among players and spectators a regret that Antrim had to be the ones to suffer because of the hunger that was part of the aftermath of the famine. But it was a regret that did nothing to subdue the abandon of the moment. In the past Tipp had the reputation of having a following that was phlegmatic rather than exuberant. Winning was a custom and there had been no generation which had never savoured victory. Nothing brought home that precise point to old-timers as much as the rush of blue-and-gold embroidered figures on to the field to mob Nicky English when his last goal nearly deposited the goal net in the canal. 'You'd think they never saw a goal scored before', said one disgusted older follower. The truth was they hadn't. Not in Croke Park by a Tipp player. Not one like this. And when Bobby Ryan lifted the cup to signal the final ending of the famine, there was such a scene as Croke Park had certainly never seen before from Tipp supporters. Hands were wrung by total strangers whose only common bond was the blue and gold, tears were freely shed and voices that were already hoarse summoned fresh life for just one more rendition of 'Slievenamon'.

In the Antrim dressing room afterwards, Brother Michael O'Grady, a former Tipp coach who was now in the Antrim camp as assistant to coach Jim Nelson, commented, 'You have to lose before you win.' Since the far off day in 1971 when Tadhg O'Connor had last received the McCarthy Cup on behalf of a team whose members were now in middle age, Tipp had known all about defeat. If losing qualified a team to win, Tipp were well qualified. Now it was time to celebrate.

Chapter Thirteen

THE HOMECOMING, 1989

The round of celebrations which began the moment Bobby Ryan raised the cup was to continue for many months — too many, those who were concerned with holding the team together for the following year would say. But then, the aftermath of famine is never without its problems.

Some of these problems began on the very night of the final when arrangements were completed for the team's homecoming. The expenses of the team for the duration of the championship had been borne by the Supporters Club, which put that organisation in a privileged position. Arrangements had already been made for the team to be received at a concert in Semple Stadium on the Monday night of their return home. That put the Semple Stadium committee in a privileged position. Then there was the County Board, which was the traditional arbiter of what the county team did and where it went after a victory.

But outside these groups were the great battalions of supporters who did not know or did not care who put the team on the field or brought them home as long as they got there. To Tipperary supporters the coming home with the cup and the ritual progress through Liberty Square to the Archbishop's residence was as much part of tradition as the winning itself. During the eighteen lean years the ritual had assumed an almost mystical quality in the telling to young people who had never known it. It was unthinkable that any part of the ritual should be omitted.

It was decided, however, perhaps on the night of the All-Ireland itself, that the team on its return home should avoid the town altogether and go straight to Semple Stadium. The colossal crowds which attended the homecoming of the team which had been beaten by Galway in the previous year had, perhaps, underlined the risks to public safety. But there is hardly any reason to think that the Garda authorities were entirely insistent on the procedure which was now followed. An unwise decision was taken and it would solve a lot if the mistake could be blamed on Garda fears of uncontrollable crowds.

As the team swept homeward on the Monday evening in the distinctive blue and gold bus, escorted by a cavalcade of cars with horns hooting and flashing lights, crowds were already pouring into Thurles, while along the road supporters waved and children got their first taste of what it was like to welcome home champions. As the bus reached the Tipperary border near Urlingford at 9.30 p.m., bonfires blazed and the crowds who had collected on the roadway gave the team a foretaste of what they might expect in Thurles. From the front of the bus Babs and Bobby acknowledged the reception and then it was onwards at full steam through Horse and Jockey. But all along the way there was a stream of excited supporters waving and cheering, with children decked out in blue and gold as though going to a match.

In the meantime, while the turnstiles at Semple Stadium began to click through the first of a crowd of some 25,000 who paid £5 a head for adults, the streets of the town began to fill up. It was a pleasant evening and the carnival air was infectious. Once again 'Slievenamon' was heard on all sides. Liberty Square was the heart of the action and from a blue and gold caravan songs with local appeal were played and replayed, particularly popular being 'Tipperary's 23rd'. The crowd were kept informed of the progress of the team towards the town.

When their heroes reached the outskirts of the town, they did not take the time-honoured route through the Square. Instead, with the lights inside the bus turned off, they skirted the town and arrived at Semple Stadium without delay, to be rushed inside before excited fans could block their way. The Wolfe Tones and local artists had been entertaining the crowd since 8.30, but not even the cheer which marked the sounding of full time at Croke Park could match the crescendo of jubilation which greeted the arrival of the team on the platform. One by one, players, subs and mentors were introduced, predictable speeches were made — each of them cheered as if it were the first — and there were promises that this was only the first of another three-in-a-row for the county. Finally, with nothing left to be said from the platform, Joe Dolan took over where the Wolfe Tones had left off. The night was still only beginning.

Back in the Square, however, the hordes who had been disappointed by their apparent rejection in favour of cash-paying customers at the stadium could not be expected at that particular moment to take into account the financial problems facing the Semple Stadium committee and their eagerness to turn every possible occasion to financial advantage. The *Tipperary Star* of the following week would report:

Some children with furry blue and gold caps and flags had stood with their parents in the Square from as early as 5.30. No one had told them that the team would definitely pass through the Square on their way to the homecoming concert in Semple Stadium, but the crowds felt it in their bones that this would be what would happen. Hadn't it always been the case, ever since their grandparents' time? . . .

By 9.45 John O'Connell interrupted his broadcasting in the Square to announce that he had heard unofficially that the team had actually arrived in the Stadium, having travelled in from Horse and Jockey, via Clongour and Butler Avenue. The decision to bypass the Square had been made by the gardaí who had been worried about the safety aspect of using the Liberty Square route. But no official announcement was made to this effect to the long-suffering public, many of whom had been waiting for several hours at this stage.

The reaction to the unofficial announcement was instant . . . Words like sacrilegious, scandalous and disgusting were on everyone's lips. Lifelong supporters of the GAA vowed that they would never again support another GAA draw.

As parents made their way home with tired and confused children in tow, the atmosphere around the Square was worse than if Tipperary had been beaten 24-0 by Antrim . . . No one blamed the team for what had happened but there was a groundswell of opposition to the GAA itself.

The truly amazing thing was that while the GAA itself became the target of the sharpest criticism, the euphoria of the victory was in no way at all diluted and the team even gained in popularity as they embarked on a massive campaign of public relations in visiting schools and local clubs with the cup. But the matter of the homecoming was one that had to be sorted out and at the next County Board meeting Chairman Noel Morris made a personal statement regarding it.

He accepted that those who had gathered in the Square had been snubbed; he apologised for it and he promised that it would not happen again. The arrangements for the concert had been in the hands of the Semple Stadium committee, he said, and he regretted the manner in which the entire homecoming had been handled. He particularly regretted the lights being turned off in the bus so that the team would not be recognised, and he promised: 'Next time Tipperary win an All-Ireland we will go to the steps of the Cathedral and we will go up the Square.'

It was a promise that would be kept, but in the meantime the county got properly into its stride at the business of celebrating. There was hardly a child who did not get an opportunity to see the McCarthy Cup and at least some of his or her heroes at close quarters. There was, however, something of a deterioration in relations between those who had been responsible for the gaffe in public relations surrounding the homecoming and those who would have liked somebody else to be held responsible. Quite appropriately, it was Bobby Ryan who drew attention to the unhealthy nature of this situation. Speaking at a reception in Nenagh, he made an eloquent appeal: 'I want to see all the GAA organisations behind the team, rowing in together so that we can achieve again what we achieved this year, but which will be more difficult next year. I am appealing to the County Board and to the Supporters Club to work together towards this end. We need your support. As players we need support, not just money, but the backing and encouragement of all sides.'

While these matters were being sorted out, if anyone had any reservations as to whether the famine was well and truly over, Tipp's under-21's gave the answer. Only a week after the seniors' success against Antrim, they brought yet another All-Ireland to the county by defeating Offaly by 4-10 to 3-11. The team was captained by Declan Ryan and included Conal Bonnar and John Leahy of the senior team as well as sub John Madden. Three All-Irelands in a year — what more could a county want!

Chapter Fourteen

SUPERSTAR

It is probably true to say of any successful hurling team that it must have at least one man who is widely perceived to be above average quality. He must have all the skills of the game to an unusual degree and his personality on the field must radiate all that makes one man more than another a winner. He must be able to do all that others can do but with much more style and panache. He must be a joy to watch in his mastery of the skills of the game and be capable of occasionally doing something which leaves spectators marvelling at his virtuosity. The hurley must seem to be part of his physical self.

In the course of a game he must be an inspiration to his own team, his presence on the field lifting the game of others and bringing the best out of lesser men who are with him. He must have the exact opposite effect on the opposition, making them ill at ease if not jittery, particularly if he is a forward. His presence on the field must of itself lend excitement to a game. He must be capable of holding out the chance of victory when all seems lost. The public, who are the final arbiters in such matters, will watch him more closely than anyone else and whether on any given day he performs as well as they would like him to, he will still be a major talking point. His name on the programme of a non-championship game is a guarantee that many who would not otherwise attend will be there. He has a drawing power of his own which is not all related to the importance of the occasion. He is a superstar.

When we think of superstars we most often think of forwards. Forward play is a higher form of hurling than back play. The back can pull with abandon and when he connects he may earn the biggest cheer of the day for a chance clearance. The forward may do all that the back does, but if his eye is a fraction out on a day he may be a failure. His performance on any given day is measured by his ability to score, not by his ability either to connect or to gain possession. The corner-back may be considered to have done his job if his man does not score, though he may have stretched the rules beyond their absolute limit in preventing his man from doing so. The standard of judgment applied to the forward is infinitely more severe than that applied to the back. But if he measures up to this demanding standard he is accorded a degree of public acclaim rarely accorded to a back. When one thinks of the greatest hurlers the names that spring most readily to mind are those of forwards — Ring and Mackey, Keher and Jimmy Doyle and so on. If one is asked to pick the greatest backline of all time, dozens of names will be offered as candidates. When one turns to the forwards there are fewer contestants and for most people about four of the positions are filled without argument. Occasionally there are backs who are considered superstars. But when we think of hurling superstars we are normally thinking of forwards.

Martin Kennedy, the Tipperary star of the 1920s and 1930s was widely regarded by his own generation as the greatest full-forward of all time. Legend persists of his artistry, his tricks and his scoring power. When I was a boy he was long past his best, but his presence on the field in a club game created an immediate buzz. His name was on everybody's lips and he was pointed out to youngsters because, truth to tell, he was past the stage of being readily identifiable as a great hurler. I can clearly remember the disappointment of discovering that the obviously ineffectual full-forward on the Kildangan team was the great Martin Kennedy of the Toomevara Greyhounds. Ten years later I saw him playing in goal when he was on the wrong side of fifty. Not even a shadow of the magic was left but he was still Martin Kennedy, the legendary full-forward, and there are those who grew up cherishing the memory of having seen him, though he was only in goal and not even fit enough for that. Playing well or playing badly, in his heyday or past his best, he was still Martin Kennedy. Therein is the quality of the real superstar.

If one is to look for the superstar of the Tipperary team of the post-famine years, one has to consider Nicholas English. No other player was so consistently in the headlines or in the minds of those playing against Tipperary. It is hardly belittling the stature of any other Tipp forward to say that nobody else was regarded by opposing backlines with such fear over so long a period. There are those who would say that the tragedy was that he played his best games during the famine period and Cork hurling followers speak with much respect of that golden patch during which he was winning his record five-in-a-row Fitzgibbon Cups. There are those who would list among his finest hours that against Clare in the 1984 championship and others that against Cork in the Munster final of 1985. But rightly or wrongly, the mass of Tipp supporters identify his moments of purest gold as those during the years when Babs was at the helm. For many the great games of the years of the revival are inextricably bound up with memories of spectacular scores and spectacular efforts to prevent English from scoring.

A study of the career of Nicholas English might prove rewarding to those who are truly interested in the spread of hurling. Because he belongs to Tipperary, it is generally assumed that he was reared to hurling. He was not. The village of Cullen close to the Tipperary-Limerick border where he was born and grew up, has no tradition of hurling. There was no local hurling team of long ago trailing clouds of glory to set a youngster's imagination alight and no local hurling team of his own day with whom a youngster could identify in any way; neither did he inherit a family tradition of hurling. He was a loner in his fascination with hurling from an early age and as he was growing up there was no youngster in the village with whom he could play hurling. His early practice sessions were alone at the rear of his house against the wall — left, right, left, right, just as Tony Wall recommended to be practised in a handball alley.

As a child, he was fascinated with all forms of sport and he kept notebooks of details of all sorts of sporting events, including golf and horse racing. Had his preoccupation been with any game other than hurling, it is likely that he would have reached the top in it. His physical attributes, his commitment and his mental discipline would have made him a champion in any sport to which he chose to give his single-minded attention.

Long after Christy Ring had played his last game with Glen Rovers and relied principally on squash to keep him fit, he confided in me that he felt if he were only beginning his sporting life, he had it in him to be a world champion squash player. Knowing the extraordinary athletic abilities of the greatest hurler of all and the fierce spirit of competitiveness which was part of his being, I believe that he could indeed, given the right circumstances, have been the world's number 1 squash player.

Nicholas English, too, would certainly have made his mark in any sport, though not to anything like the same extent or with anything like the same certainty. For one thing, he never did have or never could have quite the same deadly commitment as the wizard of Cloyne. Neither could anybody else. But English, with his natural athletic attributes and his unusual degree of dedication, would certainly have at least shone at any game. As a child he had an inherited fear of water. But he never let his fear be seen and he learned to swim without any of his classmates or anyone else recognising his problem. In that he showed one of the key characteristics of the born champion — the ability to make little of his psychological as well as physical shortcomings, the ability to be captain of his own soul. Had his chosen game been soccer, it is surely more than a guess that the South Tipperary Junior League would not have been the limit of his experience.

In view of the fact that English's first competitive hurling game was when he went to secondary school in Tipperary town, there may be a lesson for those concerned with the coaching of youngsters. While other children were being exhorted from the sideline by mentors and parents with more enthusiasm than good sense to 'pull on the ball' and win at all costs, young English was at home practising the skills which too much participation in games denies to many youngsters. Before he played his first game with Tipperary CBS against Doon CBS he had already mastered the principal skills of the game. What remained for him to learn was mainly about match-play. The acquiring of the necessary skills was his own doing and not the result of endless hurling games on the village green with local lads. Even today Cullen parish, with its population of 450, has no Gaelic field. At the moment of writing, it has two soccer pitches. But in Tipperary CBS there were mentors who knew their business and his parents still recall a visit to Croke Park when he was only 13½, led by Brother Moloughney, which turned the young fellow's enthusiasm for hurling into a passion.

English played minor football for Tipperary for three years — from 1978 to 1980. At that time, he was at least as good a footballer as a hurler and a display which he gave against Kerry in the U-21 grade when he almost single-handedly beat Kerry has become part of Tipperary's football lore. It was said at the time that had he been a Kerry man he would certainly have been a Kerry senior player. But like so many dual players, he opted totally for hurling, the difference between him and others better known as dual players being that he made his decision while yet an under-age player. He would continue to play football for his own Lattin-Cullen club, but no more than that, and indeed it was a feature of his hurling career that he retained his loyalty to his home club and never transferred away from it. I once heard a political argument regarding Jack Lynch silenced by a Cork man who asserted that a man who had played for his club as Lynch did for over twenty years must have extraordinary human qualities. By this yardstick, how does one view someone like English who throughout a distinguished inter-county hurling career continued to return to play both hurling and football for a not too distinguished junior club?

He won a minor hurling All-Ireland in 1980, having shaken off the disappointment of being dropped from the subs the previous year because of restrictions on the number of players allowable on a panel and after having overcome the handicap of a broken leg during the early summer. Nothing was going to prevent his getting back to hurling in record time and two days after the plaster cast was removed he was seen testing his leg by running round the hill of Cullen.

In the following year he won an under-21 All-Ireland and at the same time began a record run of five Fitzgibbon Cup successes with University College Cork. This was a period which was of huge significance to his development as a hurler. In UCC he was under the tutelage of the astute Fr Michael O'Brien and by the time he emerged from university to return to Tipperary CBS as a teacher of Irish, there was little more that he could learn about hurling. The game was the ruling passion, the consuming interest of his life. He was a superb master of all its skills and nowhere was this mastery better appreciated than in Cork. It only remained to be seen whether those skills would survive the heat at the very top of championship hurling.

While he was still at university major hurling honours came to him. He played for four years in a row with the combined universities and had already begun what was to be a sequence of appearances with the All-Stars. He had also become a target for on-field treatment of a sort that would have induced many a player to take a permanent holiday from the game. The memory of the injuries sustained by him in the Tipp-Waterford championship game in Pairc Ui Chaoimh in 1983 still rankles in Tipperary. Like so many great hurlers, English himself never resorted to rough, much less to dirty play. He was only 21 when injuries in that game necessitated twenty-four stitches inside his mouth. For some time he carried plaster of Paris in his mouth and he endured pain for months.

Throughout his career he was dogged by injuries and, suffice to say, not all were merely pulled muscles! In a sense he was doomed to injury by public attention. Beloved by the media, he was made the focus of every preview of a game and opponents were put under enormous pressure to stop him at all costs. When he was stopped, often by illegal methods, the cry was raised that he was unreliable and that he was a media creation, playing his best games against second-rate teams. When referees gave him the protection of the rules, the cry was raised, 'You can't lay a hand on English.' Hurling followers can be ruthless in their judgments. His succession of injuries was cited even in Tipperary as if they were self-inflicted and not the result of a basic weakness in the rules of hurling which in many ways fail to protect the skilful hurler against the merely determined one.

For three years before Tipperary emerged from the famine English had been selected for the All-Stars. He would be selected three more times. But after Tipp had regained the limelight and he had been adopted as the darling of the media he was subjected to harsher criteria — and probably closer marking than ever before. There are those who claim difficulty in explaining why he rather than any other should have been adopted by the media. But if there is such a thing as might be described in a player as stage presence, he had it. He was personable, educated, articulate, readily available, and he carried the clean-cut image on to the field with him. He looked good. He was a role model for children in that he never pulled a dirty stroke and never retaliated no matter what the provocation. And even in a game in which he played below his own standards, he was apt to produce a flash of brilliance that would make the game newsworthy and memorable. If he played to his own standard, he was newsworthy. If he did not, he was still newsworthy.

Perhaps it is true that by the end of the famine he had reached the peak of his virtuosity and for those who had been delighted over the years by the sheer range and quality of his skills, there would be after 1990 a gradual winding down process. In Cork, in particular, it is claimed that some of his very best hurling was played during the famine years. Johnny Clifford has said that every team needs a star; that English filled that need and that he more than anyone else raised Tipp from the doldrums. Fr O'Brien, who from close quarters charted and indeed was a major influence in his education as a hurler, spoke of him as a purist, with a first-class hurling brain, relying on hurling skills alone and abhorring all kinds of unsporting play. Jimmy Barry

Murphy, with every good reason to have a feel for such things, stressed that players of English's stature attract detractors. For him he was 'a fantastic player, a pure hurler'. For most hurlers wondering how they will be remembered long after the public memory is concentrated on other idols, such praise from such sources would be ample compensation for the awful moment that comes to every sports star when waning physical powers invite rejection from his own supporters.

In the autumn after Tipp's exit from the championship in 1994 I attended a private anniversary mass in a deceased hurler's house. After mass the congregation sat around discussing in muted tones the weather and other trivialities. The disappointment of Tipp's championship performance was referred to. Nicholas English's name was mentioned, voices were raised and immediately the mass-goers had divided into pro and anti-English factions. I asked myself at the time if any other Tipp player could conceivably have raised temperatures in such a way. Why did not Pat Fox — within a whisker of English in the score-sheet from 1987 to 1994 — Michael Cleary, Declan Ryan or any of the others generate such strong feelings?

It is ironic if, as has been suggested, English gave some of his very best performances before the revival began, that he will be best remembered for those years in which in the full glare of publicity he tried to shake off successive injuries and rise to expectations that in human terms simply could not often be met. Fitzgibbon team mates talk with awe of a day in 1983 when, in a game against UCD, he moved back to centre-back for the second half when UCC found themselves playing into a near hurricane. In this position were seen all his resources of hurling skill and strength to an extent that left those who saw it — including Fr O'Brien — wondering what a pity for Tipp that he could never be spared to play as a back. He did, in fact, play in the No. 6 jersey for Tipp's Under-21's that year, and when they were beaten by Galway in the All-Ireland final the selectors were much criticised for not having played him in the forwards!

There are other displays during those years that deserve to be better remembered. There was his pulsating performance against Clare in 1984 when he played what was described as true All-Star hurling through the hour. A seemingly safe lead having been frittered away, he led a final desperate assault along the right wing and managed to reach the penalty zone before being fouled. Seamus

Power rasped the penalty goalward to be saved, but Liam Maher sent the rebound to the net and Tipp were bound for another Munster final. As happened so often before and after, it was a foul against English which decided the outcome of the game.

One thinks of the Munster final against Cork in 1985 when, despite the closest attentions of a Cork backline playing before a home crowd, he clocked up two goals and three points. In an exciting game that lacked nothing but a close finish, Cork's backs were shuffled in a futile effort to contain him. It has been said that he never had the awesome power in his stroke which was part of Pat Fox's armoury. That day he showed with one of his goals why he never needed colossal power when he drew Ger Cunningham and sent the ball with pinpoint accuracy to the corner of the net. His forte was in the perfection of placing his shots rather than dependence upon brute force.

One thinks, too, of his vital personal part in bringing to an end the long night of the famine in 1987. It was another desperate raid by him along the right wing which produced against Cork in Thurles the point from a free by Pat Fox which gave Tipp the right to a replay in Killarney.

When Tipp were trailing by seven points in Killarney in the first half and in danger of falling so far behind that nothing would pull them up, it was a magical goal by English which kept them in touch. He was as closely marked as he could possibly be, but his speed in the single act of rolling and striking the ball in one movement was such that he could not be hooked. And the shot was perfectly placed away from Ger Cunningham.

Again it was he who, when all seemed lost at the stroke of time that day, made the individual foray downfield and took the lightning decision not to test Ger Cunningham, not even to risk being hooked, but to lob the ball over the bar with his hand. It was another stroke of genius, another fusion of superhuman physical effort and shrewd mental calculation that gave Tipp another thirty minutes in which to try to topple Cork.

There were other days when he showed all the qualities of the superstar. One thinks of the defeat by Galway in the 1987 semi-final when, despite the closest possible marking, he raised six flags from play. There was the day of the defeat by Cork in the 'donkey' Munster final in 1990 when he showed some of his finest touches and scored 1-4 from play. There was the performance against Waterford in the Munster final of 1989 when he scored thirteen points, including eight from frees, many of them for fouls against himself, before retiring injured.

To those who complain that there were occasions when English was only moderately good, it might be said one cannot climb Everest everyday. Perhaps, though, what he will be remembered best for in years to come will not be individual games but individual scores. Forward play is about scores, not about pucking the ball around. And if any forward ever supplied more than his share of spectacular scores, it was he. Many hurling followers of the 1980s and early 1990s have etched in their memories pictures of scores by English, the details often quite forgotten, only a hazy blur of pure magic remaining. Such a memory is before me as I write of a League game in Thurles on a mild drizzly day (the year and even the opposition forgotten). But I can still see him on the new stand side playing into the town goal, in a standing position, turning twice until, his man floundering on the soggy ground, he sent a graceful left-handed stroke over the bar with no apparent effort. It is the possibility of such moments of magic that make it worth forsaking the fireside on a winter's day.

There are, too, the magical scores whose every detail is quite unforgettable — the kicked goal against Cork in Thurles, the palmed point in Killarney, the goal at the canal end against Antrim in 1989 and dozens of points from all sorts of angles taken with that peculiar wrist action which was so identifiably English's.

Fr O'Brien's comment on English's possibilities as a back raises the question as to which was his most effective position. In this regard it is worth making the point that through the years he played at some time or other in every position in the forward line. His starting berth in the League of 1981/82 was at right half-forward and he stayed there until the 1983 championship game against Clare when he was picked at left-corner. He moved back to No. 10 for a few years before he began to figure at full-forward and left-corner in 1987/88. From 1989 to 1993 his preferred position with selectors was the No. 15 spot. The point has been made that he never had the devastating force behind his shots that some other famous forwards had and that he depended more on pinpoint accuracy — hence the belief that he was at his most lethal when near the goal. It was from a starting position of No. 15 that he scored 2-7 against Antrim in the 1988 League and 2-11 against Waterford. But his speed made him a headache to backs whether in the half or full-forward line. When close to the goal he could be 'bottled up' by numbers, but any failure to do so was fatal; when operating in the half line it was less easy to bend the rules in containing him and his accuracy at long range created its own problems for opposing backs.

With Pat Fox he struck up a dream partnership. Each complemented the other — tall rangey English jumping high for a dropping ball, Fox with a low centre of gravity at times seeming to hug the ground, relentlessly punishing every lapse by a back in dropping a ball or carelessly clearing; English the spectacular master of all the skills, Fox the dour terrier opportunist who never gave up and made every ball in the vicinity of the goal a back's nightmare. Communication between the two seemed at times telepathic. Over-attention to one provided the other with the opportunity to make hay.

Forward play, as well as being about scores, is also of course about winning matches. The mantle of immortality associated with such players as Ring, Mackey, Keher and Jimmy Doyle was secured by proven ability to win finely balanced games against all odds, at times almost on their own. Some will claim that after Killarney English never again showed in a major game against a major hurling county the ability to bring his team from behind to victory. Of course it may be pointed out that he can hardly be blamed if it became a feature of Tipp's years at the top that when he personally did not rise to superhuman proportions Tipp sagged; and that supporters felt that if he did not produce his best, Tipp did not win. Given the slightest room by backs — and indeed often when given no room at all — he retained through Tipp's years at the top the ability to produce on a regular basis brilliant scores and to display on occasion a virtuosity which would have earned approving nods from the ghosts of Ring and Mackey.

Even his meanest detractors will admit that without English the famine would not have ended when it did. For many it was his brilliance which restored Tipp to its place in the sun. Had any other forward been in his place Tipp would not have reached Killarney. And had any other forward been in his place at Killarney, there would have been nothing to celebrate.

Nobody ever sustained harder knocks in hurling than English. Perhaps learning his hurling, when he mastered the most difficult skills of the game, through lone practice was in a sense to his disadvantage. The skills of the game must be second nature to the hurler by the time he is in his teens and one of the vital skills is the ability to use the hurley for protection. A child-hurler in a hurling area will learn the art of self-preservation in a way that he is unconscious of. He will protect his head, his hands and his feet without thinking. Whether the instinct for self-preservation was ever as important to English as it might have been is a matter for argument.

Quite apart from the superlative skill which made him a natural target for hitmen, his fierce courage led him to take on backs to a degree which made frequent injury inevitable. Where another player would be content to gain possession and part with the ball quickly, he was at all times scornful of personal safety. His was a style that at times appeared almost to invite robust handling from backs and all too often he showed a touching faith in the wisdom and fairness of referees — qualities which were not always in evidence. The sheer lightning quality of his acceleration and body swerve were in themselves to his disadvantage in that his muscles were a dozen times in any one match put under a strain that invited injury. Altogether, it is not to be wondered at that so much of his career was punctuated by periods when he missed games because he was nursing injuries.

Nicholas English's hurling career will continue to be a subject for controversy as long as hurling men revel in the discussion of games and players. Whether he will be classed among the great hurlers of all time is a matter that only time will decide. But one thing is certain. As long as the golden days when Tipperary's famine was ended — and the golden days that followed — are discussed, tens of thousands of hurling followers will cherish their own recollections of moments when a young fellow who had learned to hurl against the wall of a house in the village of Cullen brought crowds to their feet with an artistry that, for those of us who regard hurling as an art form, seemed to belong somewhere between earth and heaven.

Chapter Fifteen

OH, WHAT A FALL, MY COUNTYMEN!
1989-90

I was visiting an old friend in a geriatric ward of a County Tipperary hospital on an evening in October 1989, when there was much excitement outside and in came two of the Bonnar brothers with the McCarthy Cup. Formally dressed in their team blazers, they visited every bed in the ward and old men from some of Ireland's most famous hurling parishes sat up and fondled the coveted trophy as if this were the crowning moment of their lives. I personally found it a tremendously moving scene. Afterwards I learned that the two young men had visited every ward in the hospital.

Similar scenes were repeated throughout the county in schools, hospitals and nursing homes in the months following the victory over Antrim. Seldom if ever did a winning team undertake this public relations exercise on such a wide scale. Local bodies, GAA clubs, pubs and groups who had no connection at all with sport competed for their presence and in many cases were surprised when only a few of the team managed to turn up. And the young men who had cut themselves off from all sorts of social activities and given their lives over to the achieving of a superlative level of fitness for an entire year found themselves regarded as ungracious if they were not answerable to the beck and call of a public that grew more, not less, demanding as time passed.

But there were those who disapproved of the high public profile enjoyed by the players. Increasingly there was talk of the good old days when a team won an All-Ireland, came back to Thurles, showed the cup to the Archbishop and went home to make up for the few days work that had been missed on the farm. Too much time was being spent in being entertained, it was whispered, and the celebrations would undo all the good of the victory itself. Perhaps the explanation was that though the supporters wanted to celebrate the new-found prestige, some were secretly ashamed of their own excitement. Tipperary supporters were not supposed to go overboard with the celebrations. To do so was the mark of the Johnny-come-lately. It was not traditional in Tipp. It was not done 'in me father's time'.

But if it gave the begrudgers any pleasure, they got grist for the mill when Tipp turned out, minus six of the All-Ireland side, against Dublin in the first round of the League in mid-October. They were also short English after only twenty minutes when he retired with an aggravated tendon injury which he had picked up in a club game the day before. But that was no excuse for the slippage which allowed them to lose the seven point lead they had at half-time to a team which had only just been promoted from the second division. When it came to the crunch in the second half, Dublin, with the wind behind them, took their chances in fine style and nobody could begrudge them their point win. But back in Tipperary the defeat was seen as the inevitable result of the continuing celebrations and not many were prepared to take into consideration the gruelling club games which so many of the players had been involved in since the All-Ireland. With county players not being freely available to clubs until September, there had been a telescoping of club games into the autumn. For many players this meant that after the All-Ireland they had to face into fiercely contested club fixtures which were at times running concurrently with celebrations — hardly the perfect recipe for physical well-being!

It's one thing to be beaten by a Dublin team for whose good fortune there would be a certain amount of pleasure, but it's quite another thing to be beaten by Cork in one's own backyard. When Cork came to Semple Stadium a fortnight after the defeat by Dublin, they were foolishly regarded as the team that couldn't beat an inferior Waterford in the Munster championship. Tipp paid dearly for their mistake. Captained by John Kennedy whose club, Clonoulty-Rossmore, had won the county final the previous Sunday, they rarely looked like a team that had only recently won an All-Ireland. Cork shook the Tipp net five times — three times per Kevin Hennessy and twice per John Fitzgibbon — and won by 5-8 to 0-15. Without English or Fox, the Tipp forwards, despite valiant efforts by Cormac Bonnar — who was now hampered by the new experimental rule forbidding handpassing to the net — rarely looked dangerous and long before the final whistle the team were a thoroughly beaten lot.

More complaining about the effects of the celebrations followed, more exhortations to the team to return to 'hard work', and a tiny voice here and there suggested that any Tipp team ought to know better than to take Cork less than seriously. Once again, it had been proved that it is a great advantage to a reasonably good team to be the underdogs — and particularly when the team is Cork. Defeating the All-Ireland champions at this time was going to do wonders for Cork when they met again.

Two defeats put a new complexion on Tipp's next game against Antrim and despite the margin which separated them in the All-Ireland, there was a certain amount of apprehension as the champions headed north to Casement Park. While Antrim were short a number of their All-Ireland side, so too were Tipp and among the absentees were Fox and English, who to the accompaniment of much publicity, had got married the previous week. Also missing was Ken Hogan, whose performance against Cork had set tongues wagging — perhaps unfairly since none of the five goals he had conceded had been entirely his fault. But Antrim on their home ground would not be easily beaten and there were some wry comments in the Tipp camp at newspaper hints of 'arrogance' in sending out a substandard team.

Tipp survived by the skin of their teeth in a game which was far livelier than neutral commentators had anticipated. They were two points ahead at half-time and for the remainder of the game it was a tit-for-tat struggle, with excitement mounting to fever pitch at the end. In the dying moments of the game, with Tipp two points ahead, Ciaran Barr was fouled in possession and a penalty was awarded to Antrim. A goal would have given victory to the home team and even the taking of the penalty had its own drama. As the referee turned to cast an eye over the placing of the defenders, Bobby Ryan took the precaution of moving the ball from where the referee had placed it, thus earning a mention in the latter's notebook. Then, with the crowd in silent expectation, Aidan McCarry lifted and blazed it — over the bar.

It was a cruel blow to Antrim hopes and a mighty relief to Tipp in whose dressing room there was the kind of atmosphere one might expect among All-Ireland champions who had barely avoided ending up with no League points after three games. Now there was Galway to face in the last game before Christmas and, following on the scares they had recently experienced, there would be no difficulty with regard to team attitude.

In view of the regard for Galway hurling which had come under such strain in recent times in Tipperary, the initial gesture of the Galway team when the two met in November at Semple Stadium was much appreciated by the home crowd. Twenty thousand people in crisp winter sunshine saw the visiting team form a guard of honour and clap their opponents on to the field. It was a gesture which put the crowd in a sporting frame of mind and did at least something to defuse the tensions which press comments had done so much to exacerbate over the summer.

With the game being of so much importance to both counties (Galway already facing relegation), a thoroughly entertaining hour's hurling was served up from which Tipp emerged victors by 1-14 to 0-11. Galway had definitely come to win and for that reason the sporting quality of the engagement was all the more appreciated. Though they were clearly in command for the final ten minutes, the margin was probably a little flattering to Tipp. Ken Hogan was back in goal showing some of his old reliability and Nicholas English was back but did little to affect the outcome.

The pleasure was all Tipp's then, having beaten the team that over recent years were seen as their principal rivals, having apparently buried the acrimony which was new to relations between the counties and having gained the points which put them back among the front-runners in the League. They could face Christmas and the post-Christmas holiday in Florida, which was their reward as All-Ireland winners, if not with complacency, at least with easier minds.

While they made their preparations for their trip to the sun, thirteen of the team received nominations for the Bank of Ireland All-Star awards. They were Ken Hogan, John Heffernan, Conor O'Donovan, Noel Sheehy, Conal Bonnar, Bobby Ryan, John Kennedy, Declan Carr, Declan Ryan, Michael Cleary, Pat Fox, Cormac Bonnar and Nicholas English. Declan Ryan was nominated for three different positions — midfield, centre-forward and right half-forward. Of the thirteen, six would receive the awards: Bobby Ryan, Conal Bonnar, Declan Carr, Pat Fox, Cormac Bonnar and Nicholas English. The last three made it an all-Tipp full-forward line and the Bonnar brothers established a record in being the first brothers to be selected in the same year. Bobby and Aidan Ryan had already been selected but in different years. As a measure of the closeness of the two counties, Galway would receive five awards: goalkeeper John Commins, Sean Treacy, Michael Coleman, Eanna Ryan and Joe Cooney.

The fortnight in Florida was a break from hurling which many had not experienced for many a long day. But there were team talks designed to keep them in mind of what was left of the League and what lay beyond. Otherwise it was all relaxation and fun.

There was the occasional reminder, too, of the smallness of the sporting world. Outside the hotel, while waiting for some of the lads going on a sightseeing tour, Noel Morris explained to a huge Negro that they were members of a hurling team from Ireland. 'Hurling!' exploded the Negro. 'Is that guy Christy Ring still playing?' He had worked with Terry Leahy for many years in New York and the great Kilkenny star never tired of telling him of the wonders of hurling and of the wizard of Cloyne.

The fortnight in the sun did much to relax the team which resumed the League in mid-February. The strain of celebrations could hardly be blamed for anything that went wrong from now on, though in lining out against Wexford it can hardly be disputed that there was an element of over-confidence in the Tipperary camp. On the Wexford side there was a warm cordiality in the welcome they gave to the champions. Before they arrived on the pitch the band had set the atmosphere by repeatedly playing 'Slievenamon' and again the Tipp team were handclapped on to the field by their opponents. Later there would be a presentation from the local GAA club to John Kennedy.

But the off-the-pitch cordiality did little to blunt the edge of the sharp exchanges on the field. Conscious of the drubbing they had administered to Tipp in similar circumstances two years before, Wexford set about making the running right from the throw-in. Without Fox and Leahy who were both nursing injuries, Tipp were shortly left without English, when a finger injury forced him to retire after only six minutes. Thereafter the attack seemed to have little bite and for twenty minutes of the first half Tipp, playing against a steady breeze, failed to raise a single flag. Midway through the second half Tipp were behind by five points when the episode occurred which might have changed the game. Joe Hayes dropped a high ball on to the edge of the square and Declan Ryan got possession only to be pulled down. A penalty was awarded and Declan took it himself, only to see it saved and delivered to safety. After that, Wexford's tails were well and truly up. Conor Stakelum, who had replaced English, and Michael Cleary worked hard and Cormac Bonnar hit the upright but, were it not for Wexford's poor marksmanship, the margin at the end — Wexford 0-13 Tipp 0-9 — might have been greater.

Too much being made of them, said the begrudgers. Too much Florida, too much celebrating. With half a forward line what do you expect, said the majority. All were agreed that Limerick would have to be beaten. Tipp needed a steadying success.

At home to Limerick at Semple Stadium only a week later, the joy was all Limerick's. Reinforced by Paul Delaney who only the previous night had benefited from an amnesty to suspended players, Tipp were again without English, Fox, Leahy and Declan Ryan. Nevertheless, the defeat was generally seen by their dispirited supporters as very much their own fault. They did not match Limerick in commitment or sharpness and the defence gave a present of two easy goals in the first half from which they never recovered. Playing with wind and rain, Tipp were a point down at half-time and nobody was prepared to be optimistic about the outcome.

Misfortune too made Tipp the butt of bitter jibes from their own supporters. Ken Hogan travelled the length of the field to take a 21 and drove it whizzing over the bar. Limerick goalkeeper Tommy Quaid, quickly sizing up the situation while Ken raced panting upfield, drove a mighty puckout which could easily have brought trouble before Ken arrived back at base. On another day the humorous side of the incident would have been appreciated. On this occasion, few Tipp supporters saw anything even mildly funny in it. It was not a day for laughs.

Tipp revived and went three points ahead in the middle of the second half, only to have Limerick hit back with a period of power hurling during which they showed an appetite that Tipp simply did not have. In all, Terence Kenny contributed three goals to his side's four point win in a game that must have been a nightmare for Conor O'Donovan after his majestic performance of a week before.

With this, their fourth loss in the League campaign, it was becoming more difficult for supporters to reassure themselves that this was not the real Tipp. But the fact remained that not since the All-Ireland had a full-strength team fielded in any game. Paul Delaney had been the best of the backs against Limerick. Who knows what the addition of one or two of the missing forwards would have made? Or so went the argument. In the meantime, the possibility of a drop to Division 2 was being discussed more and more. 'Oh what a fall there's been, my countymen . . . From the heady heights of All-Ireland glory and celebration, Tipperary have come to the brink of League relegation. Reasons aplenty there are, from multiple absentees to lack of real ambition in the current competition, but it is certainly no fun to see our name just above that of pointless Antrim', commented Culbaire in the *Tipperary Star*.

Now Tipp looked to their away game with Kilkenny to redeem themselves. But in the meantime there was another sorrowful 'station' to be endured. Between Semple Stadium and Nowlan Park there was the matter of the Oireachtas final to be settled with Galway. At Ennis on the Sunday in between those two League games, Galway handed them a drubbing which was the worst they had sustained in three years. With only Michael Cleary of the regular forward line, the team performed lamentably and could only raise eight points against Galway's 1-19. There were times when Galway appeared to be doing what they liked and the biggest cheer of the day went up when near the end of the game Tony Keady came on at centre-back. With Paul Delaney and Keady both on the field it seemed that an unhappy chapter of events was being closed, but Tipp would like to have seen the chapter closed in happier circumstances.

Seldom can a group of supporters have set out for a venue with a more nervous disposition than did those who followed Tipp to Nowlan Park on 11 March 1990. It would be Tipp's last League game. There was no question of advancing to the semi-finals, but it would decide whether or not Tipp was to endure the ignominy of relegation to Division 2. Adding bite to the occasion was the inexplicable revival of ancient Tipp-Kilkenny hostility which may well have originated in those decades when Kilkenny failed time and again to defeat Tipp in anything that mattered.

Still short Pat Fox and with Ken Hogan, John Kennedy and Michael Ryan on the sick list, Tipp fielded a team which, while not its first string, had a fair amount of experience: John Leamy; John Heffernan, Noel Sheehy, Bobby Ryan; Conal Bonnar, John McIntyre, Paul Delaney; Declan Carr, Joe Hayes; Michael Cleary, Donie O'Connell, Aidan Ryan; Austin Buckley, Cormac Bonnar and Nicholas English.

But if Kilkenny were through to the semi-finals and consequently lacked the same motivation that fired Tipp, the temptation to consign their old rivals to the dustbin of Division 2 was much too attractive for them to resist. The result was an extremely competitive game.

For the first time since the championship of the previous summer, Tipp supporters saw some of the qualities which had brought home the McCarthy Cup. With a fire and determination that had been almost forgotten, they put Kilkenny on the defensive for the greater part of a thrill-packed hour. John Leamy was in brilliant form in goal — it was well for Tipp that he was — and Declan Carr was in fine form at centre-field, so that as half-time approached Tipp were three points ahead. Then, from a movement initiated by English, Cormac Bonnar crashed his way towards the square and lashed the ball to the net. Despite two quick answering points the home team went into the dressing room four points in arrears: 1-6 to 0-5.

It did not take Kilkenny long to strike back after the resumption and John McIntyre, not yet entirely fit, was replaced by John Madden, allowing Conal Bonnar to take over at centre-back, while Conor Stakelum replaced Austin Buckley. Kilkenny had whittled the lead back to a point and had the Tipp defence under heavy pressure when John Madden cleared up to Conor Stakelum who, quite against the run of play, slipped the Kilkenny defence and slapped in a goal which was followed by an equally spectacular point from Declan Carr. Now Tipp were five points ahead again and seemingly coasting to victory.

I was quite a young fellow when the great Jim Barry of Cork, coach to six All-Ireland winning teams in a row, five hurling and one football, confided to me, 'You can never tell with Kilkenny. There are fifteen men on the field and fifteen that you don't see at all.'

Now the tornado struck and Tipp battened down the hatches to withstand the final assault. All the action was in the Tipp half and at times it seemed that both teams were playing only half the field. A point from Murphy, who had come on as sub for Phelan, followed by two from frees from Mick Cleere and D. J. Carey brought only a Michael Cleary point in reply. It was into injury time and Tipp were still a goal ahead when John Leamy brought the Tipp crowd to their feet with a wonderful save from John McDonald. But Kilkenny were not going to deny their supporters. Liam McCarthy blazed and again John Leamy saved only to be bundled into the net, while McDonald made sure that the ball arrived there too. They were level.

With the puckout the game was over, and while Tipp disputed the legality of the equalising goal, Kilkenny could point to their own hard luck when a vicious drive from Lester Ryan which nobody would have saved had bounced back off the crossbar midway through the second half.

As the players trooped off the field, Kilkenny mobbed by their supporters, a Kilkenny player turned back to Nicholas English and said, 'And ye're the fellows they charged five pounds to look at!' a reference, presumably, to the night in Semple Stadium when they had brought back the McCarthy Cup.

The jibe rubbed salt into the wound and in the dressing room the Tipp players looked in despair at one another, bitterly regretting the misfortune of the final goal. Then came the magic news that in New Ross Jimmy Houlihan had snatched a dramatic win for Wexford over Galway. It was Galway and not Tipp who were to be relegated. A cheer went up and suddenly all was positive. Babs spoke encouragingly. He pointed out the extent of the difference between what they had just served up and what they had been providing for months past. They should have won, but even if they hadn't, they had risen to the occasion. Nicholas English, understandably in view of the effects of his lay-off and injuries, had been barely visible and yet they had been unlucky not to win. And there were others who would be returning to the panel. Next week they were off to the Skydome in Toronto to play the All-Stars. When they returned they would really get down to work. Babs said so. Phil Conway said so. Everybody said so. It was still early in March, but already their entire attention could be focused to the exclusion of everything else on the championship. There was much to be said for being finished with the League.

Chapter Sixteen

TOWARDS A MUNSTER FOUR-IN-A-ROW
1990

Somebody made the comment as the Tipp team mingled with the All-Stars at Shannon two days after the game at Nowlan Park, 'If this is for staying in Division One, what would they do for us if we won the League!'

The trip to Canada had, of course, nothing at all to do with the League. The idea of a game in Toronto between the All-Ireland champions and the Bank of Ireland All-Stars had been the brainchild of John Dunne, the Tipperary-born Managing Director of A. & P. Dominion, a major supermarket chain which undertook sponsorship of the event on the synthetic pitch in the famous Skydome. In the wings giving encouragement was the thriving Tipperary Supporters Club of Toronto whose chairman was Jim Keating, a prominent Toronto publisher and a cousin of Babs.

Built over an area of nearly eleven acres at a cost of over $700 million, the Skydome has a retractable roof which is opened back in summer. A permanent staff of 200 service the entire complex with its huge hotel and the 600 seat tiered restaurant overlooking the playing area.

For those who were to play in the big game, the principal interest was in how the astro-turf surface would reproduce the qualities of the grassy sod at home and there were three practice sessions to allow players to familiarise themselves with it. Journalist John Guiton would later describe the experience as 'like hurling on the carpet of your sitting-room' and indeed many players found considerable difficulty in controlling the ball and in keeping their footing.

Despite late nights in the company of some of the many supporters who had travelled with them from Ireland and who made the staff of the Sheraton Hotel more than a little familiar with the strains of 'Slievenamon', the business of the game was taken seriously. With live television beaming it back home, there was no question of playing before an audience which wouldn't know the difference. Anyway, there had grown among the team a determination to put on their best possible display on this occasion. Babs had made it clear that they had a duty to those who had followed them from Ireland, to the Irish in Canada who wanted to see something they could be proud of, and to the television audience at home. Only the best they could provide would do.

The best they could provide was to beat the All-Stars by 5-15 to 3-11. In a humid 70 degrees Fahrenheit the two teams served up a sparkling standard of hurling which gave the close on 30,000 spectators and the huge television audience little idea of the difficulty they had in controlling the ball on the unusual surface. With their team confined to the All-Ireland panel, Tipp were confronted literally by a star-studded side, most of whom they had met in close encounters over the previous twelve months: John Commins (Galway), Aidan Fogarty (Offaly), Eamon Cleary (Wexford), Dessie Donnelly (Antrim), Liam Walsh (Kilkenny), Jim Cashman (Cork), Sean Treacy (Galway), Michael Coleman (Galway), Ger Hegarty (Limerick), Eanna Ryan (Galway), Joe Cooney (Galway), Tony O'Sullivan (Cork), Olcan McFettridge (Antrim), Brian McMahon (Dublin) and Shane Fitzgibbon (Limerick). Under the rule which allowed five substitutes, the All-Stars introduced during the course of the game Terence McNaughton (Antrim), John Conran (Wexford), Derek Finn (Dublin), Shane Ahearn (Waterford) and Mark Corrigan (Offaly).

To cope with the abnormal heat, it had been decided to introduce two intervals of two minutes duration together with the normal half-time break and it was only in the last quarter that Tipp began to draw away from their opponents. The scoring list shows the contribution of all six forwards to Tipp's victory: N. English 2-4, Cormac Bonnar 2-1, Michael Cleary 0-6, John Leahy 1-1, Declan Carr, Aidan Ryan and Donie O'Connell 0-1 each. But the entire team took seriously the business of providing a spectacle that would give value to those who had undertaken the financial burden of the venture. The supporters at home were well satisfied, particularly with the performance of English who established a unique record in being top scorer as well as being first and last to score.

At the end of the game the team engaged in a colourful bit of public relations. As they made their victory jaunt round the pitch, they pucked sliotars up into the crowd, so that many Canadians brought home an unusual memento of their first hurling game. It was a fitting end to an occasion that was a sporting and financial success but which has, regrettably, been repeated only once.

A few days after the team's return to Ireland, Congress passed a motion which would seriously alter the character of play around the square and perhaps Tipp would in the short term suffer more than most from the change. No longer could a score be handpassed. The ball had to be struck with the hurley. For those who appreciated the lethal quality of Cormac Bonnar's bulk when only a few yards from the goalkeeper and who remembered all too vividly Nicholas English's handpassed point and Donie O'Connell's and Mick Doyle's handpassed goals in Killarney, it was from Tipp's point of view an unwelcome change.

From a spectator's point of view there is a strong argument in favour of the handpass. One of the many characteristics of hurling which combine to make it such a spectacular game is the frequency of scores. Anything which tends to reduce scores can only be to the disadvantage of the game as a spectacle. Yet here was a rule which gave a new advantage to the backs. A mediocre back could stop an exceptionally talented forward from scoring from close quarters by simply staying with him and preventing him from striking the ball with the hurley. The proposal had come from Cork and, inexplicably, Galway and Wexford delegates, who were opposed to the move, did not speak on it.

Back in Ireland after their fortnight in Canada, the team had two months in hand to prepare for the championship and for the achievement of the four-in-a-row Munster titles — something which, despite all the honours that had been won by the county, had never been done before. It was, from the manager's point of view, an ideal situation: no League to provide a distraction; a clear two month run to give Phil Conway his head in the matter of team fitness and no real stress of club demands; and a few tournaments to allow a look at players who might need looking at. The word began to circulate that this was what Tipp had been angling for all the time — the championship was the thing and the League was merely a preparation for what was really important. If success came in the League, it was welcome; if not, well the League performance would be forgotten as soon as the championship began. True or not, it was a good story.

From Pat Fox there was some good news. A knee operation for a difficulty which had been troubling him for a very long time and which had kept him in dry dock since the All-Ireland seemed to be successful. When a depleted Tipp side lined out against Offaly a couple of weeks later for the opening of a new pitch at Mucklagh, near Tullamore, he was the only one of the six forwards who had played against Antrim in the All-Ireland final the previous September. But his presence gave a definite lift to the forward line and he showed some of his old skill in contributing a goal and two points of Tipp's total of 3-13 to an experimental Offaly side's 1-9.

In mid-May Tipp played Galway at the opening of a new field at The Ragg, near Thurles. Both sides were well below full strength — Galway more so than Tipp — but the keenness of the contest showed the healthy competitive spirit between them. Galway led throughout most of the game, but were caught in the last quarter for Tipp to lead at the end by 2-12 to 1-13. Had each side been aware that they were not destined to meet in the championship, they might have regarded the game with even more seriousness. But for the first time in a long time the scorers' names looked encouraging for Tipp supporters. They included English (1-2), Declan Ryan (1-2), Paul Delaney (0-3), Pat Fox (0-2), Joe Hayes, Declan Carr and Conor Stakelum (0-1 each).

The last of their pre-championship preparation matches was again at a field-opening — this time at Lisronagh, near Clonmel. A makeshift Kilkenny side who approached the game with a nothing-to-lose attitude held Tipp to a draw and left both Tipp supporters and selectors pondering on the incredibly mixed form which so many members of the panel had been showing since September. It left many wondering, too, about the dependability or otherwise of the full-back line.

Such had been Cork's performance in losing their League replay against Wexford that there were even those in Tipperary who regretted that they would not provide sufficiently formidable opposition for Tipp when they met — if they met. Cork were not at all certain of beating Kerry and Waterford, or so many foolishly thought. Tipp might find Limerick their major obstacle in Munster.

It was one of the ironies of 1990 that Tipp probably treated Limerick with more caution than they did Cork. There were numerous reminders of the occasions on which Limerick had proved the bogey team and there was no need to delve into history for them. The defeat at the hands of Limerick in the League still rankled and the problem of injuries still kept everyone on edge. 'I think the attitude is right now and all I wish for is that our injury situation will not hinder us. John Leahy is just back after a hand injury; Nicky

English has a lingering hamstring problem; Conor O'Donovan has ankle trouble and, of course, Pat Fox is still nervous of his old knee problem. All we can hope for is that everything will go right for them. We need everybody in right shape in order to win', was Babs' comment shortly before the team was picked for the game. But, in addition, John Kennedy had had his collar-bone fractured in a club game and he too had been counted out for some time back.

Conor O'Donovan's problem was not solved by the time the team was named for the meeting with Limerick. Though formidable enough on paper, it was not the one that would have been named, had everything been as wished. Colm Bonnar was named in the unusual position of corner-back and Bobby Ryan was at centre-back. The team was: Ken Hogan; Colm Bonnar, Noel Sheehy, John Heffernan; Conal Bonnar, Bobby Ryan, Paul Delaney; Declan Carr, Joe Hayes; Michael Cleary, Declan Ryan, John Leahy; Pat Fox, Cormac Bonnar and Nicholas English.

Seldom can a winning team have been less satisfied with a game than the Tipp team who trooped out of Limerick on 10 June, having beaten the home team by six points. Once again ammunition was provided for those who wanted to belittle their track record. Once again it could be thrown at them that they had made heavy weather of beating a team that was a man short.

The game was only seventeen minutes old when Limerick full-back Mike Barron was sent to the line for a wild pull on Cormac Bonnar. There were those — and they were not all from Limerick — who contended that the referee's decision was severe and indeed Bonnar made no attempt to pretend that he was any worse than he was. From the referee's viewpoint, however, it was necessary to declare his standards early in the game and the remainder was trouble free.

While Tipp would afterwards claim that the extra man made no difference, it is true that they were reeling in every sector for much of the first twenty minutes. Ger Hegarty and Mike Reale were in charge at centre-field and the result put pressure on the Tipp full-back line with which it was not always able to cope. At the time Barron departed, Limerick were four points in front and it was only then that John Leahy got Tipp's first point from play. With the loss of a man, Limerick had to regroup and John Heffernan was left unmarked, but even then Tipp were labouring until half-time when the dugout men were able to assess the possibilities offered by the extra man. The

116

solution adopted was to introduce John Madden for John Heffernan. Conal Bonnar took over from Bobby Ryan at centre-back and Bobby moved back to corner-back, with Colm Bonnar moving out to left half-back.

John Madden worked like a beaver as the extra man, operating behind the half-back line and sweeping up anything loose that was going. Declan Carr and Joe Hayes came alive at centre-field; Declan Ryan began to dominate things in the half-forward line; and as soon as the Limerick pace slowed, Tipp began to get the upper hand. Even still, Limerick managed to double their half-time lead of two points and it was well into the second half before that upper hand was asserted; and perhaps it was as well that Ken Hogan had one of his inspired days. Goals from Declan Ryan and Dinny Ryan, who had come on for Cormac Bonnar, were badly needed as, with spirits flagging and legs tiring, Limerick still managed to come at them. Tipp composure finally took control, but a last-minute goal by Mike Galligan took the one-sided look off the scoreboard to leave it reading Tipp 2-20 Limerick 1-17.

Among the Tipp players there were mixed emotions at the final whistle. There was the inevitable excitement at having won and at the prospect of having cleared the decks for a meeting with Cork. There was satisfaction that those who had been carrying injuries had survived. But there was something approaching bewilderment that with an extra man they had made such heavy weather of overcoming Limerick. It was clear that either Limerick were a very formidable side or that Tipp were anything but.

By way of explanation there was much talk of the injury problem and of how a number of players had consequently been unable to participate in the full training programme. There was even talk of the peculiar difficulty of playing Limerick on their own pitch. This had been the result of Tipp wanting to honour a sixteen-year-old agreement. Babs mentioned that this was 'a burden that future Tipp teams will be relieved of', but this was all for press consumption. The fact of the matter was that Tipp had not played well and had not looked good and they were told this in no uncertain terms while they were still steaming from the ordeal.

Still, they had won, and before the dressing room emptied the attention of the entire squad was focused on the coming game with Cork. It was obvious that Babs' own thoughts were already with the

Cork game and a resounding cheer greeted his final words: 'There is only one team that can deprive you of achieving something no other Tipperary team ever achieved, four Munster titles in a row, and that is Cork. We have five weeks to get ready; we are all in this together and we know what has to be done.'

Chapter Seventeen

THE DAY OF THE DONKEYS, 1990

On the run-in to the Cork-Tipp Munster final at Thurles all the talk was of injuries. Cork would be without Teddy McCarthy and Tomas Mulcahy, though Tony O'Sullivan would be sufficiently recovered from recent injury to be available. Tipp would be without — well, until the team was actually announced, it seemed at times that rumours of injuries attached to almost half the team. Bobby Ryan was suffering from an arm infection; Declan Carr was still recovering from a leg infection; there were worries over John Kennedy's collar-bone, John Leahy's finger and Pat Fox's knee. Cormac Bonnar was said to be not fit.

And still, despite all the talk of injuries and despite the fitful form of Tipp in the previous twelve months, there was a degree of confidence that had not been apparent in a Tipp-Cork encounter for many years. However, it was remarked that the crowds which turned up to see the team training in the last few weeks weren't of the size they had been in previous years. Around Thurles there seemed at times to be as much interest in Ireland's performance in the World Cup and particularly in the performance of Niall Quinn, whose father had been the Tipp hero of a National League final against Kilkenny in the 1950s.

Afterwards the question would be raised — what exactly was the basis for the confidence? Those of older vintage knew well that the margin between Tipp and Cork at any time is a thin one and is often determined by attitude. An erudite Tipp follower once expressed the opinion that Shakespeare had Tipp and Cork in mind when he wrote,

> And you all know security
> Is mortal's chiefest enemy.

The degree of confidence — or of over-confidence — can be the factor that tips the scales.

When the Tipp line-out was announced more than a few eyebrows were raised. On was John Madden; off was John Heffernan; at centre-back was John Kennedy; on was Conor Stakelum and — biggest surprise of all — John Leahy was at full-forward instead of the reportedly unfit Cormac Bonnar. The team was: Ken Hogan; John Madden, Noel Sheehy, Bobby Ryan; Conal Bonnar, John Kennedy (capt.), Paul Delaney; Joe Hayes, Declan Carr; Michael Cleary, Declan Ryan, Conor Stakelum; Pat Fox, John Leahy and Nicholas English.

On the day before the game the burial took place in Thurles of John Maher, one of the best-loved personalities of Tipperary hurling. He had captained the Tipp team to All-Ireland victory in 1945 when he was in his late thirties. He had already won All-Irelands in 1930 and 1937. His father before him had captained Tipp in the early part of the 1887 campaign. On the pathway outside Thurles Cathedral a hurling group stood around Denis Conroy, Chairman of Cork County Board, who had come up early for the funeral and would be staying over for the game.

'Who's going to win tomorrow, Denis?' somebody asked.

'Cork, of course,' replied Denis and added, 'Janey, ye think I'm joking. I'm not!'

It was regarded as another example of Denis's rich wit.

A couple of hours later, while John Maher was being laid to rest in Killinan, Babs Keating was talking to Ger Canning in a television interview that was destined to take its place in the archives of Tipp-Cork relations. Yes, Tipp had the healthiest respect for Cork, he said, and anything could happen when the pair met. The interview flowed along on predictable lines and somewhere along the way Babs made the interesting point that neither of his fellow selectors, Theo English or Donie Nealon, had ever lost a championship game to Cork. What about Fr Michael O'Brien's and Gerald McCarthy's management of Cork? Canning asked. Enormously talented men, was the import of Babs' remarks, and in a rush of modesty he remarked, 'Several managers in recent weeks got credit for being great motivators.' To those who knew Babs, his meaning was clear enough — that he was among those who had been given credit as a manager when the main credit should perhaps have gone to the team. But then, his guard dropped, he lapsed into the racing terminology with which he is so often apt to pepper his conversation: 'Donkeys don't win Derbies', he opined.

There were those who, watching the interview, realised immediately that the Tipp manager had said something which could easily be taken out of context and probably would be. It was. Somebody in the Cork camp, not pausing to look a gift horse in the mouth — if the phrase in the circumstances is not inapt — seized on the unfortunate words with a glee that was entirely understandable. The words were used, though not by Fr O'Brien, to intensify the degree of motivation that was to play a big part in Cork's splendid performance the following day. Before the game and its aftermath had faded into memory, Tipp followers never again wanted to hear anything about the chances of donkeys winning anything.

There is something special in the air during Tipp-Cork encounters that makes almost palpable the feeling that this game today will be special. With a team that, according to bookies and many judges of hurling, were rank outsiders, Cork followers on 15 July 1990 behaved as if defeat was out of the question. With a bewildering assortment of flags — everything from the Swastika to the Stars and Stripes, as long as it had a dash of red — they massed under the scoreboard at the town end and gave their team the kind of backing that is worth several points. They can't have known that they were about to blow to smithereens Tipp's most ardent dream or that they were about to take a giant step towards the incredible hurling and football All-Ireland double (in the year of the Cork man Michael Collins's centenary), but they behaved exactly as if they did. A commentator remarked during the playing of Amhran na bhFiann that he had never before heard it sung with such fervour. Something was stirring in Cork blood that had nothing to do with watching Tipp win their fourth Munster final in a row.

From the throw-in Cork were obviously the hungry ones and they went after every ball as if the outcome of the game depended on it. Tipp were sluggish, giving the impression that they had time on their side, reacting to Cork rather than dictating the play. By the 22nd minute they had only two points on the board, both by Conor Stakelum, to Cork's four and only a superlative block by Ken Hogan, when Ger Fitzgerald had rounded Bobby Ryan, had saved the Tipp net. Michael Cleary and Mark Foley, growing in confidence, exchanged points and David Quirke, hotly pursued by Paul Delaney, chased goalward until, about fifty yards later, he decided he was not going to get a swing and booted the ball over the bar. For Cork it was exhilarating stuff, with the score standing at six points to three.

Then came the passage which left Tipp supporters — and possibly many of the players — convinced that everything was in hand and that the second half would see what Tipp could really do. Joe Hayes, working like a Trojan, drove a low ball into the left corner and Michael Cleary, with Ger Cunningham alerted to a left-hand shot, turned and coolly drove the ball on his right side waist-high to the net. John Leahy, now out on the wing, pointed from long range and Nicky English, foraging away out on the left wing, collected a ball, raced across the centre before he could get in a puck to drive high over the bar. A moment later English was again in the wars in an incident which, had it occurred in different circumstances, might have brought appeals to the referee from Tipp players. Grabbing a ball far out in the right corner, he accelerated towards goal, eluding the first red jersey to come at him. He was within yards of the goal when, now receiving the attentions of three backs, he booted the ball as the feet were taken from under him. Ger Cunningham caught the ball easily and drove it upfield. Had the incident occurred at the end of a tight game, a major protest would have ensued.

The game was now thirty-two minutes old and Tipp were ahead by two points. John Leahy drove wide and, equally uncharacteristically, Tony O'Sullivan did likewise after a determined Cork attack. In the centre of the field Declan Ryan, not at all doing well in the exchanges with Jim Cashman, with his back to the Cork goal handpassed to Declan Carr who lobbed a high ball towards goal. English, at the left side of the square, soared high and connected. Down and across, perfectly met and perfectly directed, it went to the Cork net, the kind of shot that no goalkeeper can be expected to save. Now Tipp were five points ahead and seemed on course for victory. Half-time was due and that lead would do nicely.

Had the whistle been blown even half a minute prematurely, the subsequent course of the game might have been different. Had Tipp gone to the dressing room with such a substantial lead after a half in which so many of the team had played so indifferently, it is difficult to resist the conclusion that their game would have been raised in the second half. Had Cork gone in five points down despite having dominated the play during the first half, it would surely have been a heavy blow to their morale. But they did not go in five points down.

In those hurling circles in which the finer points are not always appreciated there is nothing so sure to draw a cheer as the back who relieves a pressing situation by driving a high ball into the crowd. Very often it is done with such a devil-may-care attitude that many fail to realise that a sideline cut will send the ball back into the square, possibly with greater advantage to the forwards.

Cork stormed into attack and drove wide. Ken Hogan pucked out and, with fifteen seconds left, David Quirke from centre-field dropped a high ball back in. John Madden, up until then having a fine game and doing some impressive clearing, cannily dropped behind Noel Sheehy and caught the hopping ball. Unable to clear directly ahead, he opted for a low ball out to the wing where perhaps in normal circumstances or with a little bit of luck it would be collected by a wing-back. But there was nobody to run on to it and the ball dribbled out over the sideline. Kieran McGuckian ran up, quickly placed it and struck it perfectly a little over head-high across the front of the goal. Mark Foley jumped and batted it to the net.

Seldom does a team get such a tonic at precisely the time it is most needed. Cork, now only two points behind as the half-time whistle blew, ran towards the dressing room displaying the kind of energy they would hardly have shown had the whistle been blown even twenty seconds earlier.

They showed the same kind of energy right from the start of the second half. Within two minutes Tony O'Sullivan had driven over two points and in the 4th minute John Madden experienced the kind of nightmare that haunts every back. Reaching up for a dropping ball on the corner of the square, he let it drop and John Fitzgibbon, till then reasonably contained, had it in the net in a flash. Cork were cock-a-hoop and Mark Foley, gaining even further in confidence and showing some of the cool skill that would make his display remembered as one of the outstanding features of the game, shot over superb points. By the 15th minute Cork were six points ahead

Fox had gone at half-time to be replaced by Dinny Ryan who never got an opportunity to make his mark on the game. But even with all those whose fitness had been in question beginning to look the worse for wear, Tipp began to fight back. Declan Carr made way for Colm Bonnar who brought a new vigour which made itself felt in the middle of the field and through the half-forward line. Cleary pointed three times and English and Declan Ryan had a point each.

But just as the Tipp supporters felt that their moment had come, disaster struck again in the person of Mark Foley. A movement in front of the Tipp goal saw Kevin Hennessy parting to Fitzgibbon who in turn parted to Foley. His shot was saved, but in the skirmish which followed the ball broke and Foley kicked it to the net. John Leahy pointed and the four point lead still looked manageable, though only four minutes remained. Then came the hammer blow. John Fitzgibbon, with only two minutes remaining, took advantage of a bit of scrappy play by the Tipp backs and drove to the net. Cork supporters erupted on to the goal area but the game was not over. Ger Cunningham saved a pile-driver from John Leahy and, appropriately, it fell to Mark Foley to take the last score of the day with a point that brought his personal tally to a magnificent two goals and seven points. If ever a Cork victory had been marked by a single outstanding performance, it was this.

'We went down like champions', the County Chairman told the team, and that was the consensus among Tipp supporters. All were agreed that the fault had not been in the forward line. Apart from frees, Michael Cleary had scored 1-2 from play and Nicholas English 1-4. John Leahy and Conor Stakelum had scored two points each and Declan Ryan, who did not enjoy the happiest of times at the hands of Jim Cashman, had scored a point. Neither Pat Fox nor his replacement had scored. But it had been an unfortunate day for the backs and questions were being asked as to why John Kennedy was left struggling so long at centre-back. Perhaps the answer to that was that when the change was made, it didn't appear to make much difference.

In the meantime there was a mood of *nil desperandum*. There was no question of a return to the famine days. Nobody was due to retire. And even on this day of unparalleled misfortune they had looked like champions till the end. They had been beaten by a team that was, on the day, unquestionably better, even if the margin of defeat did not reflect the margin of superiority. There would be another day. The recriminations would come later.

There was a considerable traffic hold-up in Cahir that evening as jubilant Cork supporters made their way home. Some Tipp people who had not seen the television programme with its reference to 'donkeys winning derbies' were more than a little puzzled by voices from Cork-bound cars shouting, 'He haw, he haw!'

In the weeks following, many Tipp people received in the post a print of a cartoon drawing showing Cork's Fr O'Brien astride a red and white donkey. Others received an imitation memoriam card reading, 'In Loving Memory of the Tipperary Hurling Team. Born Croke Park 1989. Died Thurles 1990. Sadly Missed by Tipperary People Everywhere. Will Always be Remembered by the Champions Cork.' From a Cork point of view it was great fun.

HOW MANY REMEMBER WHO WON THE LEAGUE? 1990–91

1990 was not a good year for Tipperary. In the middle of September Kilkenny, who early in August had decisively beaten Tipp's juniors in the All-Ireland final, repeated the performance by defeating the under-21's by a single goal. A year in which Tipp could, with a slice of luck, have repeated the feat of 1989 by taking senior, junior and under-21 All-Irelands, saw failure in all three — two at the last hurdle.

The astonishing thing is that the triple failure did little to dampen the mood of optimism in the county. The roller-coaster which had begun in Killarney had never ceased rolling. The worst feature of the famine years was the feeling that Tipp simply did not count. Now, whether winning or losing, Tipp could not be ignored. Nobody in serious quest of any hurling honours could fail to take them into the reckoning. A defeat might be unpalatable, but it was not the end of the world. Things would be different next year.

Thus, Tipp looked forward to the commencement of the League as a prelude to the championship of 1991. The first League games appeared to justify the optimism. By Christmas they had full points, having beaten Clare, Dublin, Cork and Limerick. They had also captured the Oireachtas for the first time since 1972. Things were looking good.

The opening League game against a Clare side that ex-Tipp star Len Gaynor was in the process of reshaping was remarkable only for the fine performance of Conor Stakelum who scored seven points from play. Tipp dominated the game from the beginning and the final score of 0-22 to 1-10 was no more than a fair measure of their superiority.

A week later Tipp trounced Dublin whom they had only barely beaten by two points in the Oireachtas semi-final a couple of weeks before. This time they scored 2-22 to Dublin's 2-6.

But it was the victory of the third Sunday on the trot that gave their supporters the greatest satisfaction. At Ennis on 17 November they defeated Galway by 1-15 to 0-7. Due to injuries and club commitments, Tipp were considerably depleted and Galway were equally so. A defeat at the hands of Cork in the All-Ireland had left the westerners in a state of demoralisation and, besides, they also were in the process of rebuilding. But until they appeared to throw in the towel towards the close of the hour they showed much of the craft which had made them the bogey team of the Tipp revival. In the first minute of the game Ken Hogan had to dive full length to save a rasper from Martin Naughton, and it was only when Michael Cleary kicked a goal on the call of half-time that the omens began to favour Tipp. But notwithstanding the fact that neither side was at anything like full strength, the win was of considerably more significance to Tipp than it was to Galway. The maroon jersey was beginning to be a dangerous symbol to young supporters in the same way as the red jersey had been to their fathers.

When the red jerseys came to Thurles for their League game with Tipp (Tipp's fourth busy Sunday in a row), the greater part of the 9,000 crowd were delighted by a 3-13 to 0-13 win for the home side that showed a hunger unusual for late November. Playing a first-time game which suited the conditions and did not at all suit a Cork side obviously the worse for the post-All-Ireland celebrations, they never looked like being anything but winners. Cormac Bonnar was rampant in attack and scored two of the three goals, thus reviving regrets that he had not been on the first fifteen for the Munster final. Pat Fox, not far behind, scored the other.

From Tipp's point of view the game was an interesting study. Cork were in precisely the same situation as Tipp had been twelve months before — All-Ireland champions and going badly in the League. There was even a note of sympathy in the comments of Tipp mentors and players after the game, and Cork trainer Gerald McCarthy was speaking to the converted when he said, 'You cannot keep hounding players from one end of the year to the other in an effort to maintain their enthusiasm. I think we have lost our appetite now after the All-Ireland celebrations.' It was like music to Tipperary ears to hear somebody else say it.

The last League game before Christmas was against Limerick in Limerick and it was taken so seriously by Tipp that they came together for a practice session on the Sunday morning. On an unusually mild afternoon with barely the hint of a breeze, they beat a Limerick team which, though they never got in front, provided excitement all the way and might have considered themselves somewhat unlucky to be six points behind at full time: 1-12 to 1-6.

In the dressing room afterwards there was high jubilation — full points with four wins out of four games was a performance to be satisfied with and few would deny the players their moment of self-congratulation. But there was a note of reserve in Babs' own comments on the performance and his last words before they scattered were: 'Go and enjoy Christmas, but remember you are back training on Sunday, 13 January, at 11 a.m. sharp.' County Secretary Tommy Barrett, veteran of more leagues and championships than anyone in the dressing room, warned, 'I did not think today's performance was our best so far in the League . . . It's good to be winning but we have tough games ahead.' The old dog for the hard road! Few could have anticipated that Tipp would win only one more game before making an ignominious exit from the League.

Considerable surprise had been caused after the All-Ireland by the announcement that Babs had dispensed with the services as selector of his old team mate Theo English. Like Babs, Theo was a man of strongly held opinions and when the two no longer saw eye to eye there was little room for manoeuvre. At the County Board some heat was generated by the change, but the terms of Babs' original appointment were that he had the right to nominate his own selectors. This made discussion pointless and former goalkeeper John O'Donoghue was appointed by Babs to fill Theo's position. Like the man he was replacing, O'Donoghue had a brilliant career behind him, having played between the posts for Tipp in four All-Ireland finals. He had also been Tipp's football goalkeeper during the same period and had been selected for Munster in both codes. He was based in his native Tipperary town and there was a feeling that, in view of the new importance of west Tipperary clubs, his appointment would give something of a geographical balance to the selectors. Like Babs, Theo English was from the Clonmel area, though there were many ready to point out that he had coached Cappawhite (west Tipperary) to victory in the county championship which made him as much a representative of west Tipperary as anyone could be. There was now a representative from south and west Tipp, with Donie Nealon from north Tipperary. Ironically mid-Tipperary, which for decades had entirely dominated Tipperary hurling, was not represented among the selectors. Nobody complained, or if they did, nobody listened.

During the Christmas recess the All-Star awards were announced and Noel Sheehy and Michael Cleary were among the chosen fifteen. For Tipp it was something of a comedown from their six of the previous year and eyebrows were raised at the exclusion of Nicholas English who had been nursing an injury during the pre-Christmas League games. But it was generally realised that it would have been difficult to leave out John Fitzgibbon who had made such a magnificent contribution to Cork's All-Ireland campaign. However, English, Conal Bonnar and Declan Carr would travel with the All-Stars as replacements. In all, nine Tipp players received nominations.

Word that Eanna Ryan, who had done so much to sink Tipp's hopes and raise Galway's so often, had sustained a severe head injury in a club game brought a great wave of sympathy in Tipp. On a bitter February day a bus set off from Cashel followed by a number of cars to attend a benefit function for Eanna in Galway. Raffles had been run by a number of Tipperary clubs and the proceeds were handed over at the Galway function. The Tipperarymen's Association in Galway also ran an Eanna Ryan benefit function. So much for the Tipp-Galway animosity which had provided miles of newsprint!

A couple of tournament games as pipe-openers for the resumption of the League gave the Tipp panel little rest during February and when they fielded against Waterford in their first New Year League game there was no question of cobwebs. Joe McGrath, to the accompaniment of much publicity, had taken over as Waterford's manager and he would have a point to prove.

His team had a point to prove, too, and they provided for a crowd of 8,000 at Semple Stadium as fiercely contested a game as one would get in any championship. Tipp won by 2-14 to 2-8 mainly through the return of English who booted two goals — one from his hand and the other from the ground. And having effectively won the game, he retired. It would prove to be Tipp's last League victory.

Suddenly there was talk of numerous injuries and of a place in the quarter-finals being assured, with the result that those who travelled to Enniscorthy on the first Sunday in March were not quite sure what Tipp's attitude to the game was. Whatever the attitude, they sustained their third League defeat at the hands of Wexford since 1989. Trailing by ten points at half-time with a team which included several from the substitutes bench, they rallied brilliantly and drew level. It was heart-throbbing stuff for the last five minutes and injury time was well advanced when the referee awarded Wexford a free from sixty yards out. Jimmy Holohan — who owed Tipp nothing, since it was he whose winning point against Galway the previous year had saved Tipp from relegation — coolly drove the ball between the posts in the face of a strong breeze. The Wexford crowd, resigned to a draw, were ecstatic; the Tipp crowd, annoyed at the last free — which they deemed unjust — were nevertheless consoled by the fighting performance of the second half. Now Wexford shared the top of the table with them.

When Kilkenny, the League holders, came to Semple Stadium at the end of March they needed a win to remain in contention; a draw would do Tipp. Kilkenny got their win by a decisive 2-17 to 0-13, leaving bewildered Tipp followers asking, 'Were we trying?' It seemed impossible that a team that could clock up full points before Christmas should be dismissed with such apparent ease. Ironically, the defeat acted to Tipp's advantage in that it put them into what seemed the easier side of the knockout draw.

Easier side! Now the only Munster team in the last four, they travelled to Limerick to play Offaly in late April. Paul Delaney, who had been away for some months, was back at corner-back beside Conor O'Donovan and Noel Sheehy; Ken Hogan was back in goal; John Madden and Bobby Ryan were wing-backs on either side of Declan Ryan who had been playing at centre-back for some time; John Leahy and Conal Bonnar were at centre-field; Declan Carr, Joe Hayes and Conor Stakelum were the half-forward line and Dinny Ryan, Cormac Bonnar and Michael Cleary were the full line, English and Fox being injured.

Tipp put on what was best described as an insipid performance and were beaten by 1-7 to 0-7, the low scoring indicative of the poor quality of the fare. Michael Duignan got the vital goal which sent Tipp packing and, despite his excitement at the win, Offaly manager Padraig Horan had graceful words of consolation for the vanquished. 'This will be the making of you for the championship', he assured them. Prophetic words. Babs, trying to make the best of a bad situation, echoed his sentiments. 'Look at what happened to Cork in the League last year, and how many remember who won the League? But we all know who won the All-Ireland', he reminded the crestfallen players.

It was a real consolation to Tipp that Offaly went on to win the League. In the meantime they could reflect on Padraig Horan's words.

So much did the players reflect on their own situation in the weeks that followed that reports began to filter out of dissatisfaction in the camp. It is to the credit of players and officials alike that details of players' gripes were never allowed to become the subject of press sensations. Thus, when a players' meeting with the selectors, some weeks before the beginning of the championship, took several hours to air all their grievances, there were no leaks afterwards regarding the course the discussions had taken. But the discussions did clear the air on a number of issues and the result was that training for the championship took on a note of urgency that put everyone in the right frame of mind for what lay ahead.

What lay ahead was a meeting with Limerick in the Munster semi-final to which Tipp had got a bye. Limerick disposed of Clare with some difficulty in their first-round game, winning by only three points, but in doing so they scored the huge total of twenty-one points. It was not a game which Tipp were in any way disposed to take for granted.

The topic of injuries had become as much part of life since Killarney as the games themselves and while English, Fox and John Kennedy were deemed fit, injuries had knocked both Colm and Conal Bonnar out of the reckoning. There were reservations, too, about John Leahy and neither he nor Fox togged out for the final training session, although both were included on the team which read: Ken Hogan in goal; Delaney, O'Donovan and Sheehy; Madden, Bobby Ryan and Kennedy; Declan Carr and Joe Hayes; Cleary, Declan Ryan and Leahy; Fox, Cormac Bonnar and English.

There was some surprise that Bobby Ryan was chosen as centre-back, as it was felt that he was never as much at home there as on the wing. But through the years of Tipp's revival, the failure to come up with a centre-back of classic standards was a continuing problem. There was never a Pat Stakelum or a Tony Wall, a Mick Roche or a Jim Cashman who would provide anchorage for an entire backline and a feeder point for the half-forwards. Declan Ryan had performed well there during the League but, if for no other reason, it was felt that his drive and strength were needed in the forward line.

Limerick, too, had their injury problems and were obliged to field without Ciaran Carey and Shane Fitzgibbon, a crippling blow to begin with. Nevertheless, they went into the game bubbling with enthusiasm, perhaps too much enthusiasm. The game was not long under way when there was a dreadful flare-up in the Tipp square. Following a few further minor incidents, the referee, having obviously made up his mind that a strong line would have to be taken, sent Limerick's Anthony Carmody to the line for a pull on Michael Cleary. It was a cruel blow to Limerick, particularly since John Leahy, taking over as a third midfielder, turned in a sparkling display. The Tipp man, whose groin injury had made him a doubtful quantity starting, would be chosen by RTE as the 'man of the match'. Falling back into defence and leaning forward into attack, he made Limerick feel the misery of playing fourteen men against fifteen, and before the final whistle left the score at 2-18 to 0-10, spectators were already leaving.

The two goals scored by Tipp were of first-class quality. In training Cormac Bonnar had practised kicking the ball with accuracy and he gave a demonstration in the first half when from a pass by Pat Fox he booted the ball firmly at full speed past Tommy Quaid. Twelve minutes from the end Nicholas English, with that acceleration which was the despair of inside backs, chased a running ball from Bobby Ryan-Joe Hayes to the left of the Limerick goal and, having made the yard ahead of Brian Finn to avoid the hook, drove it hard along the ground to the net with a short, left-handed stroke.

Five Limerick players, including the one sent off, were booked and two Tipperary men, thus leaving a slightly unsatisfactory taste to the afternoon's proceedings. But Limerick's misfortune in being beaten by Tipp for the second year running with only fourteen men could hardly be laid at anybody's door but their own. In the Tipp camp joy at having won their way to the final was entirely unconfined. Strangely, apart from their victories over Clare in 1983 and 1984, it was Tipp's first championship win in Thurles since they had beaten Waterford in the first round in 1973. Now everybody's attention was focused on Cork. All talk of dissension in the camp had suddenly evaporated. In any case, said Donie Nealon, the reports had been all balderdash.

THE GAME OF THE GODS, 1991

A couple of weeks before Tipp met Cork in the Munster final the two counties' juniors met; Tipp were chasing their fourth junior provincial title in a row. In a game of tremendous excitement in which the sides had been more or less level all the way through, Tipp began to pull away in the last quarter. With five minutes to go they were eight points ahead and it seemed as if they could not be overtaken. It proved otherwise. Cork clawed their way back and with the final puck from a free made the game a draw at 4-13 to 5-10. In the replay there was none of the excitement of the drawn game and Tipp proved easy winners: 2-20 to 0-11.

The lesson was not lost on the seniors. With a team which the replay later proved to be inferior, Cork had almost snatched the provincial title because Tipp had eased up when they thought the game was won. Hadn't our fathers always told us — never relax against Cork until the final whistle!

It would be easy to say that there never was a build-up to a Cork-Tipp game like the one in 1991. The truth is that to the hurling followers of both counties every championship meeting between the two promises to be unique. And very often it is. But to Tipp, in the last days of June, there was the challenge of proving that the disastrous defeat of the previous year — the year of the donkeys — had not been a true reflection of their worth. It was as if Killarney and all that followed would be proved meaningless if there was a second defeat by Cork.

It was an ideal dressing room gimmick and it was used for all it was worth. The followers caught the spirit of the challenge and the atmosphere in the county was of a never-to-be-forgotten mixture of apprehension and confidence, and good humour.

As the blue and gold hordes swept south for the game much of the talk was about the outcome of the epic Dublin-Meath football marathon the previous day. In the third replay, Dublin with three points to spare in the 70th minute went down by a point. In the space of fifty seconds of extra time Meath had scored a goal and a point to bring to a final resolution the most memorable series of football games of recent times.

In a final interview with the *Tipperary Star* before the game, Babs had voiced the feelings of many veteran followers of Tipperary teams:

> What I fear most about Cork is that you can hurl them off the field but they have the ability to get goals from nothing — Cork goals, I call them. John Fitzgibbon got eight goals for them in last year's championship, and you can go back to the days of the greats like Christy Ring, and you won't find too many equalling that. They were beaten out the gate by Waterford in the semi-final, yet they got two goals when it mattered and they won. This is what I am afraid of. Cork can play real lack-lustre hurling but still come out winners. You cannot really plan for that sort of thing.

Justin McCarthy, former Cork hurling star and coach, put it somewhat differently. Tipp, he considered the better team, but he thought Cork, with the pressure of local pride, would win.

They nearly did, but not quite. What the 46,695 supporters who crammed into Pairc Ui Chaoimh saw had all the excitement and tension that had gripped Croke Park twenty-four hours previously, with the additional ingredients that only hurling can provide. On a day of mist and drizzle and the sod as soggy as a Leeside surface can be made by summer rain, the two sides provided a contest that was truly heroic and would be remembered as one of the great contests between the two counties. But this time it was not a case of Cork making a late arrival to snatch victory or even a draw. It was quite the opposite, and by evening Cork were the ones who had best reason to think they had been hit by an irresistible force when they thought the game had been won.

It started badly for Tipp. Winning the toss and deciding to play against the wind, they had managed to score three points to Cork's two when, in the 7th minute, Kevin Hennessy rammed in a goal that was followed a couple of minutes later by another from Ger Fitzgerald. Babs' nightmare goals were materialising. Cork would not be led for the rest of the game. The Tipp backline was wobbling, only Bobby Ryan showing signs of steadiness, and Cork appeared to be scoring from almost every attack. Wave after wave washed against the Tipp lines and there were miraculous escapes as Hennessy bustled and Fitzgibbon foraged like a terrier around the square. Tomas Mulcahy laid the ball on for Ger Fitzgerald to take Cork's third goal in ten minutes. Tipp were seven points down before their backs began to show signs of taking hold.

Joe Hayes figured increasingly in proceedings at centre-field and in the 20th minute John Leahy, as if personally taking the game in hand, ran towards goal and parted to Nicholas English. Uncharacteristically, English fumbled, but Leahy had kept coming and, picking it up again, he hammered the ball to the Cork net. It was precisely what Tipp needed at that moment. From then to half-time things improved for them, but there was the frustration of seeing English and Michael Cleary between them send six shots sailing harmlessly wide. In the entire first half Cork sent over only three wides and the game had been ten minutes old before the first of these had come.

At half-time Tipp, four points behind, retired Conor O'Donovan who had been injured. Noel Sheehy moved into the full-back position and into his corner came Michael Ryan. The defence tightened and the Upperchurch man lent some of the strength of his native hills to the entire line. After thirteen minutes Tipp reduced the lead to two points. Ken Hogan miraculously saved from Mark Foley and then Cork had another glorious patch. Tony O'Sullivan pointed a free and John Fitzgibbon pointed from play. To and fro the great tussle swayed; Fitzgibbon flashed once more and the ball was behind Ken Hogan. Cork were seven points ahead again.

Tipp struck back. Like a storm coming down from Knockalough, Mick Ryan burst out and sent a long ball upfield. Pat Fox, like quicksilver, slipped in behind Bonnar and Browne, and with a blessed left-hand stroke drove past Ger Cunningham. The game was in its 60th minute. Tipp were on a rising tide, Cleary, Leahy and Fox looking increasingly dangerous, but still failing to get in front. English fumbled at one end and Fitzgibbon at the other. Michael Cleary pointed two frees; the sides were level and the tension was unbearable. Cunningham saved a blaster from English and one from Fox who sent the rebound narrowly wide. Then Kevin Hennessy, with only a minute left, sent a great point over against the breeze and excitement was piled upon excitement as Nicholas English, as so often before, sped goalwards minus his hurley. It was not the first time Tipperary's day had been saved by the boot of the flying corner-forward, and the cheer that rent the sky as the ball went sailing high might have been heard in Cashel. The sides were level again. But wait. Then came one of the most dramatic incidents of the day. The umpire waved the ball wide. Wide, wide, wide!

Whether it was or not we will never know. The consensus is that it was a point. English, not one to make a fuss, protested vehemently, as did Fox. Camera shots seem to justify their claims. But the referee had little choice but to accept the umpire's decision.

Luckily, hurling being the game played by the gods, there is a divine ordinance to Cork-Tipp games. While the Tipperary supporters were still venting their anger and the Cork followers their jubilation, Pat Fox's magic hand grabbed the ball and this time there was no mistake. The game was twelve seconds into injury time when the referee blew the final whistle.

Handshakes were exchanged in the spirit that has characterised Cork-Tipp games for a hundred years and relief was tempered with satisfaction at having provided a game that could stand on its merits with any of the greatest games in the past between the counties. For Tipp there was the consolation that they had won without a major contribution on the scoreboard from Nicholas English. Nothing had gone right for him. He had dropped a ball in front of goal, had fumbled, had sent an easy shot at goal and had finally been deprived of the vital point. 'If I had ducks they'd drown today', he complained.

The teams which provided the heart-stopping exhibition were *Tipp*: Hogan in goal; Delaney, O'Donovan and Sheehy; Madden, Bobby Ryan and Conal Bonnar; Hayes and Carr; Cleary, Declan Ryan and Leahy; Fox, Cormac Bonnar and English. Subs: Michael Ryan for O'Donovan; Aidan Ryan for Hayes.

Cork: Cunningham in goal; Considine, Browne and O'Gorman; McCarthy, Jim Cashman and Casey; B. O'Sullivan and P. Hartnett; Mulcahy, Foley and T. O'Sullivan; G. Fitzgerald, K. Hennessy and J. Fitzgibbon. Subs: D.Quirke for Hartnett; P. Buckley for B. O'Sullivan; T. McCarthy for Quirke.

The replay was first fixed for Thurles on Saturday, 20 July, but the Munster Council thought better of the arrangement and changed it to Sunday. That morning, with traffic already making its way to Thurles, the Tipp squad had a workout in Templemore, ten miles away, and it was decided that with Nicholas English only 70 per cent fit as a result of his hamstring injury, he would not start. The question at issue was whether it was best to start with him and face the consequences of his going off during the game, or to start without him and introduce him if it was felt necessary. Either option was not palatable, but in the event the decision taken was proved correct.

The team that fielded, then, saw Donie O'Connell substituted for English and playing at centre-forward, with Declan Ryan moving out to the wing. Colm Bonnar was introduced at midfield instead of Joe Hayes who was deemed by many to be unlucky to be dropped. Before the day was over, however, he would prove his worth as a substitute. While Tipp were fielding a team which on paper appeared not as strong as that which had played the drawn game, Cork were strengthened by the introduction of Teddy McCarthy at centre-field and the other dual player Denis Walsh at corner-back to keep Pat Fox out of mischief.

Going back as far as the 1920s, Thurles has always been a favourite venue with Cork, even when playing Tipp. It is considered a lively sod, with its open spaces suitable to the type of hurling traditionally favoured by Cork. The love affair with Thurles began in 1926 when Tipp, with an ageing squad, chose to play the up-and-coming Cork team in Cork where the heavier sod would allow them to slow the game to their own pace. The Cork supporters took a hand and when they flooded on to the pitch the referee called the game off, with Tipp leading by five points. The replay was in Thurles and it was a draw. In the third game, again in Thurles, Cork's youth — and an extra man for fifty minutes due to the sending off of a Tipp player — told, and they won. They went on to win the All-Ireland and a few more with it in the years following.

Sentiment and tradition apart, however, Thurles is only an hour's train run from Cork, which is conducive to maximum support from the city itself. For Tipp, Thurles is home. But it is also the place where they are most harshly judged, and when they fielded on the sunny afternoon of that July day in 1991 they had not won a Munster title there in thirty-one years. Not for the first time, blue-and-gold robed ghosts looked over their shoulders.

It is a great pity that the logistics of ticket allocation have apparently dictated that hurling followers are segregated on the terraces. For many of us, one of the most inspiring things about GAA games is how supporters passionately devoted to their counties can mix so good humouredly in the stands and on the terraces. It is a pity that administration, as a matter of convenience, makes it impossible for television viewers to be made aware of this wonderful aspect of our games. Other than for administrative convenience, there is no need to segregate Cork and Tipperary followers, Tipp and Galway followers, Cork and Kilkenny followers, or Kerry and Down followers.

The town end which was allocated to Cork supporters had little to cheer about for some minutes after the opening of the game. Cormac Bonnar, hurleyless, sailed high to catch and patted the ball to Pat Fox who stood facing him, reading his intention perfectly. Fox drove over and a moment later, after Donie O'Connell had dropped the ball, Cleary picked it up and sent it over the bar. Tony O'Sullivan pointed a free, something that would be repeated too often, and John Madden made a long run to deliver to Cormac Bonnar. The clearance from him was picked up by John Leahy at centre-field and sent over. Another Bonnar — Colm — handpassed to Leahy who again drove it high between the posts. The home crowd were ecstatic — a four points to one lead.

Cashman pointed a 65 and now the town terrace made itself heard above the Killinan end. Ger Fitzgerald jumped high, came down in possession and was pulled closer to earth. O'Sullivan pointed the free and, following a momentary flare-up, Jim Cashman pointed a free from midfield. Now the sides were level, all Cork's scores having come from frees. Sooner or later Tipp's eagerness to shut down every Cork move would cost dearly.

In the 19th minute Cork lunged ahead when a typical opportunistic pull by John Fitzgibbon from a ruck in front of the goal beat Ken Hogan. Seconds later Ger Fitzgerald pointed and a Cashman free was sent into the hand of Tony O'Sullivan who slotted it over the bar. Now Cork were ahead by five points, but big Cormac Bonnar, collecting a ball in the corner, came pounding towards goal, turning and swerving and twisting until he had attracted enough Cork defenders to him. Then, in a flash, he parted to Michael Cleary, momentarily alone in front of the goal. A lightning pull and the Cork net shook to bring much needed relief to Tipp at a time when they were beginning to struggle.

To and fro the battle raged, every moment producing its own ener-gised magic. Cashman pointed a 65 and Cunningham saved a deft flick from Bonnar. From centre-field Carr drove over a mighty point and then a sideline cut by Hartnett found Ger Fitzgerald on the edge of the square and once again the town end went wild as the green flag waved. As the clock showed the game thirty minutes old Declan Ryan, with a seemingly effortless stroke, pointed and Bonnar booted a ball through for Fox to point. Now a goal separated the sides and as Paul Delaney took too long to clear after a dangerous raid by Mark Foley, his stroke was blocked by a vigilant Fitzgibbon. Once again Foley was in possession and his point could not have come at a more opportune time for his side. The half-time whistle blew as the scoreboard read 2-8 to 1-7 in favour of Cork.

In the Tipp dressing room there was pressure to bring in English. The pressure would later increase when the situation deteriorated further. The selectors opted for Aidan Ryan for the moment instead of Donie O'Connell, who always had the reputation of performing well against Cork and having the knack of making the ball available to the wingers. He was now 31 and work commitments had made the business of achieving total sharpness increasingly difficult for him. The wisdom of bringing on Aidan Ryan would be proven in a dramatic manner.

That there was an element of unease in the Tipp lines was made obvious, if by nothing else, by the fact that six of Cork's points had been scored from frees. All Tipp's scores had come from play. The second half resumed with a further point from a Tony O'Sullivan free and within five minutes John Madden and Declan Ryan had been booked. A long free from Pat Hartnett, who had come on for Brendan O'Sullivan, gave Tony O'Sullivan another point and from almost on the sideline the will-o'-the-wisp forward pointed yet another free. Cork were now seven points ahead, but there was no sense of desperation in Tipp's game.

John Madden limped to the line and to a thunderous cheer Joe Hayes bounded on. Tipp lifted. Cleary had his second point from a free, and there followed a brilliant passage of pure hurling. Without a hurley, Aidan Ryan gained possession to toss to Cleary — another point. At the other end Tomas Mulcahy replied. Fitzgibbon, dodging and weaving goalward, drove over the bar leaving Colm Bonnar and Paul Delaney on the ground, having crashed into each other. Again Fitzgibbon ran and threw to Hennessy who, trying to shake off the attentions of Noel Sheehy, turned out from goal. Blue and gold jerseys were all around him when, incredibly, he struck and Ken Hogan never saw it. Tipperary were momentarily struck dumb as the scoreboard read: Cork 3-13 Tipp 1-10.

Leahy, ranging upfield, drove a rocket which Ger Cunningham turned out, but Fox received from Aidan Ryan to point. Then Declan

Ryan pointed. For a vital period Leahy was everywhere, now defending, now attacking. He drove a long free to Fox who pointed again, but the sight of English warming up on the sideline was a reminder that a goal was needed. Twenty minutes had gone and Tipp were two goals down. Points are fine in their own way, but there comes a time in a game. . .

At centre-field Leahy and Joe Hayes combined to send a ball up to Fox. Closed in by two Cork men, the wily corner-forward accelerated with that burst of speed which the sight of a rolling sliotar seems so often to endow him, and with a one-handed flick he sent the ball past Ger Cunningham.

Once again a generation of Tipp supporters who, growing up in the years of the famine, were never used to taking dramatic recoveries for granted, were an embarrassment to their elders. Over the paling at the Killinan end they poured in their frenzy and on to the pitch, the invasion led by a man in a wheelchair. A youngster landed on Pat Fox and in a moment there was a struggling mass of spectators mobbing the scorer of the life-saving goal. Their elders remembered a day in Killarney forty-one years before when Christy Ring, the greatest hurler of all, and Jack Lynch, the future Taoiseach, tried to coax their supporters off the pitch to allow them to get on with the business of winning the game. Cork did not win that day and neither would they win this time. But Babs Keating had no way of knowing that as he used all his powers of persuasion to move the Tipperary supporters back from Ger Cunningham's lines. Tipp were now only two points behind (3-12 to 2-13) and fifteen minutes remained.

Cleary pointed and Casey replied with a point from a magnificent sideline cut. This game had everything. Ten minutes to go and a ball dropped from the sky on the square for Declan Carr to connect and send it rocket-like to the net. Once again the supporters were in on the field and a string of gardaí arrived to support Babs in controlling them. The sides were level and Aidan Ryan pointed to put Tipp ahead for the first time since the early minutes of the game. Pat Buckley replied and now every ball was vital, any mistake a potential match-loser. Cormac Bonnar finished a great penetrating run by shooting wide. Three minutes to go and Michael Cleary, inside the Cork backs, raced on to a running ball, but Ger Cunningham got there first. At the other end Hogan saved from O'Sullivan.

Two and a half minutes left and Bonnar ran again, this time to point — Tipp two points ahead. The clock was on time when Tony

O'Sullivan from a free dropped the ball on the Tipp square. Hurleys flashed and Pat Buckley's shot hit the post. This was assuredly the game of games. On came Cork again like a great wave. Declan Ryan's hand went high and he cleared from his own 40. Declan Carr caught it and drove. Cork's Sean O'Gorman stopped and pulled, but Aidan Ryan thundered up in time to block the shot and the ball rolled on ahead, leaving him pounding in pursuit. 'Safe!' cried thousands of Cork hearts as Richard Browne moved across to connect with the moving ball, but by then the fair-haired Aidan was closing the gap. As Browne connected, Ryan arrived in time for another masterly block, and now the ball was rolling again in front of him and only Ger Cunningham to beat. Now the Tipp man had the ball in his hand and without breaking his stride he drove it from his left side past Ger Cunningham. Between the initial block and the final delivery the crowd had witnessed a bewildering array of hurling skills from one man. The score was Tipp 4-17 to Cork's 3-15.

But it was not over yet. Cork surged back. Three minutes into injury time John Fitzgibbon had a goal from a free. Still it was not over, and once more it was Tipp's turn to attack. Aidan Ryan again ran and parted to Cleary to point and as referee Terence Murray, who was taking charge of his fifth Tipp-Cork game since 1987 handled his whistle to blow an end to the epic, Michael Cleary scored the final point.

It was over, a game that would live in the memory of those who were there and in the imagination of those lovers of hurling who were not. Handshakes were exchanged between men who had for the past hour and a half been bitter foes. Their fathers and grandfathers had done so. The Cork-Tipp saga would go on.

In the Cork dressing room there was silence. No real hurling follower from Tipp or elsewhere could fail to understand. But Cork was Cork. They would be back. In the meantime, the rest of us would carry memories intertwined with blue and gold and red and white.

Chapter Twenty

A SHADOW OF GALWAY, 1991

While there was silence in the Cork dressing room after their defeat, it was not so in Tipp's. But after the first moments of careless rapture, it was back to business. They might have beaten Cork in exciting circumstances, but they had been along this road before without winning an All-Ireland. So a listener might have heard the resonant voice of Babs Keating calling, as if in a litany, the names of Finnerty and Cooney and Lynskey and Naughton and the others who had caused Tipp such nightmares in the past few years: 'Remember '87 and '88 and remember these names!' The championship was a matter of unfinished business.

If there was a consensus that Tipp were on the way up while Galway were on the way down, it was generally felt that their recent years in the wars of top-class hurling had removed from Galway whatever was left of the lingering inferiority complex that was so often associated with them. In its stead was now a firmly based self-confidence that comes only with success. But the sturdy side which had punished Tipp in 1987 and 1988 was breaking up, new players were being introduced and this time they would be facing Tipp with a number of new faces and without Eanna Ryan whose deadly goals had cost Tipp so dearly in the past and whose recovery from injury was as much wished in Tipp as in his own county.

In the fortnight before the Tipp-Galway meeting, Tipp's juniors reversed the defeat of the previous year when they beat Kilkenny by 2-13 to 0-10 in the All-Ireland 'home' final at Limerick. It was hoped it might prove an omen of good things to come for the seniors.

As the big game drew near there was increasing comment by press pundits regarding suggestions that Galway were at a disadvantage against Tipp because of the team's lack of championship practice. In Tipperary this was interpreted as a sign that the steely Galway self-confidence was waning, but the time was past when anyone in Tipp dared to take anything for granted regarding Galway. Every night in training the Tipp squad were reminded of the power Galway had been capable of turning on in recent times. The controversial aspects of the Tipp victory in 1989 — Galway having only thirteen men at the finish, the Tony Keady suspension and Galway's much publicised criticism of the referee at the time — were emphasised over and over until it was clear to everyone that nothing less than another win would give a conclusive answer to the criticisms of the verdict of 1989. Now was the time to lay to rest for once and for all the ghosts of the previous victory.

Despite early reports to the contrary, Tony Keady fielded again, but the Galway team showed a number of names that had not figured in the games that had written themselves so splendidly into hurling history over the previous few years: R. Burke; B. Dervan, P. Finnerty, S. Treacy; G. Keane, T. Keady, G. McInerney; M. Coleman, B. Keogh; R. Duane, J. Cooney, M. Naughton; M. McGrath, B. Lynskey and J. Rabbitte.

In the Munster final replay Tipp had resisted the temptation to introduce the injured Nicholas English at a vital stage of the game. He had now recovered sufficiently to be included in the attack, much to the pleasure of the media who still found him the most newsworthy hurler in the country. John Madden's Munster final injury had not yet come right and Aidan Ryan came in at midfield. The Tipp line-out was: K. Hogan; P. Delaney, N. Sheehy, M. Ryan; Colm Bonnar, B. Ryan, Conal Bonnar; D. Carr (capt.), Aidan Ryan; M. Cleary, Declan Ryan, J. Leahy; P. Fox, Cormac Bonnar and N. English.

Sadly, the game did not live up to expectations that had been based on the meetings of previous years. With five new faces, Galway were only a pale shadow of the mighty side which Tipp — and everyone else — feared so much; the ten point victory of Tipp (3-13 to 1-9) was probably a fair reflection of their superiority. Combinations such as had fielded in the maroon and white during the latter half of the 1980s are not easily put together but, ironically, the failure could not be laid at the door of the newcomers. At times Galway supporters must have sighed for a full muster of the old guard of forwards under the old conditions, as Keady rained balls on to the Tipp lines, only to have them returned as quickly as they arrived.

'Galway never rose above the mediocre yesterday', wrote Donal Keenan in the *Irish Independent* the following day. 'It was not that Cyril Farrell's gamble in introducing five newcomers failed. Quite the contrary. The debutants played smartly and justified their inclusion. It was the older heads, the ones which have brought so much honour and glory to the county, who failed to find the form which made them one of the most feared teams in the game since they came to prominence in 1985. With the exception of Joe Rabbitte, the forward line failed dismally to deliver yesterday. That was a result of their own lack of form and the best defensive display by a Tipperary team in years.'

This was a day when the Tipp backs finally came off the field leaving their supporters little to complain about. Apart from a single mix-up which gave away a goal to Michael McGrath, the full-back line of Delaney, Sheehy and Ryan never wobbled. Beyond them, the half-line consistently refused to oblige the old Galway tactic of drawing the backs, so that the wonderful passing movements which had tormented Tipp defences in the past never materialised on the anticipated scale.

After twenty-five minutes, Tipp led by the incredible margin of 2-5 to 0-2 — and against the wind. English was getting more attention than a mortal deserved, but the goals came from Cormac Bonnar and Cleary. Then Galway came and in eight minutes they scored 1-3, McGrath's goal being reminiscent of the very best 1988 vintage. But Leahy came back with a point and Cleary with two more, so that at half-time Tipp were two goals clear.

By half-time English, his jersey spectacularly splashed with blood from a five-stitch cut over his left eye and a two-stitch cut beneath, had been forced to the line by a recurrence of his hamstring trouble. He was followed eleven minutes into the second half by Cormac Bonnar who had by then given a virtuoso performance at full-forward. But though the half was only two minutes old when Declan Ryan beat two men to lash in Tipp's third goal, the lethal quality went from the forward line with the departure of Bonnar. The *Irish Independent* commented: 'The fearsome full-forward scored one goal, created a second and generally caused havoc in the Galway defence before limping from the fray with a calf injury when the battle was already won.'

The tension had gone out of the game, but Galway battled gamely on and the remaining minutes were remarkable only for the tenacity of the Tipp backs in resisting repeated Galway efforts to open them out as had been done so often in the past. By the time referee Dickie Murphy of Wexford blew the final whistle, it was clear that the game would be the least remembered of the Tipp-Galway encounters of those years.

In the Tipp dressing room the jubilation was of a subdued order. Babs' criticisms were about the performance of the forwards after the departure of English and Bonnar, but he did not appear to have his heart in the complaints. Tipperary had reached their third All-Ireland since the ending of the famine. Nobody but the most demanding — and unreasonable — could complain about that.

Chapter Twenty-one

YOU LEARNED SOME OF THE KILKENNY CRAFT, 1991

On a morning at the height of the Anglo-Irish War young Tommy Leahy of Boherlahan saw a pony and trap carrying a number of men coming along the boreen leading to the house. One of them had the unmistakable face of one of the great Kilkenny hurlers. He rushed in to shout to his older brother Johnny, 'There's men coming and I think one of them is Sim Walton!' Then, while his mother bustled round giving the kitchen a quick tidy, he waited with the greatest respect to open the gate into the yard for the visitors.

Among hurling men everywhere, Sim Walton was already a legend. Now at the end of his career, he had won six All-Ireland medals and had captained Kilkenny to victory in 1912. He had also captained Kilkenny in 1916 when, at the end of one of their periods of glory, they fell to up-and-coming Tipperary. Johnny Leahy had been captain of Tipperary that day and would be for many more years to come. He was a full-back and a corner-back, Walton a full-forward, and to the end of his days he would always say that Walton was the only one who might have had the edge as a full-forward on the great Martin Kennedy of Tipperary.

The two captains met in the yard with a firm handclasp and the other men were introduced. They were republicans who had escaped the previous night from Kilkenny jail and they had made their way to Sim Walton's in Tullaroan. It had been considered wise to move them as far as possible from the Kilkenny area, hence their arrival in Boherlahan.

The two great opponents sat at the kitchen table throughout the day, and hurling games in the dim past and in the recent past were discussed until, coming towards evening, the Tullaroan man with a 'Ye'll want to be getting on with the milking!' rose to go. The pony and trap were brought out, and as young Tommy Leahy once more opened the gate out of the yard, the great Sim called back to Johnny, 'Will ye send this lad over to us for a few weeks and we'll teach him some of the Kilkenny craft?' Then with a flick of the whip, he was off.

A decade later Tipp had beaten Dublin for the county's eleventh All-Ireland win when Tommy Leahy, who had played wing-forward, felt a firm hand on his shoulder and turning round he found himself looking into the moustached face of the former Kilkenny captain. 'You learned some of the Kilkenny craft after all', was the greeting.

Kilkenny craft. It was a commodity which over the decades was envied by Tipperary, although it was a commodity for which Tipp bone and commitment had, as often as not, proved a match. When the two captains shook hands after the epic 1916 final the Kilkenny man said, 'We were better hurlers, Leahy.'

'But we were better men, Sim,' replied the Tipperary man.

It was more than just a smart answer. It was the firm conviction of a man who believed that in hurling total commitment can often win over craft. And so, over the years, while there was the keenest admiration in Tipperary for the stylists of Kilkenny, there was also the belief that Tipp grit, bone and first-time ground hurling was the answer to the fabulous Kilkenny craft. Shortly before he died in 1981, the Tommy Leahy referred to above was talking of John Joe Hayes, a wonderfully effective and stylish Tipperary half-forward of the 1920s. 'John Joe went to school in St Kieran's. That's why he was such a tasty hurler', he said. Implicit in the comment was the deference to Kilkenny craft.

Despite their great rivalry, the two counties had met in only thirteen finals before 1991 and of these Tipp had won eight. Kilkenny beat Johnny Leahy's men in 1922 — with two goals in the last three minutes — and they did not beat Tipp in a final again until 1967. When Johnny Leahy died in 1949 Dick Grace of Tullaroan, the man who had beaten Tipp in 1922, was there with Lory Meagher, the greatest Kilkenny stylist of them all, to carry him to his last resting place. It was an eloquent reminder of the fierce loyalties which the great games between the two counties had engendered between opponents.

But on the day in 1967 when Kilkenny reversed the verdicts of forty-five years there occurred the tragic accident in which their flying half-forward Tom Walsh lost an eye. It was an incident which was cruelly twisted in the telling, and the telling was not to Tipp's advantage. Then during Tipp's famine years currency was given in Kilkenny to the theory that the rules had simply caught up with Tipp. Now that there was no third-man tackle, now that the goalie could not be charged, now that there was greater restriction on the body-charge and on the rules of obstruction, Tipp would not be a force any more. It was an interpretation that was peddled by those who did not know their hurling or their Tipperary, or perhaps their Kilkenny, and it would be no help to Kilkenny when they took the field against Tipp on the first Sunday in September of 1991.

Tipp's last All-Ireland before the famine had been against Kilkenny in 1971. In goal for Kilkenny that day had been one Ollie Walsh, now Kilkenny's manager. Playing corner-forward for Tipp had been Babs Keating who scored both of Tipp's goals in a 3-8 to 2-7 victory. The other two Tipp selectors had played in the 1967 final when Kilkenny had pipped Tipp by four points. John O'Donoghue had been in goal and Donie Nealon had played at wing-forward.

Except in patches, Kilkenny had not impressed on their way to the 1991 final. They had been lucky to beat Wexford, had looked as if they weren't going to get past Dublin and had been lucky again to beat Antrim. But whatever their championship performances, the statistics of their meetings with Tipp since the ending of the famine were creditable. In five League games between the counties Kilkenny had won two, Tipp one, and there had been two draws. Yet, the bookies' odds as they took the field were 3/1 against Kilkenny and 1/4 on Tipperary. Only a handful of the Kilkenny side had previously won All-Ireland medals.

The Tipp team that fielded to win the county's 24th All-Ireland was the same as had beaten Galway. English and Bobby Ryan, who had been carrying injuries were declared fit, but Cormac Bonnar's fitness had been in doubt until the last minute. He was still not able to participate in training when the team was picked on the Sunday before the final: Ken Hogan; Paul Delaney, Noel Sheehy, Michael Ryan; Colm Bonnar, Bobby Ryan, Conal Bonnar; Declan Carr, Aidan Ryan; Michael Cleary, Declan Ryan, John Leahy; Pat Fox, Cormac Bonnar and Nicholas English.

Kilkenny fielded: Michael Walsh; Bill Hennessy, John Henderson, Liam Simpson; Liam Walsh, Pat Dwyer, Eddie O'Connor; Richie Power, Michael Phelan; John Power, Christy Heffernan, D. J. Carey; Eamon Morrissey, Liam Fennelly and Liam McCarthy.

The extraordinary thing about Tipp-Kilkenny finals is that since Dick Grace's personal triumph in 1922 they had not produced a real classic. In 1937 Kilkenny had completely collapsed to be beaten 3-11 to 0-3. In 1945 Tipp won by two goals what 'Carbery' described as a 'clean, honest, hard-fought game'. In 1950 they had slugged it out over a dour hour to produce the uninspiring result: Tipp 1-9 Kilkenny 1-8. In 1964 Tipp had a whopping fourteen points to spare, and the Kilkenny victory in 1967 had been overshadowed by Tom Walsh's injury. Nor did the Tipp victory in 1971 fit into the category of classic. Good games rather than great ones seem to have been the norm since that far-off day in 1922 when some Tipp supporters left before full time thinking Tipp had it won, only to find out later that they had been mistaken.

For the neutral observer the final of 1991 would fit into that same moderate category. It did not produce the heart-stopping sequences of heroic hurling each of the counties had produced on their way to the final, but it did have its moments and the outcome was in doubt until referee Willie Horgan's final whistle.

For Tipperary folk, conscious of the aspersions cast on their 1989 All-Ireland win, it was the final proof that the win of 1989 had been well and truly deserved. They had beaten Limerick and Cork in Munster, they had beaten a formidable Galway team, and now they had beaten Kilkenny. What criticism could now be raised? Those who had insisted that they could not do without English had their answer when they finished not alone without the superstar but without Cormac Bonnar whom many considered their single most effective forward.

The minor game in which Tipp were also confronted by Kilkenny provided a bad omen. Despite being on top for most of the hour, the Tipp lads wilted in the face of a last-quarter Kilkenny flourish and went down by two points: 0-15 to 1-10. Typical Kilkenny, said the Tipp followers. You can never consider them beaten until you hear the final whistle. If the seniors get a lead they will have to hang on to it — no late rallies for Kilkenny this time. It nearly happened just as Tipp feared. But not quite.

Within seven minutes of the throw-in, Tipp had clocked up three points without reply. Kilkenny had only three wides to show in return. It was the tenth minute before, with the first of the nine points he would score altogether, D. J. Carey raised Kilkenny's first flag. Three minutes later Kilkenny, again through Carey, were ahead and they would remain ahead until Tipp drew level just before half-time.

From the beginning it was evident that the much publicised injuries of the big two — English and Cormac Bonnar — were no pre-match ruse by the Tipperary selectors. Both were operating under obvious difficulties and, being tightly marked, never looked like producing the kind of magic which on other days left defences in disarray. Kilkenny were leaving nothing to chance and even Pat Fox seemed to be getting little of the ball.

For some twenty minutes of the first half, Delaney, Sheehy and Ryan, the last line of defence, was the only Tipp line that was clearly in control. But despite the Kilkenny edge along every other line, there was still an air of confidence in Tipp's performance and Kilkenny, notwithstanding the wind advantage, were unable to convert that edge into real terms on the scoreboard. Then, nine minutes from half-time, Aidan Ryan signalled a pre-interval recovery which would lay a firm foundation for a Tipp victory. A point from the Borrisoleigh man, who had swopped places with John Leahy, gave an immediate lift at precisely the moment it was most needed. Eamon Morrissey replied with a wonderful point from the wing and then came what was for many the most memorable score of the day. Big Cormac Bonnar, chafing under the restriction of the heavily bandaged knee, raced out and threw himself skyward as a hard shot screamed overhead. As he hit the deck, sliotar in hand, to commence bursting, burrowing and weaving through black and amber, it seemed as if the very best he could hope for was a free. But in a split second's inspiration he spotted Pat Fox, momentarily and for the first time in the game, unmarked. The pass was perfect and Fox's drive was lighting fast — it had to be, since as he swung he too was overwhelmed by black and amber. But the ball was on its way over the bar, and for the first time that day Tipp supporters felt that the old magic was there, only waiting for the right circumstances to be produced. Tipp tails were up, but the Cats were fighting back as Michael Cleary sent two frees over the bar to bring the sides level at 0-9 each.

As the whistle blew for the interval both teams sprinted for the dressing rooms. Thirty-five minutes of gruelling physical endeavour had indicated the commitment to victory of both sides, but Kilkenny who had enjoyed superiority for most of the half had nothing to show for it on the scoreboard. They had enjoyed the slight wind advantage which the sultry, slightly sunny day had provided. They had thrown everything they had at Tipp. Yet Tipp were on level terms. With such thoughts Tipp supporters comforted one another during the interval. If only there could be a few encores of the magical combination between Bonnar and Fox, or if English could spark just once. He was

149

not getting his share of the ball. But in the past that had never stopped him being involved.

As soon as the second half commenced it was obvious that there would be no dramatics from English. Fox, challenged by three backs, belted over a point and then the Lattin-Cullen man, by now limping badly, eluded Bill Hennessy, only to drive inexplicably wide. Cleary pointed. John Leahy was like an avenging angel falling back to his own half-back line and with long, swift clearances putting his forwards on the attack. A severe charge on D. J. Carey gave Kilkenny another point from a free.

Nicholas English was in possession and trundling towards goal. What happened next will be argued over for a long time. Bill Hennessy flung his hands wide and appeared to be guilty of what many, particularly those from Tipp, would call obstruction. Others, particularly those from Kilkenny, would claim he was within his rights. The referee interpreted it as the former. It was the 10th minute and Tipp were a point ahead when Michael Cleary stepped up to take the free. Were it not that the moment is forever frozen on film there would already be a hundred versions of what followed. But the picture remains to tantalise Kilkenny hurling followers for years to come as they see the bizarre score which gave the McCarthy Cup to Tipperary. Cleary, slightly over-reaching, sent what appeared to be a feeble attempt for a point which ran the danger of being pulled down. But in the flick of an eyelid the ball was in the net, the result of a deflection from Liam Walsh's hurley.

It was a cruel blow to Kilkenny at a vital stage of the game — a shot that in a hundred years would not again find the net. It was hurling's version of the Mikey Sheehy-Paddy Cullen goal, the type of score one holds in contempt except when it is for one's own side. However, no team wins an All-Ireland without luck on their side. Michael Cleary's goal was lucky and it won Tipperary's 24th All-Ireland. It gave Tipp a huge psychological boost at a vital time; it gave them a feeling of fortune being on their side — always an important factor in a tight game — and it gave them a lead of four points. For the first time since the opening minutes of the game Tipp looked like winners. Now blue and gold flags fluttered more often and more vigorously than black and amber.

D. J. Carey (again!) pointed a free to leave only a goal between the sides, but the Tipp backs were becoming more confident and, in front,

Pat Fox was becoming more unmanageable. Michael Ryan, increasingly noticeable in defence, drove a long ball for Fox to point and a moment later Fox repeated the performance. Now the pressure was on Kilkenny and Eddie O'Connor was moved back in an attempt to curb the wily corner-forward. Eamon Morrissey pointed; Mick Ryan again cleared and at a moment when there was a rising Kilkenny tide, D. J. Carey drove a free wide from near the sideline. Then he pointed a close-in free, but — often a sure sign of a winning team — the puckout was caught and pointed at the other end by Aidan Ryan.

Then came one of the golden moments of the game. Michael Cleary ran along the line at the Cusack Stand side heading towards the Railway end. Step for step Kilkenny's Liam Simpson kept pace with him, and as the Nenagh man was about to strike, Simpson reached and caught the ball. It was one of those magical moments which only hurling can provide, but again it went wrong for Kilkenny. Declan Ryan moved in to intercept Simpson's pass and sweep it over the bar.

Cormac Bonnar had already called it a day, to be replaced by Conor Stakelum, and now he was followed to the bench by Nicholas English who was replaced by Donie O'Connell, veteran of many battles. It is indicative of Tipp's commitment that the substitutions hardly caused them to pause in their stride. Now Pat Fox was at his most dangerous best and the full-forward line was being fed with increasing fluency.

D. J. Carey had pointed two frees, one brilliantly from near the Cusack Stand sideline, to reduce the margin again to a single goal when the moment came that might have made Kilkenny's dream come true. Liam Fennelly, boxed in at the corner of the square, succeeded in getting in a shot which Ken Hogan, on his knees, saved but could not control. D. J. Carey, flying across, was a tiny bit too far ahead and could not turn quickly enough, so that the rebound was picked up by Colm Bonnar. Hearts on both sides stood still, but at that moment a bird of omen might have begun its flight to the Nore with grim news. Had the ground been firmer under Carey; had Bonnar not been there; had Hogan been unsighted; had Fennelly got in a full-blooded stroke.

Tipp hearts missed a beat once more as Kilkenny raided again but Liam Fennelly drove wide. Closing on full time Conor Stakelum blocked down a Liam Walsh clearance and Pat Fox, capping a wonderful performance, sent over a point. Now Tipp were four points ahead (1-16 to 0-15), but as they moved into injury time Kilkenny swept back with all the power and fire which has characterised the black and amber for nearly a hundred years. It was a thrilling finale, worthy of the two counties, and it seemed as though the ghosts of Sim Walton, Lory Meagher, Matty Power, Jim Langton and so many others who had adorned Croke Park in times past, clustered round the Tipp goal. Liam Fennelly, as if to make up for his previous wide, burst goalward. Conal Bonnar blocked and Michael Ryan cleared. Michael Phelan was fouled and Adrian Ronan lobbed in a high ball. It was do or die for the men from the Nore. Eamon Morrissey sparkled; Ken Hogan saved and was awarded a free out. Declan Carr won the puckout and sent Tipp attacking as the final whistle blew. It had been a dour struggle from the start, but in its closing moments it had been evocative of all the pride and skill which had characterised the two counties since their paths had first crossed in championship hurling. Now Tipp and not Kilkenny had taken second place to Cork on the roll of All-Ireland winners. The final score was: Tipp 1-16 Kilkenny 0-15.

If relations between the two counties had not been improved by press reports over the previous few weeks, there was no sign of begrudgery on the field as Tipp supporters first trickled and then flooded over the wire on to the pitch. Players shook hands and embraced and in some cases walked off the pitch together as befitted heroes of neighbouring counties who appreciated that, in other circumstances, the verdict might have been different. There was, however, a general acceptance that Tipp had been slightly the better team and that they had deserved their victory.

There was one man who believed that it might not have been Tipp superiority or even luck that had made the difference. Ollie Walsh, Kilkenny's manager and once-superstar goalkeeper, was bitterly critical of referee Horgan's handling of the game. In the *Cork Examiner* he was quoted as stressing in the immediate aftermath of the game that he had no criticism of Tipperary but added: 'Tipperary did nothing to us. It was the referee who did not give us fair play.'

However, the normally placid manager had partially recovered his composure when he visited the Tipp dressing room to tell the victors, 'We gave ye a right good rattle!' The Kilkenny chairman Nicky Brennan, himself a winner of three All-Irelands, generously assured Tipp that they had not received sufficient credit for winning the 1989 All-Ireland. He hoped that they would now get the recognition they deserved and that their injured players would recover satisfactorily.

Interestingly, it was an injured Kilkenny player who paid Tipp the tribute they most appreciated. John Power, the dashing wing-forward, had crashed into a hoarding in the first half and in an effort to save himself had badly cut his finger on adjacent barbed wire. Despite a deep cut and having lost feeling in his hand, he had courageously played on with total commitment until replaced in the second half. 'If it was against any other team I would have gone off, but against Tipperary you never throw in the towel. They always bring out the best in us and they did so in this All-Ireland final', he said. There would have been approving nods in graveyards from Tullaroan to Boherlahan.

When the team arrived in Thurles on the following evening, they found 20,000 people waiting to welcome them in Liberty Square. Through Kilkenny villages on the way they had met with good-humoured banter and one man had stuck his head into the bus to point at the cup and warn them, 'Mind that. We'll want it next year.' At Urlingford, on the border between the two counties, the joviality was at its best as supporters of both counties mixed and collected or paid on their bets. There was little evidence of the rancour that was supposed to exist between the two counties.

In Thurles things were done as they had always been done — except in 1989. The bus made its way with great difficulty through the crowds. The Archbishop was on the platform to greet the team. Speeches were made and there was much singing of 'Slievenamon'. The pubs were open for some considerable time, but people who had no interest in pubs just strolled about the streets savouring the atmosphere. The All-Ireland cup had come back and there was nobody to dispute the manner of its winning or its coming.

NEVER BRING THE MCCARTHY CUP TO THE LEE, 1991–2

The celebrations which followed the winning of the 1991 All-Ireland in Tipperary were of a more restrained order than those that had marked the 1989 win. Lessons had been learned and there was a conscious effort, not always successful, to keep demands on players to attend functions to a minimum. Nevertheless, the requests from GAA clubs and other bodies for players to make themselves available generated a considerable strain, particularly on those still involved in club championships.

Victory in an All-Ireland always gives additional bite to a county championship when spectators feel they can see their county stars in a different dimension. Perhaps they feel, too, that whereas in the early stages of the League they may or may not be seeing players at their best, in the final stages of county championships they are seeing their true worth under real pressure.

Tipp's first League game against Limerick towards the end of October was played at a time when the county's main focus of attention was on club affairs, and eight or nine of those who had figured in the proceedings at Croke Park on the first Sunday in September were not available. Limerick were not at full strength either, and under their new manager Phil Bennis they put everything into the game and with a couple of late goals managed to beat the champions. Despite the absence of so many regulars, Tipp had the winning of a game which was played before a mere 4,000 spectators and there was no attempt to belittle Limerick's win. That Limerick could do even better would be proved before the League was over.

By the time Tipp played Kilkenny in the League a fortnight later the county was talking not about their League prospects but about the impending county final in which Cashel, with its cluster of Bonnars, would lock horns with Declan Carr's Holycross. Nevertheless, there was general pleasure when Tipp, with only seven of their All-Ireland side, beat Kilkenny, who had eight of their regulars, by 2-18 to 1-11.

The winning continued after Christmas with victories over Offaly and Down. In the meantime there had been a fortnight in Florida where the happy warriors basked in sunshine and swopped ideas with the Meath footballers who were also reaping the just rewards of summer toil. But there was no let-up in the demands of games, and on the Sunday after their return they had to turn out for a tournament at Semple Stadium where, no doubt, some spectators were annoyed that they did not show the same eagerness as might be expected in mid-summer.

By the end of March the spectators were more likely to see something like summer fare and those who went to Rathdowney to see Tipp play Laois were treated to a game which for passion and commitment belonged more properly in July. Trained by Tipp's Paddy Doyle, brother of Jimmy, Laois played with a wind advantage in the first half and succeeded in leading by 1-8 to 1-2 at half-time. Nicholas English came on in the second half, but such was the closeness of the marking that he failed to raise a flag. When John Leahy, who had blasted in two goals, hobbled off injured, he was replaced by Pat Fox who in turn did not figure on the scoreboard. Tipp drew ahead in the last few minutes, but Laois made one dying attempt and a rocket by Christy Dunphy was turned over the bar by Tipp goalkeeper Jody Grace of Toomevara to leave the final score Tipp 2-10 Laois 2-10. Everybody was pleased, honour satisfied on both sides. Tipp, who had earned the point that gave them a place in the League semi-final, were pleased for Laois and particularly for Paddy Doyle.

Once more they faced Galway and some keenness was added to the meeting by the spring saga of Cashel and Kiltormer who had played three times in the All-Ireland club semi-final before the Galway club emerged victorious. A new set of selectors had taken over in Galway — Cyril Farrell having called it a day — and among them was a former Thurles player Michael Fogarty. The absence of Finnerty, Fahy and Naughton would, it was anticipated, weaken Galway, but Tipp would be without English, Leahy, Colm and Cormac Bonnar, John Kennedy and Michael O'Meara.

By now Tipp's sights were fixed so firmly on the championship that there were those who thought there was nothing so important as avoiding a meeting with Cork. If Tipp were to meet Cork in the League, went the argument, they would be showing their hand too early. But Cork and Limerick were to play in the other League semi-final. What if Cork were to win and Tipp were to beat Galway? The rumour began to gain currency that Tipp intended soft-pedalling the game against Galway, in other words, going as near as they could to 'throwing' the game.

That this was no more than a rumour was amply demonstrated on the field at Ennis. Twenty thousand spectators saw a whole-hearted game in the course of which three players were booked, two Galway men and one Tipp man, and Michael Ryan was stretchered off with a leg injury that would keep him out of the championship. But despite the knife-edged rivalry and the keenness of the exchanges, it was quite a sporting encounter which sent spectators home with the feeling that they had seen a game in which two teams were determined to give value for money. Tipp won and maybe Bobby Ryan spoke for all the players when he said, 'If it was only a game of tiddly-winks, both teams would want to win it. Defeat dampens your morale against an old rival.'

Playing against the wind in the first half, Tipp managed to stay level at half-time and by full time they were seven points ahead. But the margin flattered somewhat, since a feature of the game was the performance of goalkeeper Ken Hogan. It seemed that at last Tipp had attained a slight psychological advantage over their great rivals, but it was clear that Galway would soon be challenging strongly again for anything that was going. Had Tipp known that this would be their last major victory for twelve months, they would have experienced more than mere satisfaction at the outcome.

Limerick, not Cork, emerged from the other semi-final and Tipp were ever so pleased that they would not be 'seeing red' for another month. Besides, Limerick were not considered as formidable a challenge as Cork would have presented for the League final and a win over them would put Tipp in the right frame of mind for the championship.

But the League Final did not at all turn out as anticipated. Unfortunately for Tipp, the first half appeared to confirm their superiority, and by half-time they were ahead by 0-11 to 0-3. In the dressing room during the interval Babs was in the position of having to stress the importance of keeping up the momentum in the second half. In the Limerick dressing room Phil Bennis had the paradoxically easier task of appealing to Limerick's pride before a home following.

Whatever spark Bennis ignited, Limerick came out a different lot for the second half. Within fifteen minutes Tipp's lead was down to three points, with Ciaran Carey from centre-back leading attack after attack on the Tipp lines, where only the solid George Frend and Ramie Ryan (who had stood in for Michael Ryan and Colm Bonnar) offered any solace. At the other end, the Tipp inside line at times appeared starved. John Leahy was brought on for Joe Hayes but, whipped on by the enthusiasm of local support, there was no stopping the Limerick juggernaut. Victory went to Limerick in the end as a result of Sampson deflecting a cross from O'Connor over the bar. It was a sensational end to a game which from a Tipp point of view was nothing short of inexplicable and which for Limerick was a triumph of second-half courage over overwhelming half-time odds.

Nobody would begrudge Limerick their well-deserved victory, but for Tipp it was not so much the result as the manner of the defeat that was worrying. Most of the team were long enough in the tooth not to be lulled into a false sense of security by a half-time lead. And the wonderful display of goalkeeping by Tommy Quaid was hardly a good enough explanation of the failure by the Tipp forwards to score a single goal.

There were those, of course, who were ready to remind anyone ready to listen that Tipp had stressed all along that the championship was their main objective. In the circumstances, it was as good an excuse as any. Now they could focus all their attention on the Munster championship meeting with Cork and there could be no excuses about the outcome.

There is a school of thought in Tipperary which insists that Cork is a dangerous venue for Tipp when they are All-Ireland champions, and they can point to a number of occasions when they lost their crown there. 'Never bring the McCarthy Cup to the Lee', might be their maxim. The zest with which Cork will take on a visiting team from anywhere before a home crowd is widely recognised, not just in Tipperary, but wherever hurling is taken seriously. Authorities on the game in Cork will consider the home venue worth anything up to five points in a game with Tipp — perhaps more when the home team is the underdog.

In recent times Tipp have been increasingly nervous of Pairc Ui Chaoimh, but at a time when financial considerations were getting a progressively higher profile as a result of the problems of Semple Stadium, they deemed it worth entering a home-and-away agreement that would at least bring Cork to Thurles for every second meeting. It meant that in 1992 Tipp had to go to Cork at what proved, with hindsight, to be a bad time to enter the lion's den. Cork's footballers had already been beaten by Kerry. All their hopes rested with their hurlers and now here were cocky Tipp coming with the McCarthy Cup to further humiliate them in their own backyard. It was an invitation to Cork men to show what they were made of.

Babs Keating himself was obviously nervous of the occasion, or at least uneasy about the degree of confidence that was visible everywhere in Tipp. Beside a photograph which showed him sitting in the stand in Thurles in pensive mood, the *Tipperary Star* on the day before the game published his warning: 'It is as simple as this: you cannot really plan any tactic with certainty going into a championship against Cork . . . It does not matter what the records say. Every game against Cork is a new game in every sense of the word and I expect Sunday to be the ultimate test of Tipperary's character after four years on top in Munster.'

Since Tipp's breakthrough in 1987 they had won three Munster championships to Cork's one, and two All-Irelands to Cork's one. It was a dangerous concoction to feed the Cork supporters behind the city goal and they were never in better voice than on this occasion. Every Cork score was cheered as if it were a match-winner. Every Cork clearance was cheered as if it were a score. On the terraces, as on the field, Tipp were outgunned.

Earlier in the year, Denis Mulcahy had kept a tight rein on Cormac Bonnar when Cashel met Middleton in the club championship. Now Bonnar found himself facing Mulcahy again. Flanking Mulcahy were Brian Corcoran and Sean O'Gorman to make a rock-like line on which Tipp's ambitions would founder. Tipp's line-out was, on paper, an impressive one: Ken Hogan; Delaney, Sheehy and Frend; Bobby Ryan, Colm Bonnar and Conal Bonnar; Aidan Ryan and Carr; Cleary, Declan Ryan and Leahy; Fox, Cormac Bonnar and English. But if Tipp's line-out was more impressive on paper, Cork's would prove more impressive on the field: Ger Cunningham; Brian Corcoran, Denis Mulcahy and Sean O'Gorman; Cathal Casey, Jim Cashman and Denis Walsh; Sean McCarthy and Teddy McCarthy; Tim Kelleher, Tomas Mulcahy and Tony O'Sullivan; Ger Fitzgerald, Kevin Hennessy and John Fitzgibbon.

The tussle between the dugouts began as soon as Cork won the toss and opted to play against the wind. Bobby Ryan moved in to centre-back, leaving Colm Bonnar to police Tony O'Sullivan. At the other end Corcoran and O'Gorman switched corners and so well did Corcoran police Fox that he was generally voted 'man of the match'.

It was a dour struggle from start to finish, with close marking by the backs of both sides disposing of any expectations of a classic and ensuring that goals would be hard won. Tipp led by 0-6 to 0-5 at half-time following a flare-up, unusual at meetings between these counties, which resulted in a booking for Kevin Hennessy and Declan Ryan. When the sides resumed Cormac Bonnar was absent, being slightly concussed from a high tackle midway through the first half. He was replaced by Conor Stakelum.

Cork went on the offensive immediately in the second half, and within six minutes John Fitzgibbon had the ball in the Tipp net. But goal or no goal, Cork were dictating the run of play. Tomas Mulcahy got a touch to a sideline ball from Casey and Cork had their second goal. Colm Bonnar, injured, was replaced by his club mate Ramie Ryan, but by now Tipp's forwards were starving and when Nicholas English, in a situation in which normally he would have taken all responsibility himself, handpassed to Pat Fox who failed to collect, the writing was well and truly on the wall. By the time Declan Ryan got his team's only goal, it was irrelevant and Cork were on their way to the Munster final. The final score, Cork 2-12 Tipp 1-12, hardly did justice to Cork's superiority on the day. They would go on to win the Munster title, but Kilkenny would take the McCarthy Cup.

It is much harder to motivate a champion team than one that is considered an underdog, somebody kindly told the Tipp team as they sat disconsolately in the dressing room. But the truth was that on the day the decidedly better team had won and the surprise was that they had not won by a bigger margin. Once again Cork had been braced by Leeside air and by the knowledge that they were considered outsiders. For red-blooded Cork men, it was a potent combination.

Denis Mulcahy, who had come out of retirement the previous December, summed up the feelings of many Cork men on the occasion when he said, 'I'll say one thing . The Cork-Tipp rivalry never changes. It's as intense as ever and I suppose that's what makes victory over them so sweet.' But for Babs, reeling under the disappointment, if not the shock, of defeat, there was little comfort in the reflection that a key weapon in Cork's armoury had been the physical determination of their players. Rightly or wrongly, he spoke of it as something that was lacking in Tipperary. He referred to

'Cork's general approach which was legitimately aggressive' and he expressed the opinion that Tipp 'will have to match that type of game in future'.

That he was becoming more than a little tired of the expectations of the uninformed in Tipp was obvious when he complained publicly at year's end that there was little new talent coming on stream in the county and, despite a keenly contested county championship, he was still dependent on more or less the same panel as before. Nevertheless, he concluded, though they were now 'in a make or break situation', he felt that 'the present bunch are good enough to win another All-Ireland'. What neither Babs nor anybody else could have foreseen was that Tipp and Cork would not meet in a championship tie again during his term as manager.

Chapter Twenty-three

THE FATAL HOP, 1992–3

As Tipp looked on in chagrin while a Kilkenny team that they felt, rightly or wrongly, they could have beaten had they met them, took home the McCarthy Cup, there was, inevitably, a rumble of discontent. Declan Kelly of the *Cork Examiner* was merely voicing a widely held opinion when he said of Kilkenny:

> Tipperary would almost certainly have beaten them had they been in the final instead of Cork. Or at least they would have made a much better attempt than the Rebels did . . . On reflection, that can now only be seen as an indictment of those who were responsible for what happened in Cork on the first Sunday in June. To be frank, it was a combination of unwise management on the day, plus a lacklustre contribution from many of the more established players which cost Tipperary their Munster crown.

If this did not represent a widely held view in Tipperary, it was not far from it. Surprise that Cork should have stolen a march on Tipp for the second time in three years was not confined to Tipperary. But further and bigger surprises were in store for both Cork and Tipp before the McCarthy Cup was raised aloft again.

Like men with something to prove, Tipp went into the League in the autumn with all guns blazing and by Christmas they had beaten League-champions Limerick, All-Ireland champions Kilkenny, and Offaly. With All-Ireland winner of pre-famine days, Noel O'Dwyer, replacing Donie Nealon as Babs' second selector, there seemed at times to be a fresh determination to prove in every way possible that the mistakes of the summer had been no more than mistakes. In the *Tipperary Star* a correspondent, while expressing slight dissatisfaction with Tipp's performance against Limerick, summed up: 'But it's the result that counts.' Better a bad win than a good loss.

The game against Kilkenny was played at a time when attention in Tipperary was focused on the county final replay between Thurles Sarsfields and Toomevara. Kilkenny, short of six of their All-Ireland side, nevertheless took the proceedings seriously, but once again — as he had done in the 1991 All-Ireland — Michael Cleary sank the Cats with a free. This time it was not a mishit but a volley from the 21.

If the 'year of the twin troughs' — so dubbed because of the county's failure in League and championship — had been one of bitter disappointment to Tipp, it ended on a reasonably promising note, with full League points and no apparently insurmountable obstacles barring the way to entry to the final stages of the competition. Down and Antrim were both beaten and later Kerry, Tipp performing in the process the seemingly impossible feat of winning three games and scoring only one goal (against Antrim). Even with the old reliable forwards, Cleary, Declan Ryan and Leahy, Fox, Cormac Bonnar and English on duty for the game against Kerry, no single green flag had been raised. Perhaps there was a message in those three post-Christmas League games that might have been given greater attention.

When Tipp advanced to meet Cork in the League semi-final, neither side was particularly pleased. Not too often in recent decades have they clashed outside the championship and each side has developed an inclination not to show its hand to the other more than is necessary. In 1993 it was assumed — at least in Tipp and Cork — that the sides would be meeting in the Munster final. Tipp had drawn a bye into the semi-final, to meet Waterford or Kerry. Cork, it was assumed, would come out of the other side. That things might not work out that way had not yet occurred to anyone in either county. But now that the unexpected had happened, both sides saw it as an opportunity to gain a useful psychological advantage for the championship.

Thurles was the venue for a double bill that included Wexford and Limerick and in true League fashion the heavens opened as the Cork-Tipp game began. Cormac Bonnar slipped the full-back line for Tipp's only goal — their second in four games — and by half-time Tipp led by 1-5 to 0-7. Well into the second half an incident involving a Cork hurley and Nicholas English's head left Cork with fourteen men; later on television when Cork mentor Fr O'Brien, in a manner which set a headline for all other hurling mentors, expressed himself forcefully regarding the Cork player's behaviour, he made himself the target for much criticism from his own supporters. As had happened in the past, however, Tipp seemed unable to capitalise on the extra man. Twelve minutes from the end Manley goaled, but Tipp still appeared to have matters in hand even when they had lost centre-back Michael O'Meara and Ramie Ryan through injury.

Spectators were beginning to stretch their limbs, with time nearly up and Tipp two points ahead, when the ghost of 1984 appeared again and buried Tipp's hopes. A weak challenge off a Cork clearance put Kevin Hennessy in possession and with powerful strides he made for the Tipp goal, with Buckley and Mulcahy in attendance. It was the latter who drove it low past Ken Hogan leaving the Tipp supporters dumbfounded. Once again Cork had proved that they are never beaten until the final whistle. If there was a psychological advantage with anyone now for the championship, it was with Cork. But they wouldn't be needing it.

Wexford met Cork in the League final, not once but three times. They were gruelling games, two of which Wexford appeared to have won, but the title went to Cork on the third day. The marathon cannot have done Cork any good going into the championship. It is hard to begin the business of motivating a team afresh after a lapse of only a few weeks, and perhaps Cork, too, had their sights not on the first round but on the Munster final. If they had, it was a great mistake, but it was a mistake they were not alone in making.

Across the Shannon Len Gaynor, former team mate of Babs and now coach to Clare, saw the possibility of catching Cork off guard in the championship. And Clare did just that. On a muddy June day in Limerick they caused even greater surprise than Kerry had done in beating Waterford in their opening round. With full-blooded abandon they went after everything in red and displayed a level of skill with a wet ball which left spectators astounded and hurling followers everywhere with a kind thought for the underdog delighted. They also left Tipperary supporters struggling to adjust to this new situation. Was this a sign of a new spirit and a new talent in Clare or would they collapse as they had done so often in the past at the sight of the Munster cup? Had the magic of their footballers rubbed off on the hurlers?

It hadn't and Tipp, having trounced Kerry in a way they could not have done with Waterford, weren't taking any chances in the Munster final. Before 42,000 people they administered a drubbing that would have shattered the self-esteem of a more self-confident team than Clare. Next day Jim O'Sullivan would report in the *Cork Examiner*:

> This was a Munster final in name only, a bloodless victory for strong favourites, Tipperary, something of a disaster for the

game of hurling and a catastrophe for luckless Clare. Yesterday, at the Gaelic Grounds, saw the greatest mis-match in a championship decider in ten years, a game that was so totally one-sided from the early minutes that Tipperary's 35th title was secured long before half-time.

Its one saving grace was the marvellous striking on the Tipperary side, specifically among the forwards. They were absolutely devastating in the opening 20 minutes, at the stage in the game when Clare, backed by the wind, would have been expected to impose their will. But, in truth, their challenge, so full of promise after the prestige win over Cork, just never materialised.

Tipperary had a seven-points lead after 12 minutes, twice that (2-11 to 0-3) by the 24th minute and what happened after that wasn't of great consequence . . .

By the time the final whistle sounded, a substantial part of the crowd had already left, with the score Tipp 3-27 Clare 2-12.

It was a fearsome hammering and likely to do no good to either side. While few would misunderstand the natural jubilation which moved Babs to describe it as Tipp's 'best performance to date', there were those who were slightly puzzled at how an utterly demoralised Clare could still manage to score 2-12. On a day which they would remember with disgust, the Banner men had managed to compile a score which had won many a Munster title. Seldom can a Munster title have left the winners worse prepared for the next lap of the All-Ireland championship.

Perhaps it had been the nature of the draw in Munster that had left Tipp supporters counting their chickens so early. A game against Kerry and a game against Clare was all that was needed to get out of Munster. Already Galway were being discounted and the only serious challenger on the horizon for the McCarthy Cup was Kilkenny. Forgotten was how close Galway had come to beating Kilkenny the previous year, and remembered only was the manner in which Galway had folded before Limerick in the League. It is difficult in the extreme for mentors and players to be suitably motivated in the face of public opinion. The popular view was that Galway were on the way down and Tipp on the way up. And that was a view which, in the circumstances, suited Galway admirably.

Despite the auguries favourable to Tipp, there were those whose sense of history made them apprehensive about what was to come.

Never in the history of the GAA had the county won the hurling All-Ireland in a year ending in a '3'. All the other digits had figured on the blue and gold scroll of titles, but no '3'. Only once among the unlucky 3's — in 1913 — had they even appeared in an All-Ireland and then the great Wedger Meagher's Toomevara Greyhounds, who had won everything else, went down before Kilkenny. The most recent 3's had been marked by particularly bad luck. In 1963 an unprecedented run of All-Ireland appearances had been interrupted, and the glittering prospect of winning five titles in a row thwarted. In 1973 Richie Bennis had scored the magical 70 in Killarney, a feat that sank Tipp's expectations and propelled Limerick to All-Ireland honours. In 1983 they had been pipped by Waterford. For those who take heed of such things, there was a distinct chill in the air in 1993.

Since the decline of Cormac Bonnar, the full-forward position had been a worrying one, but it was considered that the problem had been solved by the arrival of Anthony Crosse. Tall and strong and good at gaining possession, though of somewhat unorthodox style, he had all the appearance of fitting well into the Number 14 berth and some saw in him one of a new set who would adequately fill the places of some of the ageing veterans.

One of these same ageing veterans who had a special place in the affections of Tipp followers since 1984 was Bobby Ryan, who had been slipping off the first fifteen, being replaced by Toomevara captain Michael O'Meara. However, when the team was announced it was seen that the captain had been dropped for the veteran Bobby who was accorded the difficult task of marking Joe Cooney. Pat Fox, suffering from blood-poisoning, the result of an injury in a club game, was absent, but English who like Bobby had missed the Clare game, was back.

Galway, at the same time, were pruning veterans and missing from their side were Peter Finnerty and Tony Keady. At centre-back was Gerry McInerney, normally a wing-back.

The Tipp team lined out as follows: Ken Hogan; Delaney, Sheehy and Michael Ryan; Ramie and Bobby Ryan and Conal Bonnar; Declan Carr and Colm Bonnar; Cleary, Declan Ryan and Leahy; Aidan Ryan, Crosse and English.

The game was only six minutes old when an incident occurred which gave Galway an immediate infusion of confidence and gave Tipp a corresponding flutter of collywobbles. A speculative lob towards the Tipp goal by 'Hopper' McGrath was approached almost casually by Ken Hogan. It was a slow ball and one that Ken would normally trap and clear in his sleep. A moment of horror that will forever remain frozen in the minds of Tipp supporters saw the sliotar bounce crazily off his hurley and finish in the net. It was exactly what Galway needed and until the final whistle they proceeded to play like men inspired.

It was Galway's day. They approached everything with a physical aggression that expressed their own commitment and the ball-playing Tipp forwards were treated with unceremonious ruggedness. A big blow to Tipp was the departure with a knee injury of Declan Ryan, one of the few forwards well equipped for a physical game. He had sustained the injury early in the proceedings but, by cruel coincidence, he signalled to the dugout his inability to continue at precisely the moment when it had been decided to replace Colm Bonnar. Thus, spectators were astounded to see two subs take the field together ten minutes before half-time. Given the physical quality of previous Tipp-Galway encounters, the possibility of Tipp running out of subs was all too real. In the event, this did not happen, but the double substitution left supporters on tenterhooks and left the dugout with not too much room for manoeuvre. Had Declan Ryan signalled his inability to continue a minute earlier, it is unlikely that Colm Bonnar would have been substituted. But the incident would remain to haunt Babs and to be used by those who were only too glad of any ammunition against him.

There are those who would claim that one of Tipp's weaknessess during the years of the revival was the failure to throw up a towering centre-back who could be depended on to dominate consistently in the style of Mick Roche, Tony Wall and Pat Stakelum. In Gerry McInerney, Galway had a centre-back of heroic stature on this one day when they needed him and time after time, bursting out of defence with ball in hand, he put the Tipp half-back line under the most severe pressure. Psychologically there is nothing, with the possible exception of brilliant goalkeeping, so likely to rouse a team as a storming display by a centre-back.

At half-time Galway were seven points up. Tipp shuffled the pack, English and Fox changing corners and Leahy was switched to centre-forward. But still Galway remained in front and nothing much went right for Tipp. A collision between Ramie Ryan and Paul Delaney, which left the former concussed and the latter shaken, occcurred at a time when Tipp had worked up an impressive momentum that was defused by the resultant prolonged stoppage. Defeat now assumed definite shape for the blue and gold, but still they failed to trouble goalkeeper Burke, whereas Ken Hogan was called upon several times. Michael Ryan fought like a lion to stave off collapse and repeatedly put his forwards on the offensive, but by the time Pat Fox drove a rebound to the net the game was lost. The final score was 1-16 to 1-14, which meant that, despite the seeming Galway superiority, it was that early tragic hop past Ken Hogan which sealed Tipp's fate.

Following a defeat that was as damaging as it was unexpected, the barrage of criticism directed against team and management was predictable. And it began with the final whistle. The players themselves realised that it was another of those days on which everything had gone wrong — a day on which Murphy's Law had ruled. Nicholas English walked across the dressing room and, without either of them saying a word, he embraced Babs Keating. There was no need for words.

With followers it was different. The kind of innocent joy that had characterised Tipp's reactions during the period following the ending of the famine was a thing of the past. Now supporters were more demanding. Babs and his selectors were criticised for having omitted Michael O'Meara from the initial line-out. They were criticised for not having taken Galway 'seriously enough'. The simultaneous substitutions before half-time were discussed, dissected, criticised. All right, it was said, it had been necessary to take off Declan Ryan, but why Colm Bonnar? And so the complaints ran on and on.

That a Munster final had been won was hardly noticed. That they had done in that year what they had failed to do for eighteen years was hardly taken into account. In the bitterness of disappointment all that was clearly seen was the defeat by Galway. It was a far cry from the days when Tipperary skies had reddened after a Munster final victory in Killarney.

UNSEEN POWERS ARE ACTIVE, 1994

Criticisms disregarded, Tipp faced into the League of 1993–94 with Babs still at the helm, probably much to the relief of the County Board. It was the prerogative of the general public to criticise team management's decisions on any given day. But it was the duty of the County Board to come up with an alternative management if the existing one was deemed to be unsatisfactory. Half a loaf was better than no bread and, after all, All-Irelands had been won. Nobody could deny that things had improved under Babs and perhaps in their heart of hearts not many believed that anyone else would have come up with more success than he had provided. Besides, the whole area of team management under him had come to embrace a lot more than just picking and preparing a team and already there was an element of nervousness as to what life after Babs would mean for the county. To encourage him to step down was a move fraught with danger for any chairman of the County Board and, anyway, there wasn't exactly a queue of aspirants jostling for the position in his wake.

By Christmas Tipp had full points, having beaten Antrim conclusively, Limerick by a goal and Waterford by a point. Then, on the coldest of cold days at Nenagh an experimental side was given a drubbing (3-12 to 1-11) by a Galway side that looked impressive enough to prompt a cautious bookie to rush away and reduce his odds against them for the championship. Few who saw the game would have thought that within a couple of months Tipp would reverse the result and even widen the margin between them. But while the Nenagh game was a deadly serious exercise, nine of the Tipp team that day would not line out against Galway when they next met.

One of that nine was Ken Hogan, for whom the Nenagh game was his last in the county colours. It is true to say that Tipp never won an All-Ireland without a remarkable goalkeeper — the same could probably be said about any All-Ireland winning team. But for many Tipp followers of the post-famine years, memories of great victories were intertwined with memories of magical saves by the bulky keeper from Lorrha. His departure from between the posts was, in a sense, the beginning of the end of an era of Tipperary hurling.

Missing, too, from the League line-up was Bobby Ryan, a wonderful servant of the county through good times and bad. He had given inspiring leadership in 1984 when Tipp had gone so close to fulfilling the dream of being in the Centenary All-Ireland, but he had to wait another five years before realising the ambition of every hurler. He would be etched forever in the memory of Tipp hurling followers holding aloft the McCarthy Cup in 1989.

Gone too was Conor O'Donovan, Limerick-born but sprung of first-rate Tipperary hurling stock. He had started Tipp on the road in 1991 with a brilliant display against Limerick, but had missed the All-Ireland because of injury. He was in the best tradition of Tipperary full-backs.

Donie O'Connell was gone, having announced his retirement from inter-county hurling before the beginning of the championship of 1994. He too had a special place in the affections of Tipp followers. His best games had been against Cork, and an abiding picture in the Tipp folk memory is of the hardy centre-forward in the Cork net at Killarney in 1987, having palmed in a winning goal, mobbed by delirious fans, kneeling as if in praise of the gods of the ancient game.

Cork came to Thurles a fortnight later to win a goalless game by two points against a Tipp line-out similar to that which had played Galway. Inevitably, when Tipp travelled to Enniscorthy the danger of their failing to qualify for the final stages was beginning to loom large in the public consciousness. But Wexford had been going badly and Michael Cleary's personal tally of 1-9 was too much for them. What was even more important than laying the bogey of the Wexford venue was that Tipp seemed to be moving towards their championship line-up. Jody Grace was in goal, George Frend in the half-back line, Pat King at midfield and Liam McGrath at centre-forward.

The game against All-Ireland champions Kilkenny was overshadowed by controversy as to the choice of venue, which fuelled radio chat shows as well as newspaper columns. Kilkenny claimed that Tipp owed them a venue and Tipp agreed to come to Nowlan Park. The GAA handed down its decision: the game would be played at Croke Park. Once again (shades of the Keady affair) Tipp were being blamed for a situation over which they had no control whatsoever. Tipp supporters, feeling as hard done by as Kilkenny, travelled to

Croke Park to see an unexciting performance which Tipp won by 2-18 to 1-12. It was an unsatisfactory business from everyone's point of view and in Kilkenny some blamed their team's poor performance on dissatisfaction regarding a promised holiday which had not materialised. But from Tipp's point of view, the most gratifying aspect of the win was that the goals had come from English and Fox — an echo of times past.

Tipp expected tougher competition from Cork in the League semi-final and they got just that. They began with as drab a display as they had ever given, being roundly beaten in several sectors and by half-time they were lucky to be only five points down, with Pat Fox having gone off injured. But what was worse, it was ten scores to three (0-10 to 1-2). Only the big hand of Anthony Cross, who had tossed a never-worse-needed goal to English, saved the scoreboard from telling a story that would have left some of the crowd wondering at half-time if they shouldn't slip away home.

Following the mandatory interval tongue-lashing, Tipp were transformed in the second half. They quickly got on top at centre-field, the introduction of Joe Hayes having brought new zest to the proceedings; the defence tightened up; the attack became more dangerous, and Anthony Crosse produced a quality goal of his own when he jumped high to catch from a Michael Cleary free, swivelled and struck to the net. In all he had a hand in about ten of Tipp's scores and few could argue with the decision which gave him the RTE 'Man of the Match' award.

But while Crosse had been industrious and dangerous from the beginning, it was only in the second half that most of his colleagues outside of the full-back line showed what they were made of. When they did, Cork had no answer and Tipp could afford the luxury of taking off Nicholas English and allowing Declan Ryan to make a brief appearance in the dying minutes. In injury time Cork showed their teeth one last time when a Sean McCarthy goal from a rebound gave Tipp a fright and a reminder that you mustn't let up against Cork until you hear the whistle. The final score, Tipp 2-13 Cork 1-13, sent Tipp home in the May sunshine with a psychological advantage over Cork when they would meet in the championship — if they met.

There was no great difficulty in motivating Tipp for their League final game against Galway at Limerick. Both Galway and Tipp were in the process of rebuilding. If experience counts for a great deal, so does the desire to make one's mark, and a number of the Tipp line-out on the day would have considered themselves under examination for the championship. With Fox, Delaney and English unavailable through injury, Aidan Ryan alone remained of all those who had answered the referee's first whistle in Killarney in 1987. Michael O'Meara was back at centre-back, with his Toomevara club mate George Frend in the corner behind him and another club mate Pat King at centre-field in front of him. Rightly or wrongly, it was believed that the inclusion of the Toomevara trio had brought to the team a new quality of toughness, a quality indeed which many would claim had never in any event been noticeably lacking. Inevitably, though, statisticians pointed out that in all the long and distinguished history of the club, only once — in 1961 — when Matt Hasset led Tipp to victory over Dublin, had a Toomevara man brought home the McCarthy Cup.

But George Frend was in no way shackled by history when he led out Tipp to create another chapter in the ongoing Tipp-Galway saga. He personally set an example of timely and vigorous tackling and all through the team there was a sense of commitment which Galway — whom the media had made firm favourites — answered but could not overcome. Liam McGrath pulled on everything that came in front of Gerry McInerney and Joe Hayes displayed form similar to that which he had shown against Cork. At midfield he and King contained Coleman and Malone in a way that Tipp supporters had yearned for in other meetings between the counties. Declan Ryan, in his first appearance since his injury in the last fatal All-Ireland semi-final, commenced the destruction of Galway with a goal after twenty minutes and finished it with another in the second half. The second was a classic which he began by working in from an unlikely position out in the corner and ended with an unstoppable shot from in front of the posts.

But the brightest star of the day was John Leahy who displayed a virtuosity associated with Nicholas English at his best, scoring points with seemingly effortless abandon. The *Tipperary Star* commented:

> The match will be remembered in years to come as John Leahy's final. The Mullinahone man turned in an impeccable per-formance, his high catching, strong running and accurate shooting demoralising Galway. This was Leahy at his best and in this mood he is unstoppable. Hopefully this display, following on the second half showing against Cork, heralds a great

championship for a man who on his day is surely the most complete hurler in the country.

Little did those Tipp supporters who remained to see George Frend collect the cup think there would be less reason to cheer through the summer, and that John Leahy would be a large part of the reason.

With their first-round championship game with Tipp looming ahead, Len Gaynor had no trouble in motivating Clare. They had not done themselves justice the previous year; now was the time to prove themselves. Besides, Tipp had laid it on when it was obvious that Clare were down and out and they had really rubbed it in by bringing on English to give him the scent of the hare. So said Clare men.

Babs, for his part, spoke as if he felt in his bones that something was wrong. The backslapping had barely ceased after the Galway game, the cup was still being admired and the crowds were still drifting away from the field, when he told the squad that whilst it was great to have beaten Galway, they must put that behind them now and concentrate on Clare. The nearer they got to the game, the more he warned. Everything had gone right for Tipp at their last meeting in 1993, he pointed out, and they had not seen anything like the best of Clare. The list of casualties now included Hayes, Delaney, Fox and English. Liam McGrath was not entirely fit after injury but would be lining out. Most portentous of all, John Leahy, the star of the League final victory, was grounded.

Leahy, the Mullinahone man, puts on weight easily and there were audible comments on 'winter feeding' and suchlike when he appeared in the spring. Consequently, when he was numbered, like Anthony Crosse, on the county football panel, it was thought there was no reason why it shouldn't actually help to maintain his general fitness. Besides, it would be nice for the county to have another major dual star — Babs himself, the county's most successful hurler-cum-footballer, would understand all about that.

So Leahy became fitter than ever, training with both hurlers and footballers. Almost certainly his presence on the Tipp team which took on Clare's footballers in the Munster championship at Limerick brought a considerable number to the game who would not otherwise have been there. Tipp won the game by a solitary point in somewhat fortuitous circumstances.

But if Lady Luck gave to Tipp with one hand, she took away with the other. Making his way towards goal, John Leahy was seen to go down heavily with a twisted ankle and he was stretchered off the field. In the Regional Hospital he was told that a bone had been damaged and his ankle was put in plaster. The news hit the county with the effect of a thunder-clap. The Tipp-Clare hurling tie was only a fortnight away and an unlucky step had done for the brightest star of the moment what liberal treatment of Connaught, Leinster and Munster ash hadn't managed to do. The result was a mighty outcry against the football selectors who became the targets of an entirely unmerited measure of criticism for daring to include the hurling All-Star in their plans. Inevitably, the folk memory was raked over for a precedent for the catastrophe. Older followers engaged in reminiscences of nearly fifty years previously when a couple of weeks before the 1945 All-Ireland final between Tipperary and Kilkenny, the colourful veteran corner-back, Johnny Ryan, twisted his knee in a junior football game and as a result missed his second All-Ireland medal. Blame swung from Leahy himself to the football selectors to the hurling selectors, and when the injured player himself told a pressman that he was 'keeping his fingers crossed' for the meeting with Clare, an ungracious follower remarked, 'It's not his fingers we're interested in. It's his ankle.'

It was soon clear that no amount of finger-crossing would have him fit for the first-round game. And the story got worse. Pat Fox was still recuperating from his injury sustained in the Cork game; Joe Hayes had pulled a hamstring in a friendly game with Kilkenny in support of the Lory Meagher Heritage Centre; and Nicholas English was still nursing a calf injury, his fitness to be decided on the day before the game. He would not be starting. And Paul Delaney was still absent.

So without Fox, English, Hayes, Delaney and Leahy, Tipp took the field at Limerick to play Clare, but still there was no sense of panic. They would just have to play up to the occasion and, after all, so many of the newcomers had played ever so well against Galway. Overshadowing all calculations was the memory of the ineffectiveness of Clare's challenge of the previous year and although there was much reminiscing on defeats inflicted by Clare in the past — 1955, 1974, 1977 and 1986 — not too much was made of it. All the signs were that Tipp would win, if not easily, without too much difficulty. Few were impressed by the astrology columnist of the *Limerick Leader* who forecasted,

In Limerick Gaelic Grounds on Sunday Tipperary are playing Clare in the first round of the hurling championship and, while the Banner have not impressed of late, nobody is telling themselves that it will be an easy game. Here is what the Rune Stones say.

The stone that comes from the Rune bag is that of flowing water. Unseen powers are active, powers that nourish and shape. Clare will put in a far better performance than perhaps would be expected, advancing to the next round at Tipperary's expense.

Tipp were not in the habit of consulting astrologers regarding their chances in games, particularly games against Clare. But though often reminded, not many recalled that it had been only a year since Clare had ended the championship prospects of the then League champions, Limerick.

Grace; Frend, Sheehy and Michael Ryan; Ramie Ryan, O'Meara and Conal Bonnar; King and Colm Bonnar; Tommy Dunne, McGrath and Cleary; Declan Ryan, Crosse and Aidan Ryan. This was the team that met Clare on a day when things went right for Clare and — Tipp's performance apart — Babs' luck was simply not in. Hurling with the kind of flair and passion that had upended Cork the previous year, Clare showed from the beginning that Tipp had a serious challenge on their hands.

Tipp's bad luck struck early. After fifteen minutes, centre-back Michael O'Meara retired with an injury and Colm Bonnar, until then faring well at centre-field, was brought back to fill a position which on the day did not suit him. After half-time Crosse — with Tipp ahead by 0-7 to 0-5 — was unable to resume because of injury and a less-than-fit Fox came on to give an indication of how much he had been missed.

Clare were growing stronger and a goal by Tommy Guilfoyle inside twelve minutes put all the warning lights flashing for Tipp. Five minutes from the end, and it was still very much in the balance when sub Mike Nolan laid on for Fox in a goal-scoring position. But this was the day when Babs' ducks would drown and Fox's rocket screamed inches over the bar. A minute later, when a long free dropped on the Tipp square, Guilfoyle's hurley was up to touch it past Grace into the net. A final Clare point to bring their total to 2-11 against Tipp's 0-13, and it was all over. Clare, as was their entitlement, were jubilant and Tipp were almost too shocked to be sad. For the neutral observer there was the reflection that for the second year in a row Clare had taken out the League champions in their first game. Clare would go on to beat Kerry before being washed out by Limerick.

For those who always begrudge success and who are delighted by the fall of a hero, there was pleasure not alone in seeing the collapse of Tipp's hopes but in Babs' discomfiture. After the defeat of Galway the previous year he had considered throwing in the towel, but had decided to give it one last try. Now, in the immediate aftermath of the game, while the cheers of the Clare supporters were still rising, and while he was still reeling under the shock and disappointment of the defeat, he announced his resignation. The gentlemen of the press were the first to get the news. He was a public figure and his departure had to be in public. Sean Fogarty, the new chairman of the County Board, urged him to do nothing hastily but was assured that it had been carefully considered. The decision had been taken and now was the time to go. The Keating years were over.

After eight years as the focus of a county's dreams, Babs' departure took a while to sink in. Tipperary had grown used to the giant oak against the sky. Just as a generation had grown up never having seen Tipp win anything, now there was a generation for whom Babs and the blue and gold were synonymous. For different reasons, youngsters and their elders had difficulty in adjusting to the new situation.

In the *Clonmel Nationalist* 'Westside', whose column had charted the fortunes of Tipp for a number of years and who had from time to time been critical of Babs' decisions, wrote with the air of one in shock:

> A season that began with high optimism crumbles abruptly. Tipp crash out to Clare. Weakened by injuries and unable to find form or replacements, Tipp's championship race ends in May. The fallout was instant with Babs' prompt though premeditated decision to quit after eight years. Rumours have suggested that some players might follow. Either way it's the end of an era . . .

The departure of Babs was too big an issue, he said, to be immediately treated and he would return to it.

When he returned a week later it was with an assessment that, despite its critical tone, reflected the sense of gratitude which all Tipperary felt towards the lately departed manager:

> Did Babs after all come Messiah-like to single handedly transform a depressed scene? It's a romantic view and like all romance ignores some important realities. There were indications in the mid-80s that Tipp had a useful pool of players and were about to

impact to some extent at least. Under-21 All-Irelands of 1979, 1980, 1981 and 1985 and the minors of 1980 and 1982 suggested that the hurlers were there if the potential could be exploited. Such was not the case in the 1970s when successive managements just hadn't similar talent at their disposal.

And the highlight year of 1987 deserves some objective scrutiny. In the barren years we had near misses . . . but in 1987 we finally got the break. And it did need a smile from the gods . . . Babs' great contribution was surely that he glamourised the unglamorous. He brought the managerial style of management to new levels . . . Players in the 1970s had refused the hassle of playing with Tipp; now they craved involvement. And that surely had an impact on the uprise of Tipperary hurling.

Also it must be said of Babs' management that there was an openness to new players. Cormac Bonnar was brought into a shaky Munster final where he scored a steadying goal and therein a new force was found in Tipp hurling that fully blossomed in 1991. Few others would have brought in Bonnar that day in Limerick.

And then 1991 was surely the crescendo of the Babs ensemble. That, I think, will stand apart as his greatest year when he turned a harmonious blend of players to a new level. The Munster replay in Thurles will stand as a truly great moment in his eight years of Tipp management. And the All-Ireland was taken by the hard route so that hindsight can never find flaw in its pedigree.

To be coldly analytical, however, one must point to the downside as well. 1990 in Thurles is not one that Babs will relish to recall. Two Bonnars on the sideline, John Leahy at full-forward and Fox called home at half-time still reads puzzling. The 'donkey' comment didn't help although skilfully used by Cork; injudicious comment has been a hallmark of the Babs years. And last August, too, represents a blemish on the record.

So when you balance the highs and the lows of the Babs years what have you got? Certainly not the romantic Roy of the Rovers boy of fiction. I doubt if Babs would even like that comic-book image. He was neither an infallible Messiah nor was he a magician. But he was a man who had a greater impact on Tipp hurling than anyone since the time of Paddy Leahy. He was a colourful personality who transformed that colour to the

Tipperary hurling team; he added glitz. And people will always debate the pros and cons of this or that aspect of his term and the unanswerable question of whether or not he achieved the maximum given the talent at his disposal. But through it all will shine the marvellous achievements: the sunny days of two All-Irelands, five Munsters, two Leagues and an Oireachtas. And those of us who remember the depression of the 1970s will especially appreciate what has been achieved. The glory will outshine the gloom and we'll forever utter a heartfelt thanks for the memories.

No one expressed that heartfelt thanks with more genuine feeling than Richard Stakelum who, on that golden day in Killarney in 1987, had managed to express so eloquently the emotion felt by a whole generation of Tipperary folk. Within days of Babs' announcement Stakelum wrote to him:

> Few people will ever know the effort you put into the Tipperary hurling scene. I think I do. Having travelled with you for a few years and seen it first-hand when we were starting out, I was always amazed at your energy and Nancy's patience.
>
> I'm sure the first few years were possibly more enjoyable from the point of view of the novelty and indeed the groundswell of support. The later years often saw the daggers drawn by those who always wait when something wonderful runs off course.
>
> I count myself privileged and always will to have been associated with the Tipperary team under your regime. The confidence that I still have in my own personality was a direct result of that involvement. The loyalty and deep bond of friendship that I've built up with people associated with those wonderful times will never leave me. Do you know, Babs, I think of those things nigh on every day.
>
> You should indeed be immensely proud of your contribution to not alone Tipp hurling but to the game as a whole. So many young men who have hurled for Tipperary have gone on to become very successful outside of the game.
>
> It will only be in the future that people will really understand that what you achieved was and will remain something truly special.

Still, over the next few weeks the question of whether Babs was really serious about departing was much discussed. It was recalled that it had been rumoured twelve months previously that he was about to retire. This time, however, the *Tipperary Star* correspondent opined, 'I suppose he means it.' Indeed he did.

After the defeat by Galway in 1993, which had been a particular disappointment to him, he had decided to call it a day, but the prospect of one more All-Ireland — from the point of view of any reasonable observer of the hurling scene an achievable ambition — had appealed both to his instinct as a punter and as a sportsman. There was, too, the normal human desire to go out on a winning note. The encouragement to remain on for one last throw of the dice from those players with whom he had shared so much delight and disappointment over the years was the deciding factor, and he stayed. Nobody in his situation would have considered it likely that a succession of injuries would deprive him of the glittering last-round double prize of League and All-Ireland as a retirement presentation.

That Tipp would have gone the whole way, had they got past Clare, is at least arguable. Whether they would have survived the Dooley avalanche, had they been in Croke Park instead of Limerick, is also arguable. What is beyond doubt is that, had they and not Limerick been the victims of that avalanche, fingers would have been pointed at the Tipperary selectors. Very likely, Babs would have been blamed.

C h a p t e r   T w e n t y - f i v e

THE MONEY GAME

Only a few weeks intervened between the announcement of Babs' resignation and the appointment of Fr Tom Fogarty to succeed him. A teacher in the diocesan seminary at Thurles, Fr Fogarty had impressed as manager of the county minor team, although he had not achieved All-Ireland honours. From the outset he well appreciated the difficulty of following in the footsteps of the larger than life figure of Babs.

In games, as in business, as in life, Babs had always been a go-getter, a man who thinks while he is moving and who moves while he is thinking. Only a superbly robust physical constitution could withstand the punishing schedule he endured during his years as team manager to Tipperary. From his Dublin home near the Phoenix Park he covered the ninety miles to Thurles, when necessary three times a week, and rarely gave the impression of being in a hurry away from a training session. The man who had to face the return journey to Dublin had time for the general attention to the panel and for the particular attention to anybody whom he felt needed it. Double the age of many of his charges, he managed to relate to them as easily as if he were one of themselves. At the same time he always maintained that necessary degree of aloofness which never quite allowed players to forget that he was the boss. He could take a hurley and participate in the puck-around or even in a game during training; he could walk off the field as 'one of the lads', engage in the dressing room banter and yet never let anyone forget he was in charge. It is this quality of leadership which in a military situation — perhaps in any situation — gets the most out of men. It is a quality that is often envied by teachers.

As a businessman, it was only natural that his first attention should have been given to the matter of finance. If an army marches on its stomach, a hurling team does likewise. Where finance was concerned, he more than anybody else brought the running of the Tipperary team into modern times. The framework that was there before him had served well in its time — which extended back over several decades — but it was not suited to the demands of the television age and it was not suited to the demands of a hurling squad who were expected to close the book on a long period of unprecedented failure. It was with a clear realisation that nothing moves in modern sport without money that he turned his attention to the setting up of the Tipperary Supporters Club.

Within weeks of his assuming management of the team in the late summer of 1986, Babs had inspired the establishment of the Supporters Club which over the years of his stewardship was to play an absolutely vital role in the success story of the county. A businessman's assessment of the County Board's financial situation told him that there would be little financial joy coming from that particular direction. The previous year's take from the National League pool had been a mere £3,711, an amount hardly likely to sustain his plans for off-the-field sartorial elegance and VIP treatment for those wearing the Tipperary jersey. He flung himself with typical energy and imagination into the business of establishing a fund to finance Tipp's return to glory. The Supporters Club succeeded in harnessing the enormous goodwill that existed countrywide for a Tipp revival and within months the senior team were being treated in a manner to which they had not hitherto been accustomed. Spearheaded by businessmen, the organisation would over the period of his tenure of office provide absolute relief from financial worries through a series of imaginative enterprises. Whatever difficulties he experienced, a shortage of money was not one of them.

Some of these fund-raising activities would cause antagonism within the GAA and ridicule outside it, but for the Tipperary County Board the financial relief they provided was heaven sent. The first major effort — a raffle for a racehorse — caused heads to shake in bewilderment and cynics were heard to forecast that the horse would win the Derby before Tipp would win an All-Ireland. Babs himself, with his touch for the histrionic, made comments about Tipp winning the All-Ireland and the horse winning the Derby in the same year. And while the propriety of the whole venture was heatedly discussed, the tickets continued to be snapped up. There was no problem for the winner as to what to do with the horse. Babs' friend, jockey and trainer Christy Roche, would train him for two years. It was part of the prize.

It was all very novel, colourful and exciting. The hurling public, taken by the very novelty of the whole business, reacted favourably and the racing public invested in a good bet. And if Tiobrad Arann, as the horse was called, never won a Derby, well the joke about the Derby and the All-Ireland would fall flat when half the double came up trumps.

By the time Tipp reached the All-Ireland in 1989, the Supporters Club had collected through an imaginative assortment of fund-raising events nearly a quarter of a million pounds. While engaged in the business of actually managing the team, Babs was always at the nerve-centre of all this fund-raising activity. Indeed, many of the activities reflected his own recreational preferences — golf outings and horse racing — while his business contacts were exploited to the maximum for sponsorship of various kinds.

When the rising tide began to lift all the hurling boats in Tipperary, there were those who complained that the Supporters Club confined their activities to the glamorous side of the business — looking after the senior team. But from the beginning Babs had maintained that if there was success at senior level, then all things would fall into place and there would also be success at other levels. In this he was proved entirely correct and, while the Supporters Club would shoulder the expenses of the senior team, the money thus saved was available to the County Board for looking after other teams. Because the Supporters Club put their shoulder to the senior wheel, the County Board was able to spend more on preparing other teams, hurling and football.

On top of the saving there was the increased revenue from the team's performance in the National Leagues at the disposal of the County Board. This shot up from the paltry £3,711 figure of 1986 to £22,000 in 1987 and to over £50,000 for the two succeeding years. It dropped in 1990 and 1991 to under £30,000, but it rose again to nearly £50,000 in 1993, and in 1994 the winning of the League brought with it nearly £75,000. Thus, success was seen to pay for itself and the spin-off extended in many directions.

Despite the striking contribution of the Supporters Club in helping to finance the revival, however, there was probably no single matter more often used against Babs than the high profile of those who were doing so much to help pay the piper. When officials of the Supporters Club appeared in the dugout there were complaints and even suggestions that they had a part in some of the less popular switches made during matches. When they occasionally appeared to take precedence over County Board officials there was resentment, and when they showed signs of not being quite as answerable to the County Board as some members of that body wished, there were hints that they were usurping the authority of the Board.

Through it all, Babs picked his way as delicately as he could, making every attempt to keep both sides apart but united in working towards a common objective, never losing an opportunity to take aside anyone who might be useful in preventing any misunderstandings. It was at least in some part due to his diplomatic skills that during the years of his stewardship the Supporters Club and the County Board continued to work together without an open breach.

Apart from footing the bills for occasional weekends spent at locations in Ireland, where players and officials with their wives were treated in style while they discussed team matters, the Supporters Club was responsible for a number of foreign trips. There was the two-week holiday in Las Palmas in 1988 and the Florida holiday in December 1989. The latter included a cruise to the Bahamas and five days in Orlando. In December 1991 they were again in the Gulf of Mexico and again there was a five-day cruise, this time to Albacus Island, though for many of them the highlight was being entertained by Tipperary man Pat Dalton, a big figure in the American greyhound industry. These perks, so memorable to the players themselves as hard evidence of an appreciation of their commitment, were possible only through the hard work and generosity of the Supporters Club.

While the Supporters Club was raising money on another front, the County Board itself wisely made it its business to capitalise on the popularity which attached to hurling in the county during the post-famine period. The County Draw, which was launched in 1988 while the fumes of Killarney were still in the air, began with 8,500 members who were dazzled by a glossy brochure showing Nicholas English in full flight. Therein was contained the unstated message that this was all part of an all-out programme of training the team and winning more All-Irelands. It was certainly in aid of that objective and a lot of other things too. The number of subscribers — each contributing £60 a year — rose to 16,000 and they provided undreamed of financial resources to the County Board. In seven years the draw produced a turnover of £6 million which returned £2.7 million to those clubs whose members had canvassed for subscribers. At a time when the annual running cost of a moderately active hurling club was in the region of £8,000 — a highly successful club may cost around £25,000 per annum to run — the commission on the County Draw proved a financial life-saver to many clubs.

Quite apart from the money earned directly from commission, there were other benefits to clubs from the draw. In the first seven years of its existence, £87,000 was paid to clubs who reached the closing stages of the county championship; a figure of roughly £350,000 was paid out to hurling and football coaching schemes; £110,000 was paid out in grants to schools; £70,000 to the setting up of the GAA museum, Lar na Pairce, in Thurles; and a whopping £250,000 towards the debt on Semple Stadium. For an industrious club the possibilities offered by the County Draw were endless and one such club, Clonmel Og, through imagination and hard work, drew £130,000 in seven years which was invested in the purchase of new grounds and training facilities.

Thus, when Babs Keating was motoring from Dublin to Thurles after his own day's work had ended and while players were sweating it out on the practice pitch on winter nights, they were generating revenue for hurlers and footballers through the length and breadth of the county. The colossal success of the County Draw was due in great part to the imagination of those who launched and conducted it. It may have been due even more to the high profile of the county's hurlers with whom the entire business was tied up in the public imagination.

There was another feature of the years of the post-famine revival which generated much finance and even more public notice than either the Supporters Club or the County Draw. The Thurles Feile — the name itself caused it to be confused with Feile na nGael, the wonderful juvenile hurling festival which had been first launched in Thurles — grew out of the thoroughly praiseworthy determination of Michael Lowry, chairman of the Semple Stadium Committee, to pay the debt on the stadium which had been growing since its development began prior to the playing there of the 1984 Centenary All-Ireland final. Lowry, a TD for North Tipperary, more recently Minister for Transport and Energy and Communications, had been chairman of the County Board at the time the revival of the county's fortunes began in 1987 and it was during the period of his chairmanship that Babs had been entrusted with the management of the team. He viewed it as a matter of personal honour that the stadium debt should be wiped out and in particular he had pledged that money contributed in a 'Double your Money' scheme would be repaid.

The three-day rock festival, which grew out of Lowry's determination to see the stadium's debts paid, caused controversy of a markedly heated quality. Featuring some of the biggest names in the world of pop music, it took place on the actual pitch itself, generating a kind of atmosphere which was, despite the financial advantages, embarrassing to those who found themselves disparagingly referred to as the 'traditionalists' of Tipperary's GAA.

To some outside the GAA, as well as inside it, it now seemed that the organisation which was normally associated with a recognisable moral stance on such issues as drugs and the over-use of alcohol was departing from its own standards in staging an event marked by those very same abuses. For the entire weekend of the festival Thurles required a large police presence and Justice O'Reilly, who held court every day of its duration, was scathing in his remarks about the GAA's responsibility for the proceedings.

Opposed to the multitude of arguments against the feile, there was one huge consideration that outweighed everything else — money. Over a period of five years the event contributed roughly half a million pounds towards the alleviation of a debt which had been growing at alarming proportions until the feile itself focused attention on the seriousness of the situation. But if it contributed hugely to the elimination of the debt and helped restore the financial good name of Tipperary GAA, the feile cost a lot in terms of prestige and goodwill.

To the business community of Thurles, the feile presented an opportunity for a financial killing such as no community in its right mind could ignore. To youngsters of the locality who were casual workers, it was an opportunity to make some money. To youngsters outside the county who were into the modern musical scene, the 'Trip to Tipp' was an alternative to the Slane Castle doings. To most youngsters it was simply great fun. To ordinary Thurles folk who stood to make no financial gain from it and who liked to go about their daily business without interference, the feile was a monumental nuisance. It filled the town for days with young folk of whom a minority were badly behaved and a further minority were below the legal age for drinking. The feile patrons introduced problems such as no number of hurling games brought to the town and which no provincial town was wholly equipped to deal with.

Kerry man Archbishop Dermot Clifford of Cashel and Emly, patron of the GAA, walked from his house through Liberty Square during the first feile, got the full flavour of the proceedings and there and then set himself against any repeat performance. Few would deny the Archbishop's right to make the criticisms he made, but the need to clear the debt was uppermost in the minds of those who took the decisions. At the county convention after his public criticism of the feile, the delegates gave him a polite hearing and a polite handclap, but Michael Lowry's excellently presented case for the event won their support. If Lowry's proposals were not accepted, then it was up to those present to come up with an alternative, and there was a feeling abroad that GAA supporters in the county had been already squeezed as hard as they could reasonably bear.

The matter had, in fact, already been thrashed out at a County Board meeting (in camera), when the members had accepted by a large majority the necessity of holding the feile. An ex-chairman of the board had presented an alternative which proposed a diversion of County Draw monies to the stadium for a number of years until the debt was cleared. But in the heat of enthusiasm for what promised to be an immediate reduction of the debt, this proposal got little notice from the County Board and, because of the in camera restrictions on the meeting, it received no publicity at all. At the county convention the Archbishop's voice was the only one raised to express the widespread disquiet regarding the feile.

Few controversies in the Thurles area generated such heat over a number of years and it did much to highlight a basic change that has taken place in Irish society with regard to episcopal influence. Dr Clifford was unequivocal in his denunciation of the feile and all that went with it. There were many in the town and in the GAA itself who agreed with him. But the Semple Stadium committee and the officers of the County Board felt that, however much they might dislike it, they had no alternative but to stand by it. It was the only way of paying the stadium's debt, they argued. It was only undertaken because the stadium's financial situation demanded it. When it was no longer necessary it would be discontinued, they promised. And they had their way.

Each year's feile was going to be the last and when the next year came and another was announced, the abuses of the previous year were going to be taken care of. Each year the controls were tighter than the previous year, the sanitary arrangements were better, the garda presence was stricter — and still the complaints flowed in. But the money flowed in too, and if one chooses to put the payment of one's debts above every other consideration, then it was all in a good cause. Not even when in 1993 a striptease 'artist' was introduced as part of a musical act did the promoters wince sufficiently to consider calling it a day. But there was one more outing before the day was finally called in 1994.

When Michael Lowry announced at the county convention in January of 1995 that the Semple Stadium debt had been cleared, there was a collective sigh of relief through the county, most of all in GAA circles. The majority of those within the organisation who had countenanced the feile only did so because they felt they had to, that there was no alternative open. In doing so, they had established a standard of financial rectitude, but they had forfeited something that was of immense, some would say far greater, value.

Nobody held the Tipperary team responsible for the feile; they had, in fact, by filling the stadium on a number of occasions, helped in the most satisfying way of all to clear the debt. But for many the controversy surrounding the festival would be an abiding memory of the years of the hurling revival.

TALKING TO BABS

At the end of January 1995, six months after he had laid aside the cares of office, I sat with Babs Keating looking out over the Comeragh Mountains on a wet, miserable Saturday afternoon. The Suir was in flood, roads here and there were impassable. It was an evening for staying indoors but Babs didn't appear to notice the general misery. On such days as this over a period of eight years there had been practice sessions at whatever location in the county was playable and available. Weather conditions had rarely intervened. Months later supporters would come out in their tens of thousands to watch in summer weather the end result of all the hardship that had been undergone while they were indoors watching the English league or perhaps the winter fun in St Moritz.

He had just returned from three weeks in Dubai and was as tanned and relaxed as could be. He had played golf and gone racing with friends who shared his interests. There were no phone calls from home telling of yet another injury, of someone on the Tipp panel having played badly in a club game, of a field not being available for a practice game two Sundays from now. He had not been totally idle, but he had been totally relaxed.

Removed from the mainstream of GAA affairs, he was in the right frame of mind to look back, so I asked him the obvious question — what was the golden moment of his eight years as Tipp manager? He had to think before he answered.

'There were so many great moments, but I suppose one would have to pick out Killarney. There was a sense of breakthrough and to beat Cork in a Munster final in the circumstances that we did it was a mark of success that any hurling man would accept. The excitement of the supporters and the sense that something unforgettable was happening made Killarney unique.

But I don't agree that Tipp would never have made a comeback if we hadn't won in Killarney. In fact, it is possible that we might have won the All-Ireland in '88. The fact is that Tipp arrived at the top maybe too quickly for their own good. From being nobodies they were suddenly the darlings of the media and the hype was such that it was difficult to cope with. There was a touch of the *nouveau riche* about the whole thing and maybe if we had arrived at the top by slower stages we would have been able to handle our situation better. It is easy to forget now the countrywide welcome for Tipp's return to the "big time" and how hard it was for a team to cope with that sort of thing.

On the night after the Killarney game the team were met off the train at Nenagh by a huge crowd and in Borrisoleigh the whole population was waiting for them to arrive. Some of the lads stopped off at Shaneen's pub in Latteragh, leaving the crowd waiting. Even a thing like how to treat supporters properly has to be learned in stages. No team was ever treated to such hype with such suddenness as Tipp. Killarney was worth living for, but if Nicky had tried for a goal instead of palming it over the bar and if Ger Cunningham had stopped it and we were beaten by that point, we might have won more in the long run.

The lads were really played out after all the Munster games. They were past their peak when they met Galway, and Galway were waiting for them.'

Did he have a worst moment — one that stands out so clearly that he didn't have to think for the answer? He did. I settled back to hear, possibly, of Noel Lane's devastating goal in 1988. But that wasn't the worst for Babs.

'I'll remember until I die the evening in 1986 when Laois beat us in the League. We had been working flat out with the team and we thought we were getting somewhere. We beat Antrim in the first League game and we said, well that's a start anyway. And then, in only the second round of the League, Laois beat us by eight points. I drove back to Dublin that night and I thought, My God, are we going anywhere at all? I felt so bad about it that I almost didn't want to reach home.

When I started in 1986, it was a case of starting from scratch with everything. Even a firm financial base had to be established. The County Board hadn't a bob. In fact it was heavily in debt. So was Semple Stadium. There seemed to be nowhere that money was going to come from unless we tapped into new sources. I could see that if the team was to be treated in the way I thought they should be, I would have to organise the finances myself. It took an awful lot of time but it never took me away for five minutes of time that should have been spent with the team. The time came out of other things. The Supporters Club will never get the recognition they deserve for providing the financial back-up. They removed all the financial worries so that we could get on with the business of looking after the team.

188

People ask if Fr Tom Fogarty will be able to help with the financing of the team as I did and I say he won't have to. The structures are there and the money is there. Tipp County Board are in the black, the Semple Stadium debt is cleared and the officers of the Supporters Club are the kind of people you couldn't have a row with if you tried. I will continue to help raising money and sponsorship, though I won't be involved timewise as much as I used to be. But I will be involved through the Supporters Club. I want as much as I ever did to see Tipp on top.'

From the very beginning in 1986, it was obvious that under Babs a new style of team management had arrived and perhaps the visible sign of this was the clean-cut image of the team on and off the field and the associations of affluence. Why the emphasis on image?

'Your self-image is as important as your public image and it was a deliberate policy on our part to help players feel self-confident. The man who wears a blue and gold jersey must feel that he is somebody and that he is one of a worthwhile group. The blazer and the rig-out won't give confidence, but from the point of view of the public it says something the public understands. If you expect a fellow in his twenties to give up several nights of the week, you must be interested in everything about him — even his appearance. I would regard the lads who played from 1987 to 1994 as my personal friends. I have placed some of them in jobs and there is a bond between us. I would feel that they will be my friends for life.'

Thinking of the outrageous demands on the time of any man, especially an already busy one, which modern management of a hurling team demands, I put the question whether a manager should be a full-time paid official. There was no hesitation.

'No. Just no. By the way, I have never thought of myself as a manager but as a selector. Theo, Donie and I always worked together as a group. Later with John O'Donoghue and Donie, and later still with John and Noel O'Dwyer, it was the same. We scoured the county from one end to the other for possible county players. If any player was ever mentioned as a possibility, we made sure he was looked at, and looked hard at. The other selectors deserved any credit that was going as much as I did.

But since you use the phrase "modern management", to answer your question, I must say no. Modern management demands absolutely total commitment. I often arrived home from Thurles long after midnight and had to be at a business conference at the other side of the city at 8.30 in the morning. But I was never sorry for myself. You have to give up lots of things, put players even before family and self. That's the way it is and that's the way it has to be if you are going to do the job properly. Hardly a day would pass without my being on the phone to the other selectors and to several others in connection with the team.

But payment? No. The GAA is an amateur organisation. Pay me and you must pay the other selectors. If the three of us, why not the players? Where do you stop? Managers and selectors and players should be treated decently with expenses and they should never be out of pocket because of their commitment to the game. Further than that I would not go.'

To many it was a never-ending source of wonder that Babs could combine the demands of his own job as an area manager with Esso Petroleum for an area covering half of Leinster with those of Tipp hurling. How was it done?

'Not easily, is the answer. But I am in the happy position of working for a firm which, with a consistent market share of 24.5 per cent, doesn't mind how I achieve my targets as long as I achieve them. Esso is a firm with high standards and if I can do my job in less time than another might take, that is to my advantage. However long I could continue to do that is another question. In 1987 I had the best targets of any sales manager in Europe.

I regularly attend management courses abroad and I believe that there are management skills which you can't pick up by accident. In modern business you have to stay on top of your job to survive. The business of management fascinates me and I read a good bit about it. I like to think I bring some of the expertise of management into the dressing room too. Handling men and handling players, sometimes the skills overlap. When I was 25 I did a month-long course in memory retention and to this day it stands to me. I can remember players' performances and I never have to watch a video in order to recall an incident in a game.'

We came to the question that will forever be asked as long as the Keating years are discussed: did Tipp win as much as they should have won between 1987 and 1994?

'You can say if you like that we didn't win enough. But I made the point, when we presented the Munster medals last year in Pat Fox's pub, that since I took over in 1987 we had won two All-Irelands — on a par with Cork, Kilkenny and Galway. Look at football then — Down, Meath, Cork — they all had more firepower from under-age teams than we had and yet they won no more All-Irelands than we did. There is a perception that Meath have been up there all the time and yet they have won only two All-Irelands. Every hurling All-Ireland we saw in the last few years, there has been a Kilkenny team in it between minors and under-21's and they haven't won more senior All-Irelands than us.

I have no doubt that we would have won the '93 All-Ireland. We did everything right to have the lads right and ripe for the championship that year, but every bit of bad luck possible came to us in Croke Park, from Ken's easy goal to the injury of Declan Ryan. And when did you see two players from the same team colliding and the two being knocked unconscious?

That was followed up by the events of the past year. This was the one year (1994) that you could really say we had a team that was better than anything in the country. Offaly won the All-Ireland with a young team playing badly for most of the hour and they will improve. But there is little doubt that had we survived Clare, things would have happened for us. It is hard to perform at your very best against a team that you had beaten by as much as we had beaten Clare in 1993. Of all those injured, one injury less would still have allowed us to win — John Leahy could have won it for us. All our bad luck seemed to come together that day, although there were other days that we had no luck. But it would be hard to beat the Clare game in '94 or the Galway game in '93 for pure misfortune.'

I had noticed that Babs rarely mentioned the League and I put the question to him: is it possible anymore to win League and All-Ireland in the same year?

'It is not impossible, but it does seem to be a harder target to meet than it used to be. We never set out with the stated intention of winning the League, or even the Munster championship. Our target was always the All-Ireland and everything else was something to be met on the way. You have to get to the League semi-final or at least the quarter-final as part of your preparation for the championship. Otherwise, there will be too much of a lay-off period before the championship starts. The 1994 League almost fell to us by chance. We got near the final stages and Kilkenny seemed to have no great interest in it. Then we got through Cork and we found ourselves in the final against Galway. The rivalry with Galway was enough motivation for everyone and suddenly we found ourselves League champions. Maybe if we had been beaten before we had got that far at all we wouldn't have been beaten in the championship; but luck was against us anyway. The injuries were still there.'

One of the more controversial statements made by Babs has been that Tipp needed more physical toughness — the traditional toughness. This was said in 1993 after the defeat by Galway. Did he still stand over this?

'I do believe that many Tipp players lacked the physical toughness to cope properly with the kind of physical aggression that confronted us both in Munster and outside. I am not talking about dirty play, but simply tough physical reaction to tough physical tactics. If you are to win All-Irelands, you must be able to make it clear that you will not be "pushed around". Galway were a case in point. They were physically tough. They "acted tough" with Tipp and we had to try to get the lads to act tough, in turn, without giving away frees. There's a difference between being dirty and being physically uncompromising. At the top level of hurling, the last thing you want an opponent to think is that you can be intimidated. The proper reaction to physical aggression is something that we never got right.

When we took over in 1986 we stressed from the beginning that there was no place in our plans for dirty play, no place for the "hard man" who loved the cheer from the terrace when he floored somebody, and no place for the fellow who couldn't be depended on not to be sent to the line before the game was over. If we were to succeed, it would have to be through pure hurling. And what we provided was pure hurling. But somewhere along the way I felt that we had lost that tiny ingredient of pure steel that is necessary at the top. It's not at all the same thing as resorting to dirty, or even rough, play.'

Looking back on all the tussles against Galway, what were his feelings about the Galway team that had taken two All-Irelands from him?

'Galway were one of the great teams. They had real power — and toughness. Look at the half-back line — Finnerty, Keady, McInerney — and Malone and Coleman at centre-field. And look at the talent in the forward line. They were aggressive, at least against Tipp. They were less so against Cork. They came up the hard way and they deserved the All-Irelands they won. An ugly kind of relationship developed between Tipp and Galway and maybe it was inevitable, given the keenness of the rivalry that was there. If either county wasn't there, the other might have had a bag of All-Irelands. But Galway supporters behaved badly towards Tipp. They refused to accept that Tipp had nothing whatsoever to do with Tony Keady's suspension, even though it was made as clear as could be. Tommy Barrett stood up at the Central Council meeting and proposed on behalf of Tipp that Keady be reinstated, and no more notice was taken of that in Galway than if it never happened. I never heard before or since of a sporting gesture like that from one county to another, and still the Galway supporters managed to hold Tipp responsible.'

How did he feel about the traditional Tipp-Cork rivalry after his years of management?

'It goes without saying that there will always be something special about the Tipp-Cork relationship. It is something that is based on mutual respect. Your performance against Cork is the yardstick for judging your worth and your future possibilities. But I was a bit soured by the distortion of my words about the "donkeys" in 1990 and the way that distorted version was used. I know that Cork made use of it to motivate the team for a day, but it was the sort of thing that I would not do myself. I think there should be certain standards of behaviour between opposing dressing rooms. But Cork and Tipp always test each other and I hope it will always be that way.'

Kilkenny?

'In the '60s there was deep bitterness against Tipp in Kilkenny and I don't think it all came from the day Tom Walsh lost his eye. I don't know where it came from. It seemed to be there when I came on the team first. Even in America there was little communication between the teams, but the bad blood seems to be fading out in recent times. I didn't see it in the likes of the Fennellys and D. J. Carey and others.'

Who were the managers he feared and admired?

'A lot of them I admired; I feared none of them.'

Cyril Farrell?

'A very able manager. He had fine talent in Galway and he used antagonism towards Tipp to get the last ounce out of them. He didn't have a personal hurling record behind him and he may have felt the lack of it, but he managed to cover it up. He was a tough man driving a team.'

Ollie Walsh?

'I admired Ollie so much as a player that I always thought of him first as a goalie. I think he was the greatest goalie of them all. He beat us in '67. He was a class goalkeeper of real star quality. Everything he did had style.'

Who was the best hurler of his time as manager?

'Without doubt, Nicholas English. His skill as a ball player was a thing apart. He had it in his hands and in his head. His scoring power and the quality of his scores were wonderful. Remember the goal he kicked against Ger Cunningham, and his first-half goal in Killarney? Count up the number of his scores over the years. And despite all his bad luck with injuries, he was totally committed to the game, never hesitating to do what he was asked. You would have to go back to Jimmy Doyle for another Tipp forward quite like him.'

Were there any particular 'strokes' he had pulled which gave him pleasure to look back on?

'Well, one was playing Pat Fox at corner-forward. He had been playing at corner-back and at centre-field and we fitted him in at corner-forward. If he had stayed outfield, would anybody remember him? And playing Bobby Ryan at full-forward — a move that was much criticised but which served its purpose at the time. Do you remember the way Bobby let the ball run between his legs for English to score in Killarney? I know he was a natural half-back, but he served us well when we needed him at full-forward.

There were other moves — the introduction of Martin McGrath in Killarney, and the playing of Colm Bonnar at centre-back. Often people forget the moves that work and remember the ones that don't.

There is one thing I would like to emphasise, and this brings us back to where we started with your question as to whether we won as much between '87 and '94 as we should have. Tipp has been markedly short on minor All-Irelands in recent times. It's been '82 since we won one. And it's '89 since we won an under-21 All-Ireland.

You know the record of Tipp minors in the '50s — six All-Irelands in the decade. Then we went on in the '60s to win four senior All-Irelands. In the '60s we won no minor All-Irelands and we only won one senior All-Ireland in the '70s. There is more of a connection than people think.

You must have new talent coming on stream all the time if you are to stay at the top and there has not been that surge of top-grade new players over the past few years. The ideal situation is to have not alone a top-class player in every position, but a top-class sub for every position. We have not had that kind of luxury for years. When we took the field in '87 we had twelve new players from the team that had fielded in the previous championship. But of the subs listed for the '89 All-Ireland, none had fully made it to the team the following season.

What I am saying is that we were not as rich in talent as many would like to think and, considering everything, we did not do badly as regards All-Irelands and Munster championships. We did well in winning two All-Irelands and five Munster championships and, with any bit of luck at all, we would have had others to go with them.'

How does he see the future of Tipp hurling?

'I would worry not just about the future of hurling in Tipp, but hurling everywhere. It is the most skilful game in the world, an art form, and it should be approached as such. There must be a huge emphasis on it in schools if it is to survive, and the GAA must be prepared to invest in it to a degree that has never been done before. Modern life and the school bus are problems, but they must be faced and the skills of hurling must be imparted at the right age. There are lots of people like myself who would gladly be involved in passing on to youngsters the skills of the greatest game in the world. It is no use teaching something the wrong way. There is a huge commitment in time and manpower needed from clubs and schools, but it must be done. Otherwise we are lost.'

We had been talking for a couple of hours and on that note Babs rose to go. There had been an air of 'It's all in the past' about the entire conversation and I ventured to remark that there must be a vacuum in his life now that he was no longer at the helm. There was no hesitation in his reply.

'There certainly is. And it's a very pleasant vacuum. I've plenty of golf and I'm good enough at it to enjoy it. And there's plenty of racing. It's only when you give up something that you have been busy at for a few years that you realise how much it has taken over your life. I was living two lives in one for eight years. It couldn't go on for ever. I'm 51 now and I'm due to retire in a couple of years. I've become conscious of the physical strain of looking after a team and of my general lifestyle until now. There comes a time to make a move.'

A quick shake-hands and he was gone. He was on his way to the presentation of the League medals in Thurles. The final curtain was about to be drawn on the Keating years.

Chapter Twenty-seven

WHITHER HURLING, WHITHER TIPPERARY?

With the possible exceptions of Mick O'Dwyer, Kevin Heffernan and Jack O'Shea, none of the modern team managers of the Gaelic arena enjoyed quite the same distinguished career on the playing field before turning to management as Babs Keating. Whether his success as a manager was consistent with his record on the field is a matter that will be debated for a long time to come. But his departure from hurling management will certainly, to borrow the metaphor, leave a blank space against the sky. For eight years his presence on the hurling scene was one that could not be ignored. His absence for the foreseeable future prompts the question, whither Tipperary hurling? Perhaps closely bound up with that question is one regarding the future of hurling itself.

Alone among the great organisations which before the turn of the century were launched on the crest of the enthusiasm of the time, the GAA has actually achieved what it set out to do. It has not been an unqualified success, but it has come nearer to being so than any organisation that ever saw the light of day within these shores. It gave to Gaelic football a popularity that would have astonished its founders. It supported Irish athletics on its first tottering steps, and having seen it to the crosssroads, allowed it to go its own way. It disappointed neither the aspirations of the athletes Davin and Cusack nor the nationalist Nally. The Australian Prime Minister who watched from the Hogan Stand as the crowd of Derry supporters swept on to the pitch at Croke Park received a lesson on the politics of Irish nationalism which no amount of diplomatic manoeuvring could have given. For over a hundred years the GAA has remained the greatest single bonding force in the Gaelic nation.

Paradoxically, the revival of hurling has been both the great success story and the great failure of the GAA. The refining of the game between parishes into the media friendly spectacle it is today would have gratified the founding fathers as much as the vast crowds which flock to see it played. But the fact that its spread has never matched that of Gaelic football would have been a disappointment. After all, Michael Cusack's expressed wish was to 'bring back the hurling'.

In the 100 years plus since the first All-Ireland final was played, only twelve counties have succeeded in capturing the blue riband of hurling. Three counties — Cork, Kilkenny and Tipperary — have accounted for over three-quarters of the titles won. Offaly has been the only new addition to the list of All-Ireland winners in nearly fifty years. Take the quarter of a century before that again and one finds Waterford as the only new addition. It is against this background that one must view the significance for the game itself of the eighteen years during which Tipperary failed to win an All-Ireland.

When Christy Ring made his famous remark about the GAA being only 'half dressed' without Tipperary, he was not merely expressing a personal nostalgia for the disappearance from the front rank of the county which had contributed much to his own personal legend, he was also voicing the apprehensions of an ardent lover of hurling for the continued existence of the game itself. Take away Tipperary or Cork or Kilkenny and the game would be only 'half dressed'. Take away two of them and it would not be dressed at all. The game of hurling needs these three counties as much as the GAA needs the game of hurling.

Were Kerry to disappear forever from the list of winners of football titles, the loss to the game would be immense and would be mourned by all who truly love the game. But it would not be a body-blow to football in general. Football would survive. There might be a somewhat different situation were one of the major powers of hurling to go into permanent decline. No true lover of hurling failed to be delighted by Offaly's wonderful victory in the 1994 All-Ireland final, just as nobody failed to feel anything but sympathy for Limerick. But given the state of competition for the hearts and minds of the young, the game of hurling simply cannot afford to lose any county. Above all, it cannot afford to lose a county where it has been for over a hundred years as natural an interest for children as any ball-game can be. It would not be the end for hurling, or anything like it, but it would set alarm bells ringing among those who have the future of the game at heart.

One of the more striking phenomena of modern times is the extent to which the young are, as never before, success orientated. The entire thrust of modern society is to place success on a pedestal, whether in the market place or the playing field. Success means winning and nothing else, no matter the manner of the achievement. The dramatic spread among the young of the popularity of soccer can hardly be separated from the successes of the Charlton years any more than it can be disentangled from the packaging and the presentation of the game by the media. In the modern climate how long would hurling have survived in Galway without the successes of recent times? How long would hurling have survived in Tipperary without the successes of the Keating years? When Cork is a few years removed from a McCarthy Cup win, there is an upsurge of support within the county for Gaelic football and for soccer. That hurling is a delicate flower is a fact that needs to be taken more seriously at present than it has been in the past.

The suggestion that hurling is just another game and that its problems are shared by every other game is not entirely true. There are few examples, if any, of top-class hurlers who did not play the game since childhood. Hurling is unique in that the top-class player has physical qualities which, were he not to make hurling his first game, would give him a head-start in any other game he chose to play. The attributes of the top-class hurler, the co-ordination of hand and eye, the physical strength, the speed, the quickness of mind, the anticipation, the sureness of foot — these are qualities which no amount of coaching will of itself produce, though it may certainly hone and refine them. This is not to say that hurling skills are inherited. But the qualities which make it possible for a young person to grow into a hurler may be. And the qualities having been inherited, the skills must be inculcated and worked upon during endless hours of practice which are utterly wasted if the initial requisites are not present. Hurlers are not made; neither are they born; but the qualities necessary for the making of a hurler must be present from birth. Tony Wall, earlier referred to as one of the greatest centre-backs hurling has produced, was born in County Meath. Had his family not moved to Thurles, he would never have been heard of as a hurler if for no better reason than that he would have been playing some other game. On the other hand, though he was raised in Thurles, not all the training in the world would have given him the physical attributes needed in a great hurler, had he not been born with them.

It is that phrase 'endless hours of practice' which is causing so much difficulty for those who are prepared to spend their time coaching youngsters today. The spirit of the age has little time for anything that does not provide instant enjoyment. The mastery of the hurley itself, the grip and the swing are matters which have to be given considerable attention before enjoyment comes. From the beginning there is a lot of hard work involved. Young people are not prepared to invest in future enjoyment in the way they once were. Gone are the days when youngsters hurled from morning till night because they simply had nothing else to do. But it was those hours of putting down time that produced a level of skill that eventually delighted thousands and won All-Irelands.

Not the least difference between the outdoor recreational activities of youngsters today and those of a generation ago is the assumption that there are to be 'training sessions' only when adults are present. It is a rarity to see a group of children hurling among themselves without the presence of an adult. In other words, little hurling is done by children for pure pleasure. If it is not organised by an adult, whether in school or in a club, it does not happen. The days of seeing a group of children heading for the nearest field with their hurleys simply for 'a few pucks' are gone.

This is a development which introduces another problem. As in every other area of life, the number of adults, whether parents or otherwise, who are willing to give their spare time to coaching children in anything has declined sharply in the past decade. For those who are prepared to give up their time to the training of youngsters in the skills of hurling there is the hassle of sliotars, of hurleys, of helmets and of the minor injuries which can add a degree of frustration to the proceedings which is only understood fully by those who have been involved in them. Finally, there is the difficulty of transporting fifteen players, plus some subs — a matter which often makes hurling mentors look with envy at a soccer club which can send an entire team away to a game in a single minibus.

In the schools the declining numbers of teachers willing to become involved in the evening in teaching children the skills of hurling is already a problem. In urban areas the disappearance of Christian Brothers, whose presence on playing fields after four o'clock was taken for granted, is throwing over on to clubs, already hard pressed for manpower, a burden of responsibility which they have difficulty in coping with. Exacerbating the problem is the reduced number of male teachers. Even given the goodwill which so many ladies bear towards the game, it is hardly reasonable to expect that a young married teacher is going to be available after a day's teaching to coach hurlers before returning home to her family. The GAA is doing excellent work in sending coaches into schools under employment schemes. However, there is no substitute for the teacher of other days who instructed the pupils to bring their hurleys in the morning and who watched them hurling during lunch-break and after school. Like the snows of yesteryear, he belongs in the past and he will not be back.

Tipperary, like everywhere else, may well be facing a crossroads with regard to the game which has been so much a part of its life for over 100 years. The departure of Babs Keating raises the question as to how hurling might have stood in the county had he never taken over as manager in the autumn of 1986. It is easy to say that nothing would have been substantially different, that the county had the talent and would have chalked up victories no matter who was in charge. But the eighteen years of the famine still causes an uneasiness among those who think of the future. Nobody thought, when an open lorry carried the Tipp team of 1971 through Liberty Square to the Archbishop's residence, that eighteen years would pass before the scene was repeated. There were no warning signs. No one could have seen what lay ahead. But what did lie ahead left a scar on a generation of Tipperary folk.

If the famine years left a scar on an entire generation, the ending of the famine and the years that followed left a host of memories which will not be forgotten by the generation who were there to share them. Johnny Clifford, known to the present generation as one of the country's leading coaches but who for many of us will always be the flying corner-forward who sank Wexford's hopes in 1953, spoke feelingly of the unprecedented emotion he saw in Killarney when Richard Stakelum held the Munster cup aloft. The nearest to it I had ever witnessed in Munster was in 1952 when, having beaten Tipp for the first time in four years, Christy Ring was hoisted on Cork shoulders in the centre of the field and cheer after cheer split the sky until it seemed that one man was the focus of the emotion of all the Cork men who had ever followed the game of hurling.

Cork at the time needed such a win, even if for the three previous years they had been within a puck of the ball of Tipp. Tipp needed Killarney and if Killarney had not happened then or later, what would have become of hurling in the county hardly bears thinking about for those who regard the Tipp hurling tradition as part of their lives. The emotion of which Johnny Clifford spoke was the product as much of relief as delight, relief that a nightmare had ended.

There are those who believe that, with all the challenges of other games, any county that seriously wants to monopolise the allegiance of its youth needs to win on a regular basis. Given the modern cult of success, this will be even more necessary from now on. From Tipp's point of view, the trouble is that except for the famine years there never was a period when the effect of consistent failure on the mood of the younger generation could be accurately judged.

In the meantime, hurling in Tipperary, as elsewhere, is faced with the challenge of soccer. And this challenge is not entirely related to the successes of the national team. At local level in rural areas soccer is more of a recreation than hurling. The commitment to 'the honour of the little village', formerly the strength of the hurling club, is now becoming its weakness. Hurling demands commitment on and off the field. The spirit of the age is that recreation should be recreation. A former inter-county hurling goalkeeper who shall be nameless confided in me that he began playing soccer as a relaxation from the demands of hurling. On the morning after a club game his popularity in his parish was in indirect proportion to the number of balls he had to pick out of the net the previous day. He suddenly discovered that he could enjoy himself playing soccer without any pressure and with near anonymity. He claimed that when he began playing soccer he realised that he had forgotten how enjoyable playing a team game could be. It wasn't the same as the thrill of hurling but it had its compensation — one could have fun without pressure.

I am aware of two inter-county hurlers who played soccer with a club forty miles from their home and in another county for the same reason. They could drive to be with their soccer team, play their game and be back home within half a day on a Sunday and feel neither obliged to nor under pressure from anyone. They had no desire to play soccer in the upper echelons of a local league; all they wanted was recreation without hassle. If soccer enjoyed the same local prestige as hurling, the pressure would attach to it in the same way. But it doesn't — yet — and until it does, it will have an attraction which fierce local loyalties are taking from hurling.

At its lower levels there is possible an almost instant mastery of soccer and an instant enjoyment of the game which hurling can never offer. It is this aspect of the challenge which must make the spread of soccer among juveniles worrying in a county such as Tipperary, where it is increasingly seen as a challenge to hurling for the attention of the very young. From a starting base of a mere handful, there are at present over eighty junior and nearly as many under-age soccer teams in County Tipperary; when the hurling revival began there was only about a third of those numbers playing soccer. Few of the soccer clubs draw any strength from local loyalties of a kind expected by hurling clubs. Such strength as they have derives from the participation of the players.

There is another aspect of Tipperary hurling which, because it became noticeable during the years of success after 1987, did not attract huge attention but which might yet be a cause for worry. The map of Tipperary parishes printed elsewhere in this book shows the mid-Tipperary parishes in the immediate vicinity of Thurles as being the traditional heartland of the county's hurling successes. Declan Carr stands alone as the sole representative of this area in the championship successes since Killarney. Thurles, whose selections brought no less than ten All-Irelands to the county, has not had a representative on the Tipperary team since before Killarney. Nor has Moycarkey, nor Boherlahan, two clubs which were once known wherever hurling was discussed. There was a time when a Tipperary team, the backbone of which did not come from mid-Tipperary, would have been almost inconceivable. Sadly the last Thurles man to win an All-Ireland with Tipp was when Jimmy Doyle and Paul Byrne went in as subs in 1971. That same year John Flanagan was the last Moycarkey man to win an All-Ireland. A geographical shift of hurling power within the county may be a good thing. But it is not good to see a decline in strength in clubs that for many decades enjoyed a rich hurling tradition.

There are, of course, those who will say that hurling has never declined in the areas mentioned and that their failure to be represented on the Tipperary team is in no way a reflection of anything other than a failure to produce stars of the first rank. There are those who will say, too, that the distribution of county players reflects a universality of strength within the county that is vastly preferable to dominance by any single club or group of clubs. Certainly the quality of games in the final stages of Tipperary's county championship over the past few years has been such as would make many counties happy to claim them as their own.

But, as has already been stated, hurling is a delicate flower, and not just in Tipperary. That there are apprehensions felt regarding its continued blossoming on Tipperary soil is merely indicative of the place it holds in the hearts of Tipperary's people. There are those who live in fear of a return to days when they lived from summer to summer knowing the ignominy of defeat and of seeing the first Sunday in September come and go without a blue and gold flag flying from gable-end or from gatepost; without parties of children on the road at Kilbehenny or at Oola or at Urlingford greeting the conquering heroes as they returned from combat; without the fullness of a Christmas replete with reminiscences of summer glories. The fear that another famine may be looming ahead is intolerable. The prospect of another eighteen years during which the old slogan 'Knocknagow is gone!' might again be carried in the wind between the Shannon and the Suir, between Slievenamon and Galteemore, is one that is too unpalatable for the sons and daughters of Matt the Thresher even to contemplate.

APPENDIX

Tipperary championship record 1987–94

	P	W	D	L	For	Against
Antrim	2	2	0	0	7-39	5-19
Clare	4	2	1	1	8-70	5-44
Cork	7	3	2	2	16-120	17-106
Galway	5	2	0	3	7-75	8-71
Kerry	2	2	0	0	5-42	4-15
Kilkenny	1	1	0	0	1-16	0-15
Limerick	4	4	0	0	8-71	3-46
Waterford	1	1	0	0	0-26	2-8
	26	17	3	6	52-459	44-324

Championships 1987–94: clubs represented

7 Players: Borrisoleigh; 6 Players: Toomevara; 5 Players: Cashel; 4 Players: Nenagh Eire Og; 3 Players: Cappawhite, Clonoulty-Rossmore, Loughmore-Castleiney; 2 Players: Eire Og Annacarthy, Holycross-Ballycahill; Kilruane McDonagh, Lorrha, Mullinahone, Roscrea; 1 Player: Burgess, Killenaule, Kilsheelan, Knockavilla Kickhams, Lattin-Cullen, Newport, Silvermines, Upperchurch-Drumbane.

Tipperary championship scorers 1987–94

Nicholas English	12-94 (130)
Pat Fox	11-87 (120)
Michael Cleary	8-75 (99)
Declan Ryan	5-33 (48)
Aidan Ryan	1-35 (38)

John Leahy	2-25 (31)
Paul Delaney	0-19 (19)
Donie O'Connell	2-12 (18)
Cormac Bonnar	3-6 (15)
Joe Hayes	1-11 (14)
Anthony Crosse	1-9 (12)
Conor Stakelum	1-9 (12)
Declan Carr	1-8 (11)
Colm Bonnar	0-7 (7)
Michael Doyle	2-1 (7)
Bobby Ryan	1-3 (6)
Martin McGrath	0-5 (5)
Pa O'Neill	0-3 (3)
Dinny Ryan	1-0 (3)
Michael Scully	0-3 (3)
Liam Stokes	0-3 (3)
John Cormack	0-2 (2)
Tommy Dunne	0-2 (2)
John McGrath	0-2 (2)
Richard Stakelum	0-2 (2)
Conal Bonnar	0-1 (1)
Pa Fitzelle	0-1 (1)
John Kennedy	0-1 (1)

Tipperary All-Stars

1971: Tadhg O'Connor, Mick Roche, Francis Loughnane,
Babs Keating
1972: Francis Loughnane
1973: Francis Loughnane
1975: Tadhg O'Connor
1978: Tommy Butler
1979: Pat McLoughney, Tadhg O'Connor
1980: Pat McLoughney
1983: Nicholas English
1984: Nicholas English
1985: Nicholas English
1986: Bobby Ryan
1987: Ken Hogan, Aidan Ryan, Pat Fox, Nicholas English

1988: Bobby Ryan, Colm Bonnar, Declan Ryan, Nicholas English
1989: Conal Bonnar, Bobby Ryan, Declan Carr, Pat Fox,
Cormac Bonnar, Nicholas English
1990: Noel Sheehy, Michael Cleary
1991: Paul Delaney, Noel Sheehy, Conal Bonnar, John Leahy,
Michael Cleary, Pat Fox, Cormac Bonnar
1992: Michael Cleary
1993: Michael Cleary
1994: John Leahy

Texaco 'Hurler of the Year' awards won by Tipperary

Tony Wall (1958)
Liam Devaney (1961)
Donie Nealon (1962)
John Doyle (1964)
Jimmy Doyle (1965)
Babs Keating (1971)
Nicholas English (1989)
Pat Fox (1991)

Championship games between Tipp and Cork 1987–94

12 July 1987 at Thurles: Tipp 1-18 Cork 1-18 (draw)
19 July 1987 at Killarney: Tipp 4-22 Cork 1-22 (after extra time)
17 July 1988 at Limerick: Tipp 2-19 Cork 1-13
15 July 1990 at Thurles: Cork 4-16 Tipp 2-14
7 July 1991 at Cork: Tipp 2-16 Cork 4-10 (draw)
21 July 1991 at Thurles: Tipp 4-19 Cork 4-15
7 July 1992 at Cork: Cork 2-12 Tipp 1-12
Total: Tipp 16-120 (168) Cork 17-106 (157)

Championship games between Tipp and Galway 1987–94

9 August 1987 at Croke Park: Galway 3-20 Tipp 2-17
All-Ireland final 1988: Galway 1-15 Tipp 0-14
All-Ireland semi-final 1989: Tipp 1-17 Galway 2-11
All-Ireland semi-final 1991: Tipp 3-13 Galway 1-9
All-Ireland semi-final 1993: Galway 1-16 Tipp 1-14
Total: Tipp 7-75 (96) Galway 8-71 (95)

Munster titles won by Tipperary

Year	Captain
1887	Denny Maher (Thurles)
1895	Mikey Maher (Tubberadora)
1896	Mikey Maher (Tubberadora)
1898	Mikey Maher (Tubberadora)
1899	Tim Condon (Moycarkey)
1900	Ned Hayes (Two-Mile-Borris)
1906	Tom Semple (Thurles)
1908	Tom Semple (Thurles)
1909	Tom Semple (Thurles)
1913	'Wedger' Meagher (Toomevara)
1916	Johnny Leahy (Boherlahan)
1917	Johnny Leahy (Boherlahan)
1922	Johnny Leahy (Boherlahan)
1924	Johnny Leahy (Boherlahan)
1925	Johnny Leahy (Boherlahan)
1930	J. J. Callanan (Thurles)
1937	Jim Lanigan (Thurles)
1941	Johnny Ryan (Moycarkey)
1945	John Maher (Thurles)
1949	Pat Stakelum (Holycross)
1950	Sean Kenny (Borrisoleigh)
1951	Jimmy Finn (Borrisoleigh)
1958	Tony Wall (Thurles)
1960	Tony Wall (Thurles)
1961	Matt Hasset (Toomevara)
1962	Jimmy Doyle (Thurles)
1964	Noel Murphy (Thurles)
1965	Jimmy Doyle (Thurles)
1967	Mick Roche (Carrick-on-Suir)
1971	Tadhg O'Connor (Roscrea)
1987	Richard Stakelum (Borrisoleigh)
1988	Pa O'Neill (Cappawhite)
1989	Bobby Ryan (Borrisoleigh)
1991	Declan Carr (Holycross)
1993	Michael O'Meara (Toomevara)

All-Ireland titles won by Tipperary

1887 Thurles selection captained by Jim Stapleton
1895 Tubberadora (Boherlahan) selection captained by Mikey Maher
1896 Tubberadora (Boherlahan) selection captained by Mikey Maher
1898 Tubberadora (Boherlahan) selection captained by Mikey Maher
1899 Moycarkey selection captained by Tim Condon
1900 Two-Mile-Borris selection captained by Ned Hayes
1906 Thurles selection captained by Tom Semple
1908 Thurles selection captained by Tom Semple
1916 Boherlahan selection captained by Johnny Leahy
1925 Boherlahan selection captained by Johnny Leahy
1930 Thurles selection captained by J. J. Callanan
1937 Thurles selection captained by Jim Lanigan
1945 Thurles selection captained by John Maher

In 1949 the prerogative of the club winning the county championship to select the county team was terminated. The winning club still had the privilege of appointing the captain, if one of its members was on the team.

1949 team captained by Pat Stakelum (Holycross)
1950 team captained by Sean Kenny (Borrisoleigh)
1951 team captained by Jimmy Finn (Borrisoleigh)
1958 team captained by Tony Wall (Thurles)
1961 team captained by Matt Hasset (Toomevara)
1962 team captained by Jimmy Doyle (Thurles)
1964 team captained by Noel Murphy (Thurles)
1965 team captained by Jimmy Doyle (Thurles)
1971 team captained by Tadhg O'Connor (Roscrea)
1989 team captained by Bobby Ryan (Borrisoleigh)
1991 team captained by Declan Carr (Holycross)

PARISHES WHICH PROVIDED ALL–IRELAND WINNING CAPTAINS TO TIPPERARY

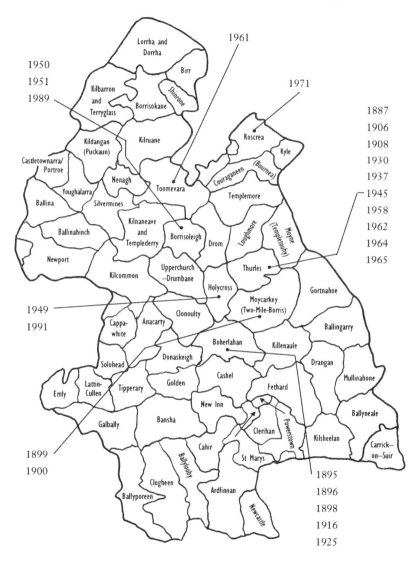

Until 1949 the club which won the county championship was responsible for selecting the Tipperary team. The winning club still provides the county captain.

209

National Hurling Leagues won by Tipperary

Year	Defeated	Year	Defeated	Year	Defeated
1928	Galway	1955	Wexford	1964	New York
1949	Cork	1957	Kilkenny	1965	New York
1950	New York	1959	Waterford	1968	New York
1952	New York	1960	Cork	1979	Galway
1954	Kilkenny	1961	Waterford	1988	Offaly

INDEX

Cleary, Michael *continued*
v. Kilkenny, 72, 110, 147, 149,
150, 151, 162
v. Limerick, 55, 116, 130, 131
Cleary, Pat, 52
Cleere, Mick, 110
Clifford, Archbishop Dermot, 185
Clifford, Johnny, 97, 200, 201
Clonmel Nationalist, 42, 175
Clonoulty, 12, 83, 104
Coleman, Martin 21
Coleman, Michael, 63, 106, 113,
142, 171
Commins, John, 40, 41, 42, 63, 64,
65, 73, 80, 106, 113
Connolly, Liam, 61
Conran, John, 48, 113
Conroy, Denis, 120
Conway, Phil, 72, 73, 77, 111, 114
Cooney, Jimmy, 16
Cooney, Joe, 39, 40, 41, 42, 48, 63,
64, 65, 106, 142, 165
Corcoran, Brian, 158, 159
Cork Examiner, 152, 161, 163
Corrigan, Mark, 52, 69, 113
County Draw, 182, 183
Cregan, Eamon, 44, 54
Crosse, Anthony, 165, 170, 172, 174
Crowley, John, 6
Culbaire (*Tipperary Star*), 34, 55,
79, 108
Cunningham, Anthony, 42, 63, 64,
73
Cunningham, Ger, 3, 6, 36, 40, 47,
56, 99, 122, 124, 134, 135,
138, 139, 140, 158
Cusack, Michael 11, 12, 197

Davin, Maurice, 11
Delany, Paul, 44, 48, 52, 60, 82, 83,
84, 171, 172, 173
v. Clare, 32, 33
v. Cork, 4, 5, 56, 58, 120, 121,
135, 138
v. Galway, 40, 41, 63, 64, 65, 66,
115, 142, 143, 165, 166
v. Kilkenny, 49, 109, 147

v. Limerick, 55, 75, 108, 116, 130
Denton, John, 59, 80, 82
Devaney, Liam 61
Dillon, Ted, 42
Donnelly, Brian, 85
Donnelly, Dessie, 85, 113
Dooley, Johnny, 52, 66
Doyle, Jimmy, 16, 19, 26, 31, 61,
194, 202
Doyle, John, 16, 26, 61, 85
Doyle, Michael (Mick), 5, 6, 23, 41,
114
Doyle, Paddy, 155
Doyle, Tommy, 22, 84
Duggan, Seanie, 61
Dungourney, 14
Dunne, John, 102
Dunphy, Christy, 155
Dwyer, Paddy, 65-6

English, Nicholas, 41, 48, 51, 52, 53,
54, 77, 83, 93-102, 105, 111,
113, 128, 135, 172, 173, 194
v. Antrim, 49, 59, 60, 85-6
v. Clare, 32, 33
v. Cork, 3, 4, 23, 36, 47, 57, 58,
120, 122, 124, 134, 135,
159, 162
v. Galway, 39, 40, 42, 45, 61-2,
66, 71, 106, 115, 142, 143,
166, 167, 171
v. Kilkenny, 148, 150, 151
v. Limerick, 31, 44, 69-70, 76,
130, 131
English, Theo, 1, 17, 29-30, 61, 74,
120, 127

Farrell, Cyril, 42, 67, 142, 155, 193
Fennelly, Liam, 48, 72, 147, 151,
152
Fenton, John, 2, 3, 4, 5, 6, 23, 33,
36, 48
Finn, Brian, 55, 131
Finn, Derek, 113
Finn, Jimmy, 26, 61, 85
Finnerty, Peter, 40, 45, 48, 63, 142,
165